Praise for Sarah E. Ladd

"Sarah E. Ladd has crafted yet another masterful story set in the Regency era, filled with intrigue and heart. The twists and turns will keep you guessing until the very end. Ella and Gabriel's story is one you'll root for, every step of the way."

—Laura Beers, bestselling author of the Courting the Unconventional series, for *An Unconventional Lady*

"With twists and turns and vivid descriptions on every page, Sarah E. Ladd's *An Unconventional Lady* will keep readers on the edge of their seats as Ella and Gabriel work together to fight for justice. Ella is so easy to root for—she is determined, intelligent, and undeniably brave for her time, and matched perfectly with Gabriel. I loved this sweet love story!"

—Megan Walker, award-winning author of *Lakeshire Park*

"A sweet Regency romance about grief, forgiveness, and being true to one's gifts. Ladd is a master of the genre, and she shines in this tale filled with intrigue, gentle manners, and lots of heart."

—Anna Lee Huber, *USA TODAY* bestselling author, for *The Cloverton Charade*

"Sarah Ladd deftly weaves her charming, rivals-to-lovers romance with antiques-filled intrigue, wonderful Regency-era detail, and an intelligent heroine who beautifully comes into her own strength. Add in a house party set in atmospheric Yorkshire and *The Cloverton Charade* is a gentle Regency romance that's an absolute delight to read."

—Celeste Connally, author of *All's Fair in Love and Treachery*

"A sweet, enjoyable second-chance-at-love Regency romance with a strong heroine, a steadfast hero, a dash of suspense, and elegant descriptive prose. I rooted for this well-matched couple from the very first page!"

—Syrie James, author of *The Missing Manuscript of Jane Austen*, for *In the Shelter of Hollythorne House*

"The Regency has found a gifted voice in Sarah Ladd, who spins magic from windswept moors and romance from a love separated but not forgotten. *In the Shelter of Hollythorne House* is a beautiful tale of lost love finding its strength again when all hope seems lost. Atmospheric and lush, readers will find themselves swooning in the manner of Jane Austen."

—J'nell Ciesielski, bestselling author of *The Brilliance of Stars* and *The Socialite*

"The swoon-worthy romance of Jane Austen meets the suspense of Charlotte Brontë in Sarah Ladd's enthralling *The Letter from Briarton Park*. As Cassandra navigates the mystery of her own life, it is absolutely clear that family—either of blood or heart—are where she, and we, ultimately find our home."

—Joy Callaway, international bestselling author of *The Fifth Avenue Artists Society* and *The Greenbrier Resort*

"*The Light at Wyndcliff* is a richly atmospheric Regency novel, reminiscent of the works of Victoria Holt and Daphne du Maurier. The storm-swept Cornish coast is a character unto itself, forming the perfect backdrop for an expertly woven tale of secrets, danger, and heartfelt romance. A riveting and deeply emotional read."

—Mimi Matthews, *USA TODAY* bestselling author of the Parish Orphans of Devon series

"[*The Light at Wyndcliff*] expertly deploys elements of gothic mystery . . . The descriptions of the dilapidated property add dark, delicious atmosphere . . . The atmosphere and intrigue keep the pages turning."

—*Publishers Weekly*

"[Ladd] faithfully depicts the rough Cornish coast of the 1820s, with its rocky coves and windswept moors, the slow-simmering romance between the attractive principals is skillfully done, the suspense is intriguing, and all is brought to a satisfying conclusion . . . This charmingly written, gentle tale of manners and romance hits the right notes."

—Historical Novel Society for *The Light at Wyndcliff*

"Fans of Julie Klassen will love this."

—*Publishers Weekly* for *The Thief of Lanwyn Manor*

"Cornwall's iconic sea cliffs are on display in *The Thief of Lanwyn Manor*, but it's the lyrical prose, rich historical detail, and layered characters that truly shine on the page. Fans of Regency romance will be instantly drawn in and happily lost within the pages."

—Kristy Cambron, bestselling author
of *The Paris Dressmaker* and
the Lost Castle novels

"*Northanger Abbey* meets *Poldark* against the resplendent and beautifully realized landscape of Cornwall. Ladd shines a spotlight on the limitations of women in an era where they were deprived of agency and instead were commodities in transactions of business and land. The thinking-woman's romance, *The Thief of Lanwyn Manor* is an unputdownable escape."

—Rachel McMillan, author of *The London Restoration*

"Brimming with dangerous secrets, rich characters, and the

hauntingly beautiful descriptions Sarah Ladd handles so well, 1800s Cornwall is brought vividly to life in this well-crafted tale."

—Abigail Wilson, author of *Masquerade at Middlecrest Abbey*, for *The Governess of Penwythe Hall*

"Lovers of sweet and Christian romance will fall in love with Delia's strength amid the haunting backdrop of her tragic past and the Cornish coast."

—Josi S. Kilpack, Whitney Award–winning author of the Mayfield Family series, for *The Governess of Penwythe Hall*

"Absolutely captivating! Once I started reading, I couldn't put down *The Governess of Penwythe Hall*. This blend of *Jane Eyre*, Jane Austen, and *Jamaica Inn* has it all. Intrigue. Danger. Poignant moments. And best of all a sweet, sweet love story. This is by far my favorite Sarah Ladd book."

—Michelle Griep, Christy Award–winning author of the Once Upon a Dickens Christmas series

"A strong choice for fans of historical fiction, especially lovers of Elizabeth Gaskell's *North and South*. It will also appeal to admirers of Kristy Cambron and Tracie Peterson."

—*Library Journal* for *The Weaver's Daughter*

"A gently unfolding love story set amid the turmoil of the early Industrial Revolution. [*The Weaver's Daughter* is] a story of betrayal, love, and redemption, all beautifully rendered in rural England."

—Elizabeth Camden, RITA Award–winning author

"With betrayals, murders, and criminal activity disrupting the peace at Fellsworth, Ladd fills the pages with as much intrigue as romance. A well-crafted story for fans of Regency novels."

—*Publishers Weekly* for *A Stranger at Fellsworth*

"Ladd's story, with its menace and cast of seedy London characters, feels more like a work of Dickens than a Regency . . . A solid outing."

—*Publishers Weekly* for *The Curiosity Keeper*

"A delightful read, rich with period details."

—Sarah M. Eden, bestselling author of *For Elise*, for *The Curiosity Keeper*

"The premise grabbed my attention from the first lines, and I eagerly returned to its pages. I think my readers will enjoy *The Heiress of Winterwood.*"

—Julie Klassen, bestselling, award-winning author

"If you are a fan of Jane Austen and *Jane Eyre*, you will love Sarah E. Ladd's debut."

—USAToday.com for *The Heiress of Winterwood*

An *Unconventional* Lady

Also by Sarah E. Ladd

THE HOUSES OF YORKSHIRE NOVELS

The Letter from Briarton Park

In the Shelter of Hollythorne House

The Cloverton Charade

THE CORNWALL NOVELS

The Governess of Penwythe Hall

The Thief of Lanwyn Manor

The Light at Wyndcliff

THE TREASURES OF SURREY NOVELS

The Curiosity Keeper

Dawn at Emberwilde

A Stranger at Fellsworth

THE WHISPERS ON THE MOORS NOVELS

The Heiress of Winterwood

The Headmistress of Rosemere

A Lady at Willowgrove Hall

STAND-ALONE NOVELS

The Weaver's Daughter

An *Unconventional* Lady

Sarah E. Ladd

THOMAS NELSON
Since 1798

An Unconventional Lady

Published in Nashville, Tennessee, by Thomas Nelson. Thomas Nelson is a registered trademark of HarperCollins Christian Publishing, Inc.

Published in association with Books & Such Literary Management, 52 Mission Circle, Suite 122, PMB 170, Santa Rosa, California 95409–5370, www.booksandsuch.com.

Thomas Nelson titles may be purchased in bulk for educational, business, fundraising, or sales promotional use. For information, please email SpecialMarkets@ThomasNelson.com.

HarperCollins Publishers, Macken House, 39/40 Mayor Street Upper, Dublin 1, D01 C9W8, Ireland (https://www.harpercollins.com)

ISBN 978-1-4003-4831-2 (epub)
ISBN 978-1-4003-4829-9 (TP)
ISBN 978-1-4003-4832-9 (IE)

Library of Congress Cataloging-in-Publication Data

Printed in the United States of America

25 26 27 28 29 LBC 5 4 3 2 1

For C.J.O.—In Loving Memory

Prologue

KEATLEY HALL, GILLHAM, ENGLAND
SEPTEMBER 1810

THIRTEEN-YEAR-OLD ELLA WILDE knew one thing with certainty: Her mother was not a murderer.

Had Leonora Wilde been eccentric? Unconventional and challenging to a fault?

Without a doubt.

But a murderer?

Never.

A bead of perspiration slipped down Ella's flushed face, and she swatted at a fly buzzing about her. The late afternoon was unusually muggy and thick, and the dazzling sunlight sliding through the west-facing conservatory's windows compounded the stifling humidity within the glass walls.

Unable to bide the conservatory's oppressive, still air a moment longer, Ella wiped her brow, removed the apron she'd been wearing to protect her crepe mourning gown, and stepped out to the verdant back garden—a vibrant, luscious extension of the exotic conservatory, with intricately shaped brick paths bordered by meticulously manicured hedgerows, brilliant amethyst Michaelmas daisies, and vibrant aureate chrysanthemums.

The damp breeze gusting down from the western moorlands met her, and she turned her face into it, relishing the momentary distraction of the rich, earthy scent. Ella lifted her long blonde hair off her neck, desperate for relief from the searing heat.

In a few short weeks autumn would creep onto the Keatley Hall grounds, quietly at first, with soft tendrils of cool air, and then suddenly, with an abrupt frost. The oak leaves would fade to gold, and the wind would sweep away all petals of color, leaving behind a gray dormant landscape.

Seven months had passed since her mother's death. Seven long, agonizing months.

Everyone had assured her that time would alleviate the tormenting ache residing in her chest—that breathing would once again become natural, and she'd no longer hear her mother's voice in every creak or puff of wind.

Initially Ella had believed them. She longed for it to be true, but as one monotone, endless month slid into the next, this new, haunting reality cloaked her like a burial shroud. The chasm of disconnected loneliness was widening, and she feared it would swallow her whole.

At first Mother's demise had been deemed accidental—a gown's hem that had passed too close to the fire, catching ablaze with such immediacy that nothing could be done to stop it.

But then . . .

Polite, feminine laughter coming from the adjacent boxwood garden captured her attention. Ella pivoted, curious as to who would venture out on such a blisteringly hot day.

The previous day, nearly fifty guests had descended on Keatley Hall—which was not only a school for boys but her family's ancestral home—for the annual symposium of the Natural Philosophers Society of London.

Normally Ella anticipated the symposium's activity and elegance. It was the one time of year when the expansive halls and corridors were teeming with people other than students. But this year was different, and for now the amber sun hung low in the western sky—so low it seemed to be staring at her, challenging her with its disorienting brightness.

Ella moved into Keatley Hall's sizable shadows, finding comfort in the ancient structure. Her gaze climbed the rust-colored ironstone, up more than three stories to the slate-capped roof and series of symmetrical mullioned windows, as she tried not to think about how her mother could often be seen standing at the windows, surveying the grounds below.

Seeking distraction from melancholy thoughts, Ella rose to the tips of her toes to reassess the voices' origin. Three refined ladies—each the wife of a Society member—stood on the far side of the hedgerow with their backs to her. Their hushed words carried on the breeze.

"You read the pamphlet, did you not? Have you any reason to doubt it?" asked one of the women. "It was written by experts in phrenology—Mrs. Wilde's very own friends."

Ella's family had long been supportive of phrenology—the idea that a person's personality and dispositions were predetermined by the shape of their head. Her mother had been uniquely passionate about it and devoted many years to the study and research of it.

Ella wished she'd never even heard the word.

"So-called friends, I'd say," responded the second lady, "for who would write such atrocious things about someone they considered an acquaintance, let alone a friend?"

"I'm inclined to believe it," the first voice replied. "Mrs. Wilde was volatile by nature. What reason would we have to doubt the men who wrote that pamphlet? What motive would they have to lie?"

Ella inched toward the hedge's edge, wrinkling her nose at the sickly sweet scent of a nearby phlox bloom and holding her breath to hear.

"I simply can't envision Mrs. Wilde intentionally setting a blaze. It's absurd!"

"Absurd or not, several of the servants insisted they heard her shouting prior to the fire, and we all know her opinions and behavior were increasingly radical and at times bizarre."

After a brief lull, the first lady spoke again. "What do you make of the pamphlet's claim that a phrenological assessment was performed on Eleanor when she was an infant? The authors state that she possesses the propensity to behave like her mother."

Ella jolted. They were speaking of her! How could she see the folly of such assumptions when all the adults around her considered them truth?

Ella could stand to hear no more.

It was as if some other power suddenly took control—as if all the grief and anger spiraled together, culminating in one overpowering force. "How dare you!" Ella sprang from the hedgerows onto the brick path, her cry disrupting the swallows on the garden's branches. "How can you say such cruel things about someone you called a friend? Your lies are far worse than anything my mother ever did. At least she told the truth. You are the bizarre, vile ones! If my mother were alive, she'd never forgive you."

With her shouted words still echoing from Keatley Hall's stone exterior walls, Ella whirled and ran. The garden's colors of sage, ochre, and saffron commingled as tears blurred her vision and the heat choked her, making each breath feel as if fire smoldered in her lungs.

Someone called her name, but she did not stop running. She raced through the garden, through the iron gate, and over the craggy meadow. She did not slow her pace until she reached the shadowy shelter of the forest's canopy.

Gasping, Ella dropped to the mossy ground, ripping her stocking on a broken stick and scraping her palm against a chunk of decaying bark. She panted for air.

She'd been rude. Disrespectful.

But she would never *ever* forgive those cruel gossips.

It didn't matter what they had said. She was not bizarre or radical or any of the other words she'd heard whispered in recent days, and neither was her mother.

Most importantly, their words were now etched in her memory, and even if it took until her very last breath, she would prove them wrong.

Chapter 1

KEATLEY HALL, GILLHAM, ENGLAND
AUGUST 1820

BITING HER LOWER lip in concentration, Ella Wilde balanced her mother's handwritten journals in her arms. She'd spent the last week poring over their pages, compiling evidence to strengthen her argument.

In less than one month, the entire body of the Natural Philosophers Society of London would once again descend upon the Keatley Hall School for Boys for their annual symposium. Preventing the event would be impossible, but maybe, just maybe, she could convince her father to discourage Mr. Bauer's attendance.

With each step along the uneven wooden planks of Keatley Hall's first-floor corridor, Ella silently rehearsed her rationale. Until now her father had met her attempts to broach the topic with lukewarm tolerance, but time was running out.

Without knocking, she turned into the open door of her father's study. The late-morning sunlight flooded the narrow room, illuminating the dust motes hovering in the stale air and splaying across a desktop cluttered with letters and haphazard stacks of books.

Philip Wilde looked up from the letter he was writing. His

attention fell to the journals in Ella's arms, and after a long sigh, he plucked his spectacles from his nose and lowered them to the desk.

"I know what you're thinking," Ella interjected energetically before he could speak. "But this is something you need to hear."

She placed the journals on the desk and scurried to the tall leaded casement window and pushed the heavy pane outward. It squeaked as it opened, and cool air swirled in.

Her father leaned back in his chair and folded his arms over his chest. "The decision's already been made, Ella."

"You might change your mind if you would but read Mother's accounts of Mr. Bauer's past actions. They're atrocious! You'll see—"

"It's out of my hands," he interrupted, his tone firm. "The Natural Philosophers Society *will* come to Keatley Hall, and Mr. Bauer *will* be the speaker."

"How can you say it's out of your hands?" Ella challenged as she adjusted the window's stay to prop it open. "Keatley Hall belongs to you, not the Society. Surely you have a say in what occurs under its roof."

"I've already given the itinerary and guest list my blessing. I know you have reservations, but I—"

"Reservations?" Ella spun from the window. "Father, that man helped to write that horrific pamphlet. He accused Mother of insanity, not to mention me. How can you even consider allowing him to step a single foot into Keatley Hall?"

With renewed energy she approached the desk. "This gathering is an opportunity to expose the true nature of phrenology. The very notion that the shape and size of a person's head could affect their behavior is ludicrous. *Everyone* will be here. A little education, healthy debate, and we can put the entire matter of phrenology to rest. I emphatically believe it is what Mother would have—"

"No." He fixed his light, rheumy eyes on her with unwavering directness in a rare display of authority. "Hawthorne's made his choice, and as the Society's leader, his decision is final. I'll not prevent it. Regardless of what we may think of Mr. Bauer personally, he is respected in his field and will be here as the Society's invited expert. And need I remind you that the Society's endorsement is the singular lifeblood of Keatley School? If they were to retract their support, where would we be? Any argument that should arise will not be ours to engage in, and you will not contradict him. Am I clear?"

Ella noisily exhaled the breath she'd been holding and peered out to Keatley Hall's still forecourt to refocus her thoughts.

Phrenology.

How she despised it.

Her mother and maternal grandfather had at one time both been passionate about studying the new theory coming from Austria, but over time its flaws and improper application became too obvious to ignore. Her mother had denounced the theory shortly before her death, but then the pamphlet was published.

And everything changed.

A week did not go by that Ella did not encounter the repercussions of the outlandish fallacy in one fashion or another, and now it had been thrust once again to the forefront of their lives. She detested living under the shadow of such rumors and was more determined than ever to prove them false.

Her father's tone softened to a gentler timbre, just as it did whenever he'd speak of Leonora. "How you continually remind me of your mother. Like you, she'd embrace an idea and refuse to let it go. I understand why you are opposed to this, but remember, nothing was more important to your mother—or your grandfather—than this school. For that reason I refuse to allow anger to affect my judgment."

Ella's gaze drifted to the large watercolor portrait of her mother hanging above the mantel. She took in the sharp mahogany eyes and an abundance of unruly raven hair that consistently resisted even the simplest chignon's hold.

Her father's words snapped her back to the conversation. "My only concern now is the school's future and what will become of it when I am gone, which also, I might add, greatly affects you."

The study's heavy atmosphere shifted as tangibly as if a cloud had eclipsed the sun, and guilt descended as the conversation took a turn she hadn't anticipated.

Father pushed unsteadily against the carved arms of his chair and stood. The white sunlight streaked through the dust-caked west window, highlighting his nose's high bridge and intensifying the shadowing of his cheek's hollow. With a hefty sigh he straightened his checked bottle-green waistcoat as he stepped to the window and looked out over the forecourt.

"I'll admit, daughter, that I failed you. I permitted—nay, encouraged—you to become engaged to Mr. Rawlston. I believed him to be a man of integrity. I was wrong, and you're forced to bear the brunt of his deception. I'm sorry for my oversight."

Ella's muscles tensed as the recollection surfaced. Her engagement to Mr. Rawlston had not been a love match, but his abrupt decision to sever the arrangement still stung like betrayal. "He made his own choice. It was not your fault."

"Yes, but a father's duty is to protect and provide. I should have been more thorough in my scrutiny."

The expectation for her had always been clear—and monumental. For Keatley Hall to stay in the family, Ella simply needed to be married when her father died. Then, as a part of her dowry, the school would pass to her husband, who ideally would assume the role of headmaster. If she was not married, however, Keatley Hall, the school, and all its holdings would pass to a distant cousin, thereby dissolving any right she had to her beloved home.

Mere weeks ago, the future had seemed so secure. Mr. Rawlston had been supportive of her goal of opening a school for girls, and work had even commenced to convert a vacant cottage on the property to a smaller school in the coming year. But after he unexpectedly broke off the engagement, every plan—every dream—screeched to a halt. Her dowry might consist of the legendary Keatley House and school, but it came with the heavy contingency of maintaining the relationship with the Society, and that responsibility ruled out many men.

"Speaking of an uncertain future." Her father's forced brightness did little to alleviate the mounting tension. "I've devised a solution to this predicament that should both satisfy the Society's need to support our plans for the next generation of students and put our minds to rest. I've been in contact with Abraham Abernathy on this very subject."

Abraham Abernathy.

The blood in her veins cooled.

The ticking of the mantel clock intensified. The air breezing through the window warmed. She could protest Mr. Bauer. She could challenge perceptions and misconceptions, but there was no abating this one.

"Father, I—"

Her father's arched brow and intense stare silenced her. "Abernathy's been at the school for years. He's proven himself loyal time and time again, and he knows the inner workings as well as you and I. I believe him to be genuine, even-tempered, and reasonable. What's more, he's amenable to helping this situation."

This situation—as if she were a problem to be solved—an offending stone in an otherwise smooth path.

The certainty in his tone evoked alarm, yet Ella refused to give in to emotion. "Let's discuss this first. I think—"

"Discuss what, Ella? Time for all such discussion has passed. You're three and twenty, and I shudder at the thought of what would happen should my heart have another episode. I'm ill. Anyone may see it, and if not already, everyone will be aware of it at the symposium. This life of mine has been gratifying and full of accomplishments, but if I die knowing that my only daughter's future is not secure, what is the point? You, my dearest Eleanor, owe it to your family's legacy to continue this work that generations have poured into, not pursue dusty journals filled with random musings and argue against a phrenologist who will be here one day and gone the next. Do you understand?"

A thousand sharp retorts lined up like vigilant soldiers standing at attention in her mind, ready to defend her. Yet her throat felt dry. The words would not form.

This resolute manner was unusual for her father. His normal attentions were on the philosophical or scientific . . . rarely on practical matters. When he did ultimately speak on them, it was not until he was determined.

For he was right.

If he died, she would have nothing: No family. Very little money. And no options to speak of.

She looked at the journals she'd dropped on his desk, almost embarrassed at the plucky sanguinity that had accompanied her into the chamber. The confidence that her father would be persuaded by them was as deflated as her optimism for her future now that Abraham Abernathy had been named as a contender—if not the *only* contender—for her hand.

"Those are exactly what I am talking about," he blurted, as if noting her shift of attention and pointing toward the dusty tomes. "You must trust me on this matter and cease this foolhardy obsession with proving Mr. Bauer's incompetence. Do not give anyone ammunition against you. Given enough room, Mr. Bauer will dig his own grave. Men like that always do."

Chapter 2

LONDON, ENGLAND
AUGUST 1820

IT WOULD BE SO much easier to pretend he'd not recently become aware of certain information and abandon the idea of this letter altogether. But he *had* heard it, and now that he knew the truth, a moral battle raged.

Gabriel Rowe adjusted his grip on the quill, rested his forearm against the desktop, but stopped short of pressing the nib to the paper. He paused, rolled the quill in his fingertips, and questioned, yet again, the wisdom of the action he was about to undertake.

Thomas Bauer, the phrenologist who had so captivated the interest of the natural philosophers of the city, was a fraud.

In a few weeks Mr. Bauer was to speak before the Natural Philosophers Society of London—an organization that Gabriel's own father was once associated with and that many of his friends and acquaintances still participated in.

As Gabriel thought about the missive he intended to write, though, it seemed absurd. Would he even be taken seriously?

The nearby candle lamp's amber light flickered against his modest office's plaster walls. Just outside, a heavy late-summer rain pummeled the bustling London street, temporarily drowning out the sounds of shouts, voices, carriages, and wagons. Gabriel tapped the toe of his boot against the planked floor as he considered his options.

He could not share this information with Mr. Hawthorne, the head of the Society, for he and Bauer were rumored to be great friends.

He could not go to Mr. Wilde, the headmaster of the school Gabriel had attended and the man whose estate was the location of the symposium, for his loyalty to both the Society and Mr. Hawthorne was famously unwavering.

The scenario left only one person who would be empathetic enough to listen and perhaps find a way to act before it was too late—Miss Eleanor Wilde. But even that seemed far-fetched.

The willful young girl with the untamed honey-hued hair, sun-kissed cheeks, and bright blue eyes flashed in his vision. They'd been friends when he was a student at Keatley Hall, but that had been years ago. Gabriel had not seen her since, but her name would be mentioned from time to time in certain circles, and she was rumored to be passionate, fearless, and obstinate.

Was it right to contact her with such information?

After shoving his fingers through his disheveled hair, which was in dire need of a cut, he blew out his breath in exasperation and glanced to the stack of paperwork he needed to attend to—wills, trusts, guardianships, and other legal documents that would eventually be signed and stored away. They were the tasks that brought in regular money, but they seemed dull and inconsequential. Gabriel's true passion was for the cases of significance, the ones that would have substantial impact.

Exposing Mr. Bauer would have just such importance.

Practically, assisting a group such as the Society would open a whole new clientele for him. With his sister now living with him and depending on him for support, he needed all the work he could get. At best he could save the Society—not to mention the Wilde family—from an embarrassing blunder. At worst he could shine light on a major mistake and risk alienating himself from some of the most influential men in London.

Regardless of the possible risks and rewards, he possessed information that no one else knew, and his honor forbade him from allowing a preventable injustice to occur.

Gabriel dabbed the quill in the inkpot once again and pressed the quill to the paper.

Dear Miss Wilde . . .

Chapter 3

KEATLEY HALL'S CONSERVATORY wrapped Ella in its warmth, and for the moment memories of the strained conversation with her father faded. She closed her eyes and inhaled deeply, flooding her lungs with the red Bengal rose's musky, sweet aroma and allowing the scent to transport her to a moment from well over a decade prior.

"The Rosa chinensis. *All the way from China!"* Her mother's dark eyes had been wide and bright when she first introduced the plant to Ella. *"It blooms several times a year. Not like the European roses, which bloom only once. Isn't that a marvel?"*

"The China rose." Ella whispered the bloom's common name as she opened her eyes and gently touched her fingertip to the soft crimson petals. This plant, with its prickly stems, lustrous dark leaves, and vibrant hue, had been her mother's final addition to the lush conservatory before her death. With each new blossom it felt as if her mother was still with her.

Returning to the task at hand, Ella smoothed the worn linen apron over her striped ivory muslin gown, secured it around her waist, then lifted her pruning scissors. Three of the conservatory's four walls were lined with broad leaded windows, and dusk's purple glow cast a long streak of light on the plethora of plants thriving within. Dahlias. Dianthus. Geraniums. Lilies. Two lemon trees. Three orange trees. A Japanese hydrangea. And dozens more.

The stillness and beauty of this space usually offered peace and a sense of connectedness, but despite the memories residing here, melancholy and loneliness prevailed.

Several days had passed since she had spoken with her father in his study, and Ella continued to wrestle with their conversation.

He'd urged her to trust him.

Ella had always trusted her parents implicitly. She had no reason to doubt that her unorthodox upbringing, which included an intense formal education that would rival that of any boy, could be anything but beneficial. She'd never questioned her parents' decision to forgo any instruction in traditional feminine pursuits that would equip her for polite society.

After her mother died, life with her father continued in the same patterns as it always had: education and study, debate and conversation. She'd long been praised for her original ideas and enduring confidence, but somewhere in the past year's murkiness and unexpected events, the tides had turned. No longer was she encouraged to forge her own path, and her once-welcome opinions and suggestions now fell on deaf ears.

Her father's new demand for compliance was demoralizing.

Ella understood his arguments—to a point. She'd been allowed much more freedom of thought and action than most young women. Would she enjoy such autonomy after he died, when she was left to contend with the world alone without his shelter and provision?

Time was not on their side, and difficult decisions needed to be made, but her trust in him, for the first time, was waning. How could she really trust anyone when the rules were constantly shifting in a game she did not understand?

She clipped a fading leaf from the rose's stem and then another. She should feel relieved at Mr. Abernathy's interest. It was no secret that she had to marry, and it never had been. If she did not, she'd lose her beloved conservatory, not to mention the dream she'd been planning for since her mother died—offering education for girls.

Her mother had been very clear: While grateful that Keatley Hall could provide such a stout education for boys, she was frustrated that young women were not given the same opportunity to develop and expand their minds. Ella mirrored her mother's abhorrence of the unequal treatment, and if she could help even a few young women find power through education, she would be gratified.

But somewhere, somehow, time had slipped by, slowly and largely unnoticed, and the practicalities of life had dwarfed urgency. Suddenly action was inevitable, and the price to keep her dreams alive would be dear indeed.

The idea of matrimony was generally agreeable to Ella, and she'd never opposed the idea of marriage to Nathaniel Rawlston. She had not loved him, but he was amiable, astute, and could engage in a pleasurable conversation. Most importantly, he shared her family's vision for furthering the natural philosophies in all forms.

But Abraham Abernathy? The idea would take getting used to.

Movement at the conservatory's glass door caught her attention. Mrs. Chatterly, their housekeeper, stood in the doorway, a shawl wrapped around her thin shoulders and a candlestick in her hand. "I thought I'd find you here."

Refusing to appear out of sorts, Ella forced a smile. "Of course I'm here! Did you see these new blooms? Aren't they lovely?"

Mrs. Chatterly had been Ella's mother's lady's maid, and after Ella's mother's death, Mrs. Chatterly assumed the role of Keatley Hall's housekeeper. Besides Ella's father, Mrs. Chatterly had been the one constant in Ella's life.

The older woman stepped in farther and wordlessly assessed the bloom in question before she spoke. "Your father informed me that he'd been in conversations with Mr. Abernathy. He also told me why."

Ella's smile faded. She knew better than to attempt to fool Mrs. Chatterly with a feigned cheery disposition. "I suppose I should be pleased. A solution at last. Father has figured it out. I shouldn't question it."

Mrs. Chatterly stepped to a small wooden worktable just inside the door, scooted a stack of empty pots to the side, and placed her chamberstick next to it. "But you are questioning it, aren't you?"

Ella's response felt heavy on her tongue, preventing her from an immediate response. Mr. Abernathy was such a diversion from the plan—a diversion that made her feel as if she'd been tricked instead of contributing to the solution. "You think he's right, don't you?"

"It doesn't matter what I think, does it?" Mrs. Chatterly tilted her graying head to the side, her eyes unnervingly direct.

"Yes. It does."

Mrs. Chatterly sighed and walked around Ella to the far side of the table, where a mature potted lemon tree stretched its glossy leaves and perfumed the air with its zesty aroma. "Do you remember when you were a young girl and you'd encounter something you didn't like or understand? What would your mother tell you to do?"

"Be curious."

The unspoken words were ingrained on her mind and heart. The phrase had been her mother's solution to any conundrum and was the first advice she would offer when faced with a dilemma—to neutralize the emotion and approach something rationally.

Mrs. Chatterly's intense gaze did not shift, and Ella knew it would not until she gave the housekeeper the correct answer. "To be curious."

"That's right." Mrs. Chatterly lifted her pointed chin, as if satisfied that her clue had incited the answer to her riddle. "And I believe she would urge you to be curious about Mr. Abernathy."

Ella's nose wrinkled in response.

Mrs. Chatterly's dry laugh filled the chamber. "He's not that ghastly, dear child. We've all known him a long time."

Ella snipped another leaf.

Mrs. Chatterly was right, she supposed, but in all the years Ella had known Mr. Abernathy, she'd barely noticed him. He was quiet. Plain. Unremarkable.

Mrs. Chatterly did not stop. "I imagine the bigger question would be, why would he *not* be interested in this arrangement? He's served the school loyally for over a decade, and becoming headmaster would be his next logical step. It would mean great social advancement for him. What reasonable man would not relish such prestige and responsibility?"

Ella's words seemed almost ridiculous as they passed her lips. "But he doesn't care about *me*."

Mrs. Chatterly shook her head. "You were not thinking of a

romantic relationship with Mr. Rawlston. Why is this different? Mr. Abernathy's a good man. No, he's not as entertaining or charming as Mr. Rawlston, but maybe he's better suited. This would hardly be the first marriage concocted for a specific purpose. With mutual respect and common interests, it will end up all right."

Ella wanted to scream at the injustice of it. How could Mrs. Chatterly condone this idea? Just because she was a woman, she was forced into this horrid ultimatum—marry or lose the life she'd always known. Her mother would be appalled.

Ella could fight it. She could cry out all the reasons why this wasn't fair, but what good would come of it?

She lifted her gaze to the leaded glass that formed the conservatory's ceiling and to the fading twilight overhead. Whether she liked it or not, she was bound to Keatley Hall by an inexplicable devotion that transcended her own personal aspirations and inclinations. She was destined to live the rest of her years here, and she'd make any sacrifice necessary to make that happen. "I cannot leave Keatley Hall."

"And there's no reason you should." Mrs. Chatterly's tone lifted optimistically, as if to signal a change in topic. "Soon we will depart for London, yes? There you shall see Miss Hawthorne. Perhaps chatting with her about this will help you find clarity."

The mention of Phoebe Hawthorne bolstered Ella's weary spirits. As Mr. Hawthorne's only daughter, Phoebe often accompanied Ella to Society events. Phoebe had been her best, and only true female friend for as long as she could remember.

"The fear of a thing is sometimes worse than the actual event. We build things up in our minds, but rarely do they meet our expectations. Don't stay down here too late." Mrs. Chatterly offered a warm smile, but as she turned to quit the conservatory, she paused and retrieved a letter from the pocket in the folds of her gown. "Oh, and merciful me, I nearly forgot. The entire reason I came to find you! A letter arrived for you."

Ella accepted the missive, and after the housekeeper had left, Ella turned the letter to identify the sender and frowned at the strong, unfamiliar handwriting. She wiped her free hand on her apron before she slipped her finger beneath the seal to pop it open.

Instinctively her gaze flicked to the signature to find out who it was from.

Gabriel Rowe.

She jerked, surprised. It was a name she'd not heard in a very long time—a man who had been a student at their school years ago.

She flipped open the letter.

Dear Miss Wilde,

I apologize for the intrusive nature of this letter, and I hope I do not offend. My only goal is to provide information that I hope may prove beneficial.

It has been a while since we last spoke, but currently I am a solicitor and work in law. I am aware that Mr. Bauer is to be the speaker at the symposium at Keatley Hall. I have reason to question Mr. Bauer's credentials and his intentions, and I am concerned that his reputation might negatively affect the school and the Society. I do not wish to cause trouble, but because of my past relationship with the school and the Society, and my respect for your family, I want to share what I have learned.

If you would like the information, please contact me at the enclosed address and I will be happy to share it with you.

Shock slowed her thoughts.

Then her satisfaction roared to a flame.

This letter validated her concerns, did it not? And if Mr. Rowe made the effort to contact her after all this time, the information must be damning indeed.

Ella tapped the letter against her hand thoughtfully before she folded it again and put it in her apron pocket. She'd promised her father she'd not intervene or act on her suspicions, but the dubious nature of her situation left her no option: If Mr. Rowe had viable proof, then she had no choice but to investigate it.

Perhaps all hope was not lost after all.

Chapter 4

ELLA GLANCED UP at the elegant Hawthorne town house, with its four stories of uniformly paned sashed windows, its fresh white stucco facade, the impressive Corinthian columns on each side of the large black entry door, and the wrought-iron railings separating its front stairway from the street. She looked down the row of impressively elegant and uniform houses gleaming in the afternoon sun.

How different this home was from Keatley Hall, with its ancient stones and windswept grounds. How exciting and modern.

"You're here at last!" cried Phoebe as she rushed from the front entrance, her nutmeg curls bouncing on each side of her fair face with each hurried step. Enthusiasm gleamed in her light brown eyes, and once she was close, she grabbed Ella's gloved hand in her own. "It seemed you would never arrive."

Ella stepped aside as a footman assisted Mrs. Chatterly from the carriage. "I'm sorry we are late. The road had flooded not far out of town."

"You're here now, and that's all that matters. Come with me," Phoebe urged energetically, unaffected by their elegant surroundings and the bevy of servants who'd appeared to welcome the carriage. "We've so much to catch up on!"

After parting ways with Mrs. Chatterly, who had accompanied her not only as a chaperone but also to speak with the Hawthorne staff regarding the symposium, Ella and Phoebe made their way to Phoebe's first-floor bedchamber.

The instant the heavy paneled door to the bright, high-ceilinged bedchamber closed, Phoebe whirled and clasped her hands together, and her animated expression sobered. "Before either of us says a single word, I must tell you how terribly sorry I am about what happened with Mr. Rawlston. I'm just sick about it."

Ella stiffened. This was the first time she'd seen Phoebe since Mr. Rawlston severed the engagement. Ella knew she'd have to discuss it, but sharing her private feelings had never been easy, not even with those close to her. "It was quite a shock, but I'm all right. Please, there's no need to be upset."

"Did he offer you an explanation?" Phoebe blinked. "An apology? Anything?"

The brief and painfully undetailed letter flashed in her mind's eye. "Only that he no longer believed us to be compatible. He thought it cruel to continue with the arrangement when he knew we could never be truly happy as man and wife."

"Oh, my dear. You must be devastated!" Phoebe dropped onto the chair next to the mantelpiece.

Devastated.

Phoebe's word choice seemed melodramatic, but perhaps no word could be more accurate—especially when she considered the predicament the situation put her in.

She'd never let anyone know how much the rejection affected her, for she refused to be pitied, and anything stated to the contrary would do just that. "No, I'm not devastated. It's merely a change in plans. It's behind me now, I assure you."

Phoebe scoffed, her jaw dropping in unmasked disbelief. "Behind you? If that is indeed true, then you're much more composed than I could ever be. I daresay it is a blessing that you found out the truth about him before the engagement proceeded any further."

Phoebe was right, of course. It would be worse to learn of his fickle nature after they were married, but now the stigma of a woman whose intended broke off the engagement haunted her. What was more, there was no hiding from it. "I only dread the comments and the stares. Everyone at the symposium will know. When we visit the assembly rooms tonight, I fear I will be a spectacle."

"Oh, who cares about them?" Phoebe waved a dismissive hand. "Most of the people who will be at the symposium are grumpy old men who have little interest in such things. And how many women will be there? A few at best. They are busybodies with little else to do besides gossip. Regarding the assembly room, everyone there will be too worried about their appearance to give much thought to anything else."

Ella smiled at Phoebe's attempt to lighten the situation. She could always count on her friend to be firmly on her side. "Enough of that. Have you news for me? I'm desperate for a diversion. I've not seen you in months! Surely there is something you haven't shared in your letters."

At the suggestion, a pretty pink flushed Phoebe's round

cheeks, and she chewed her lower lip. "Well," she began slowly as she fussed with the lace cuff of her sleeve, "since you asked, there is something I should like to share with you, but I'm hesitant to do so."

Ella frowned and sat on one of the carved wooden chairs next to the marble mantelpiece to be at eye level with her friend. "Why? We're dear friends, are we not?"

"Indeed we are!" Phoebe's high-waisted turquoise muslin gown rustled as she pivoted to fully face Ella. "But I am afraid you might not like what I tell you."

Ella took Phoebe's hand in her own to reassure her. "I can't imagine that."

"I'm happy to hear you say that, because if I don't tell someone soon, I might burst!" A girlish giggle bubbled from Phoebe, and she gave a little squeal. "I have met a gentleman. Ella, I have! A most handsome, attentive, wonderful man!"

Relief rushed through Ella. She'd prepared herself to hear the worst, but this was happy news. "Why on earth would I be upset about that? I think it's wonderful!"

Phoebe shook her head intently, sending the loose curls framing her face dancing before her expression sobered once again. "It's a great secret. No one knows. You must tell no one. Especially not my father."

"Of course, but who is the gentleman?"

Phoebe drew a shuddery breath, then exhaled it in a long, slow stream before finally making eye contact with Ella. "You might be shocked when I tell you, for I'm quite certain he is the last person on earth you'd expect me to say. He's older than me by at least two and a half decades. He'll attend the assembly rooms later, which is why I was so insistent we go there tonight. It is Mr. Thomas Bauer."

Ella's hands went numb. Every bit of air fled her lungs. Had she been struck? The name rang in her ears, and each syllable echoed in the air.

Thomas Bauer. The phrenologist.

The man Gabriel Rowe had written to warn her about.

The rosy glow faded from Phoebe's face, and she jerked her hand away from Ella's. "Oh no. I knew it would upset you. I—"

"No, no!" Ella protested, ignoring the alarming, knifelike stab that seemed to restrain her breathing. "I'm surprised, is all."

"I can assure you that no one—not even you—is more surprised than myself."

Ella shook her head, dislodging her disbelief and attempting to maintain as normal a countenance as possible. "I knew Mr. Bauer was a friend of your father's, but how is it that the two of you became friendly?"

Phoebe jumped from the chair, stepped back to the wardrobe, and lifted a gown that had been hanging just inside. "It all happened so suddenly. So wonderfully! Mr. Bauer first called on Father about six months ago when he approached him with the idea of reintroducing phrenology to the Society. At first Father was skeptical, and understandably so, given what has happened between him and your family, but over time Father came to realize that Mr. Bauer is a brilliant man—one from whom we can learn much about what is being done in other countries. Ever since then we've been in each other's company quite frequently."

Ella's thoughts raced. Phoebe was aware of her deeply rooted disdain for the man. The relationship must be serious if she would mention it to Ella. A dozen questions, demands, and even accusations balanced on the tip of her tongue, but it would not do to upset or alienate Phoebe, who was one of the only people who truly cared for her. "You said not to tell your father. If he's not aware of the attachment, how is it that you have spent time together?"

Phoebe held the gauzy lilac gown up to her shoulders and turned to assess the reflection in the looking glass in the chamber's corner. "Mr. Bauer has dined at our house on numerous occasions. We've also been together at all the usual places. Balls. The assembly rooms. The park. We've had to be so careful to mask our true feelings. He doesn't want anyone to accuse him of using our relationship to sway my father's favor, but I told him I could never keep such a secret from you."

Ella struggled to make sense of what she was hearing. "And Mr. Bauer is to be at the assembly rooms tonight?"

"He is! I've shared how important you are to me, and he's hopeful that the two of you can become friends. Oh, and he is aware of your frustrations regarding the pamphlet and all that happened, but he believes it is all a big misunderstanding and that all can be mended."

Phoebe spoke of the pamphlet as if it were such a minor issue—a small hurdle in her life's path—when in fact it had been one of the most defining occurrences of Ella's existence. This man had a hand in turning her life upside down, and he referred to it as a big misunderstanding?

Ella forced her breathing to remain slow, for what other option did she have other than to be agreeable? "I will do my best to give him the benefit of the doubt. For your sake."

Phoebe, beaming with pleasure, turned her attention back to the filmy gown and prattled on about the new satin dancing slippers she'd purchased just for their visit to the assembly rooms later that evening.

As Ella listened to her friend's happy chatter, she became even more determined: Not only had Mr. Thomas Bauer affected her, but now he was affecting her friend. If Mr. Gabriel Rowe had information about him, she had no choice but to seek him out and find out what he knew.

Chapter 5

TORCHES BLAZED AND gas lamps flickered their orange light on the slick brick street in front of the Clancy Assembly Rooms. For as far as Ella could see, carriage lamps illuminated the row of black carriages, shiny from the evening's drizzle. Pungent scents of smoke and fish drifted from the nearby Thames River and mingled with the raindrops, and a general hum of excited energy surged in the night's atmosphere.

Ella stepped from the Hawthorne carriage, ignoring how the damp air chilled the bare skin of her arms. She gathered the thin muslin skirt of her gown, now limp from the air's moisture, and hurried to follow Phoebe through the main entrance.

At the beginning of the season, Ella had attended this assembly room with Mr. Rawlston, and she'd portrayed confidence and happiness. They had just announced their engagement, and their fellow guests were eager to offer congratulations to the well-known, affable young man and his soon-to-be bride.

How different it all was now. Not only was she the marked woman, the result of a broken engagement, but she would also meet face-to-face the very man she was trying so desperately to avoid. Mr. Bauer.

As she stepped farther into the vestibule, curious stares were cast in her direction from both ladies and gentlemen alike. Were they feeling sorry for her? Wondering if the rumors about her were true?

Phoebe, clad in a gown of shimmery lilac gauze, with her hair forced into curls and piled atop her head, was blissfully unaffected as she looped her gloved hand through Ella's arm. "Do not give any of them a second thought. Tonight will be delightful. You'll see."

Ella nodded, simultaneously wishing she could share her friend's optimism and inhaling deeply to bolster herself.

As uncomfortable as she was, there was no denying the magical quality of the lively dancing music and the conversation's energetic hum once she entered the ballroom. She joined the mass of people, all searching for a place to stand or watch. She smiled apologetically at a young man who inadvertently bumped her shoulder, and she aided a woman who dropped her reticule. The loud, buoyant music impeded any sort of serious conversation, and she rose to the tips of her toes to locate the tearoom's entrance. The image of tall, awkward Abraham Abernathy flashed in her mind, and Ella tried to envision him in this environment.

"It's so stuffy in here." Phoebe tightened her arm around Ella's and leaned close. "Come, let's go to the tearoom and find Mr. Bauer. He told me that Mr. Clancy has permitted him to do demonstrations there."

Together they left the only partly watchful eye of Mrs. Nolting, their chaperone, and wound their way through the dense crowd, weaving around clusters of people and waiting for the dancing to shift so they could make their way through.

The tearoom, which was usually set with elegant tables and light refreshments, had been transformed. It was every bit as crowded as the other chambers, but it was oddly quiet, save for the echo of music, voices, and laughter reverberating from the ballroom.

"There he is!" Phoebe said softly. "There, on the platform."

Everything else faded as Ella locked her eyes on Thomas Bauer.

His broad back was to them, obscuring his face. A plump woman in saffron organza was seated before him with her brunette locks loose over her shoulders. His thick hands were placed on each side of her head, and periodically he'd whisper something to a young man next to him. He must be in the midst of a reading.

Curiosity seized Ella. She'd read everything she could find about phrenology, but she'd never actually witnessed a phrenological assessment being performed.

As Ella watched his hands glide over the lady's head, doubt crept in. Phrenology had gained popularity in several cities on the Continent. Many well-educated, critically minded people embraced the study, and judging by the comments around her, those gathered were captivated. What if she'd been wrong all along and it was a viable practice?

"Isn't it amazing?" whispered Phoebe excitedly. "Come on. Let's move closer."

As they approached, Mr. Bauer pivoted and his features came into focus. He was easily one of the tallest men in the room and cut an imposing figure, with a shock of black hair streaked with gray at the temples and side-whiskers. His square face was flushed—due, no doubt, to the chamber's exceptional heat and abundance of candles—with thick black brows, a strong, hooked nose, and thick lips.

"He's quite entertaining." Phoebe's adoring gaze did not waver. "And so insightful. Just wait until you see what he can deduce about this lady."

Mr. Bauer continued to move his hands methodically—mesmerizingly—over the woman's head. Ella recognized the patterns he employed. In phrenology the head's surface was divided into sections, and the size and shape of each section was said to give insight into a specific personality trait.

After several moments, Mr. Bauer stepped away from the woman, took the notes from the man assisting him, and, after reviewing them, turned to the crowd. "Mrs. Whetham," his deep voice boomed, "can you please confirm to these good people that you and I are not acquainted and that I know nothing of your character or life?"

Mrs. Whetham toyed with the glittering topaz pendant at her neck and, almost like a coquettish schoolgirl, blushed. "Of course not, Mr. Bauer. I've never met you before this night."

"Then I will rely on those of you present who are well acquainted with Mrs. Whetham to confirm the validity of my assessment. Based on my findings, I can attest that Mrs. Whetham has a very calm disposition and is rarely incited to anger. If she does rise to anger, injustice or mistreatment of the less fortunate is certainly the cause. Even though she has the propensity to feel emotions very deeply, she displays valiant self-moderation and controls them admirably. Loyalty is perhaps her strongest virtue, and her awareness of the needs of others often guides her generous actions. I suspect she is quieter than she is outspoken—she listens more than she speaks—and she is limited in what she shares with others."

Hushed whispers circled the crowd, followed by a burst of applause.

Surprised at the report's brevity and the trivial nature of the qualities addressed, Ella joined in the clapping.

Next to her, Phoebe applauded the demonstration emphatically. A deep rose stained her cheeks, and her chestnut-brown eyes shone with such brilliance that Ella feared her friend might cry.

Still unsure of what to make of the spectacle she had just witnessed, Ella observed the chamber. Even more onlookers had gathered, drawn no doubt by the thunderous acclamation.

The scene sparked recollections of the notes in her mother's journal—that phrenologists were using such amusing demonstrations to bring attention to the discipline. The problem was that the phrenologists were bending their findings to depict their specimens in the most favorable light, and what was more, they were even accepting payments to use phrenology as a means to mold a person's image. This had been her mother's fear—that the science and anatomical truths associated with phrenology, if they indeed existed, would devolve to nothing more than a parlor trick.

With each moment that passed, Ella's discomfort grew, and after Mr. Bauer finished speaking with some of the guests, he approached Phoebe.

At first he didn't seem to notice Ella. His attention was focused entirely on Phoebe, and his expression, which until this point had been distinguished, lightened to one much more flirtatious. "Miss Hawthorne! What a pleasure to see you. I hoped you would be here tonight."

Phoebe curtsied prettily and extended her hand. "You know I'd never miss a demonstration of yours if it could be helped."

He touched his fingertips to her gloved ones and bowed low, then leaned closer to her. "Did you enjoy it?"

"I always enjoy your demonstrations. But see? I've a surprise for you. Someone you've long wanted to meet."

He raised his thick dark brows. "Oh?"

Ella straightened her posture and lifted her chin.

Beaming, Phoebe pivoted toward her. "May I present my very dear friend, Miss Eleanor Wilde of Keatley Hall."

Mr. Bauer jerked. He stared at her, and then a captivated smile quirked his full lips, as if he were assessing a rare jewel. "Why, this cannot be! Miss Wilde, Mrs. Leonora Wilde's daughter. Of course, I would know you anywhere."

Ella ignored the statement as a mere nicety, for indeed she bore no physical resemblance to her mother. She curtsied. "Good evening, sir."

As much as she attempted to downplay the situation and avoid drawing any attention, Mr. Bauer seemed to grow larger before her eyes. His baritone voice boomed in the vast chamber and echoed from the ornately plastered ceiling. "Oh, it is my most delighted pleasure! All these years I have wondered about you. Indeed I have! There now, I see the disbelief in your eyes, but you forget, your mother was a friend of mine." Mr. Bauer lifted his gaze to glance around the chamber. "Is your father present tonight?"

"I'm afraid not," Ella responded. "He remains at Keatley Hall."

"Meeting you, then, must be enough to tide me."

Someone called his name, and he looked back over his shoulder. "If my time were my own, I would spend every moment with you ladies, but it is not. I have promised more assessments, and what better way to share my passion for this theory than to share it with the world, eh?" He bowed, ostentatiously low and formal, his eyes fixed firmly on Phoebe's. "Perhaps later we might speak again."

As quickly as he had joined them, he was absorbed back with the others.

Nothing he said would be considered inappropriate or unfriendly. Indeed, everything had happened as politely and smoothly as possible.

Ella told herself not to let her predetermined opinions interfere, especially if he was to be her dearest friend's beau, but the stilted display she'd witnessed made her even more concerned. She had hoped that meeting him in person would change her mind for Phoebe's sake, but what she had seen did little to calm her nerves.

Chapter 6

GABRIEL CHOSE THE law as his profession for one reason: his sister, Mary.

At one time, Mary's large, tawny eyes and infectious laugh had been vibrant—so full of life—but circumstances had faded her once-bright complexion and cheery disposition into something quite unrecognizable.

This was not what Gabriel thought life would be like at this age—for him or for his sister.

What sort of future would she have, living here in his small terrace house with no friends, acquaintances, or other family? Was this how she was to spend the rest of her life? But after what she'd endured at the hands of another, he could almost understand.

If he could, he would take the shame and anguish that Mary had been forced to endure on himself. Instead, he would do his best to improve her future and do what he could to make sure no other woman was in the same situation.

But what could be done?

Gabriel cleared his throat as he stepped farther into the parlor. "I'll be out late tonight."

Mary looked up from the book she was reading. "How handsome you look. I wasn't aware you were going out tonight."

"I'm meeting with a client." Gabriel reached for his cobalt wool coat and slid his arms through the sleeves. "Will you be all right alone?"

"Of course. Mrs. Menton will be here with me. And Liza."

It pained him that Mary considered their housekeeper and maid as suitable companions, but nothing could be done. He'd just received the missive from Andrew Clancy that Thomas Bauer was at the assembly rooms that night, and if he wanted to observe this man, he needed to seize this opportunity.

Clancy, a longtime friend, was the owner and one of the standing masters of ceremonies at Clancy Assembly Rooms. Despite his nonchalant persona, Clancy was a shrewd businessman. He catered to the higher echelons of society, but as with most enterprises, he'd occasionally encounter suspicious characters and contact Gabriel to discreetly track down the offending persons. Clancy often would return the favor, informing Gabriel of the comings and goings of people he was investigating.

By the time Gabriel arrived at the assembly rooms, they had already been open for hours, but even so, patrons and carriages were lined up out front, waiting to gain admittance. Gabriel bypassed the main entrance and took the alley back around to another entry to an antechamber just off the main vestibule.

He found Clancy in the ballroom, as expected, impeccably clad in a tailored tailcoat of vibrant emerald wool and buff cotton trousers. Every auburn curl was in place, and his cravat, uniquely and intricately tied to a double bow, gleamed snowy white. As the master of ceremonies, Clancy knew everyone and, on the surface, appeared friendly with everyone. The man's social aptitude was unmatched. His power lay in the fact he was intimidated by no one, and he was incredibly discreet. And his loyalty—a dying trait—propelled him above everyone else.

"Full tonight?" Gabriel asked as he approached Clancy.

"Ah. Rowe, good man. Yes, very full. You got my message, I see."

"I did."

Clancy nodded to the left. "Bauer's in the tearoom, conducting his little demonstrations, or whatever he calls them."

Noting the sarcasm in Clancy's tone, Gabriel angled his head to see through to the tearoom.

"He seems harmless at the moment, but you know how these things go." Clancy adjusted the cuff of his sleeve, cocked his head to the side, and lifted a finely arched brow in amusement. "So what are we watching this one for? Theft? Murder? Smuggling? I do love to know all the details."

Gabriel grinned and tugged at his linen waistcoat to straighten it. "Something like that. If my hunch is right, you'll be the first to know."

"I'd better be. I dare a man like him to attempt to take advantage of my patrons, and yet he's hardly the first to try captivating this crowd. I do have to admit that of all the odd attractions I've seen attempting to dazzle society, this is a new one. Phrenology. Who ever heard of such a thing? Everyone seems to love it, though. I daresay at times the tearoom has been more interesting than the ballroom."

Gabriel shook his head. "Apparently Mr. Bauer *claims* to be a serious anatomist and behaviorist."

"But you don't think that, do you?"

"We'll wait and see what the natural philosophers say about

him. He's to be their speaker at their symposium, you know. They're a serious lot. I doubt they care how entertaining he is."

Clancy clicked his tongue. "Always assuming the worst, aren't you, my friend? Ah, well. If it is the natural philosophers you are keen to sway, then you might be interested to learn that Mr. Richard Hawthorne is here."

Gabriel nodded at the name. "Is he?"

Clancy paused to bow toward a small group of women who walked by them. "Hawthorne is the one who vouched for Bauer's integrity and suggested my venue would be an interesting stage for him to share his skills. He's here with his daughter and two other ladies."

"Miss Phoebe Hawthorne?" he clarified.

"Yes, with Miss Caroline Nolting and Miss Eleanor Wilde."

Gabriel's interest flashed at the last name mentioned.

"Aha! See, I have told you something you don't know."

Gabriel quickly steadied himself. He'd written his letter nearly a fortnight prior and had received no response. "You're right. I am surprised. I'm acquainted with Miss Wilde. I attended her father's school."

"Then are you aware of the recent scuffle with her and the failed engagement? It's all that is being spoken of."

Gabriel's brow rose in question.

Clancy pivoted and lowered his voice. "She was engaged to Mr. Nathaniel Rawlston, and he was poised to take over as headmaster at the school, but he had an inexplicable change of heart after meeting Miss Catherine Hughton in Scotland. I'm told an engagement is imminent."

Gabriel glanced around the ballroom, hoping to glimpse Miss Wilde. "I'd not heard."

"But there is always more to it, isn't there?" Amusement lit Clancy's gray eyes. "With all this renewed interest in phrenology, that damning pamphlet written about Mrs. Wilde has resurfaced. I've heard through a trusted source that Rawlston was concerned Miss Wilde might follow in her mother's perceived insanity, and that is what prompted him to set his sights on greener pastures."

Gabriel searched his memory, vaguely recalling the scuffle. "Ah yes. I remember."

"Rawlston's the fortunate one, though, for society will overlook a handsome man's offenses, will it not? Poor Miss Wilde hasn't a prayer."

After finishing the conversation, Gabriel thanked Clancy and made his way to the tearoom and assessed his surroundings. The tables had been cleared to the side, and Bauer stood prominently in the room's center.

Gabriel had seen him a couple of times in passing, but this was the first he'd seen him in the role of phrenologist. Above-average height. Black hair with gray streaks at the temples. Dark eyes. A crowd was gathered around him—mostly women. He didn't recognize anyone from the Natural Philosophers Society, and Clancy had mentioned that Richard Hawthorne was present. Gabriel turned to go find him, but as he did a woman caught his eye.

Miss Wilde.

How was she not the focus of everyone in the room? Her golden hair, which was swept up in an elegant chignon, glistened in the candlelight, and even from this distance her eyes boasted an entrancing blue hue.

She shifted, and in the flickering light of the low-hanging candle lamps, their eyes met.

He dipped his head in acknowledgment and held his breath.

A slight smile dimpled her cheek.

At this, his pulse raced. She'd recognized him. He didn't know if she'd received his letter, but it didn't matter now. She was here . . . and he had to find a way to speak with her before the night's end.

Chapter 7

AS SOON AS Phoebe was distracted and Miss Nolting was nowhere to be seen, Ella stepped out of the tearoom into the shadowed corridor. If there was one thing more bizarre than her encounter with Mr. Bauer, it was seeing Gabriel Rowe.

Was his presence here a coincidence? Had he been looking for her?

She pressed her way through the ever-increasing throng of people toward the ballroom. The gathering heat, smoky haze from the candles, and dizzyingly loud voices were disorienting, and most of the other people present were taller than her, which made it difficult to see. With seemingly every man clad in a dark coat and buff trousers, how was she to find him?

She stepped back to allow a cluster of gentlemen to pass before identifying a small open path toward one of the ballroom's entrances. She scurried through the narrow opening and emerged into the ballroom, where dozens of dancers ebbed and flowed with the spirited music. She spied Mr. Rowe against the far wall and under the overhang for the minstrels' gallery.

Lifting the hem of her gown, she inched around another group.

With each step Ella reminded herself that she was acquainted with Mr. Rowe. It was not inappropriate to approach him. Was it?

He looked exactly like she remembered, and yet nothing like it. He had the same dark umber hair that curled just above his coat's high collar. Well-kept side-whiskers framed his square jaw. Every feature—his straight nose, the slight cleft of his chin—all seemed sharper and much more defined than the boyish visage she recalled. No longer was he lanky, but he now appeared athletic and strong, and he stood at least a head taller than her. Ella had always thought him pleasing to look at, with an easy, affecting smile and an approachable countenance, but time had enhanced his charm. In fact, he was handsome. Incredibly so.

Which made approaching him even more difficult.

Gathering every ounce of courage, she stepped into his line of sight. Their eyes met once again. He straightened. She ignored the flutter in her chest at his charismatic grin, for this was not a social conversation. He had information for her, nothing more.

Neither spoke as she joined him under the minstrels' gallery overhang. "I thought that was you, Mr. Rowe."

He bowed. "I had no doubt that it was you, Miss Wilde."

She moved to stand shoulder to shoulder with him and watched the dancers. Ella was rarely nervous or flustered, yet she struggled to focus her thoughts. Normally she prided herself on presenting a stoic, composed demeanor, but his nearness, combined with the emotions Mr. Bauer's presence had unearthed, affected her.

She maintained a steady tone. "I suppose it's fair to say that I have wondered, from time to time, what happened to you after you left the school."

"And?" He raised his dark eyebrows and looked slightly over at her. "Did you ever think you would see me at the Clancy Assembly Rooms while observing a phrenologist?"

She could not help but laugh at the odd example. "Surprisingly enough, no. That's not what I thought at all. I'm glad I did encounter you, though, for I did receive a very unusual letter from you."

"Ah yes." His posture relaxed slightly. "I wondered if you received it."

"I never responded to it, which now I realize could be considered rude. I am curious about what you have to say, but I don't think here is the proper time or place for such a discussion."

"I'll be at my office tomorrow afternoon if you'd like to join me there."

His unhesitating tone boasted confidence, but the thought of meeting him in private incited the odd flutter in her chest yet again. She was about to respond when she saw Phoebe standing on the tips of her toes across the room, no doubt looking for her.

Mr. Rowe saw her too. "Your friend is looking for you."

"Indeed, I think she is."

Phoebe took notice of her and headed in her direction. Once she arrived, she curtsied. "There you are! And Mr. Rowe. What a surprise."

Mr. Rowe bowed in response. "Miss Hawthorne. A pleasure."

Phoebe smiled hastily before fluttering her jewel-encrusted silk fan and disrupting her glossy curls. "My, but it's warm in here. I've been looking everywhere for you! When did you run off?"

"Oh, I didn't run off. Like you said, it's warm. I was merely in search of fresh air."

"Well, I'm glad I've found you, for there is someone else you must meet. You will forgive me if I take her away from you, won't you, Mr. Rowe?"

He smiled with an impressively unaffected manner. "Of course."

Ella, optimistic to have connected with Mr. Rowe yet confused about Phoebe's brusque attitude, allowed Phoebe to lead her from the area back to the tearoom.

Once they were out of Mr. Rowe's earshot and had been absorbed by the crowd, Phoebe snipped, "What on earth were you doing talking with Gabriel Rowe?"

Surprised at the accusatory tone behind the question, Ella winced. "We were only talking. He was a student at the school, do you not remember?"

"Oh, I remember." Phoebe's tone harshened.

Ella frowned. "What does that mean?"

Phoebe's normally nonchalant expression darkened into one quite annoyed, and she pressed her lips tight. "Mr. Rowe might be engaging, but do not be fooled. He is considered to have a dubious character. It is his profession. It would be best if you ignored him altogether."

"I thought he was a solicitor," Ella countered.

"He is a solicitor, but he—he's more than that." She lowered her voice to a whisper. "Mr. Rowe is involved with rabble who would make polite people uncomfortable. Clients pay him to track down criminals and apprehend them."

Ella wrinkled her nose. "Do you mean a thieftaker?"

Disgusted, Phoebe shook her head. "I don't know about all that, but he's rumored to be associating with people that a gentleman should avoid."

The warning rang like a bell, reverberating even as Ella tried to focus on other conversations. She'd wholly accepted that Mr. Rowe's letter had been genuine and an earnest effort to be useful. But what if Phoebe was right? What if he did have other intentions?

The thought rambled noisily in the back of her mind the rest of the evening, but she would rather put her faith in a man she once knew as a lad instead of a man she knew had written false information about her mother. For Phoebe's sake Ella dropped the subject, but as her thoughts cleared she was more determined than ever: She would visit Mr. Rowe's office the next day and hear what he had to say.

Chapter 8

BY THE TIME the carriage arrived in front of Mr. Rowe's office, Ella's stomach was in knots—mostly due to Mrs. Chatterly's palpable disapproval of their impending visit and Phoebe's warning about Mr. Rowe's reputation.

Ella should follow the advice of those around her, but it had never been her manner to do so. Instead, she relied on her own counsel to be curious and gather information before drawing conclusions.

The carriage rocked to a stop not far from the assembly rooms she had visited the prior evening, and the footman traveling with them opened the door.

Ella gathered her beaded reticule in her gloved hand, brushed a bit of dust from her pearl-gray wool traveling gown, and stepped from the solace of the carriage to the bustling cobblestone street. Refusing to be distracted, she turned her attention to the small, tidy building boasting a large bow window adorned with the words *Gabriel Rowe, Solicitor* in elegant red letters.

As Ella and Mrs. Chatterly approached the door, it swung inward, revealing Mr. Rowe with a broad smile, as if he had been waiting. The afternoon sun fell on his tanned cheeks, and the breeze lifted his hair from his brow.

The very sight of him—his energy and his brightness—confirmed that she had made the right decision. How could it not be when he appeared so confident and enthusiastic?

What was more, he appeared much more casual today, more like the boy she remembered. Instead of the formal attire he had worn the previous night, a light brown, high-collared tailcoat emphasized his broad shoulders and drew attention to the tawny shade of his eyes. A sage-green waistcoat hugged his torso, and his linen cravat was far less intricately tied than the silk one he wore the previous evening.

She fidgeted with her reticule, finding it difficult not to be affected. "I'm sorry that we are here so late in the day."

"No need to apolo—" He stopped abruptly and lifted his gaze behind Ella. "Is that Mrs. Chatterly?"

Ella turned, half expecting to see a frown of disapproval, but Mrs. Chatterly's expression was congenial. She even smiled. "Mr. Rowe."

He laughed and opened the door fully. "How wonderful it is to see you! I must say that this reunion, such as it is, has been good for my soul. Come in, please."

Ella and Mrs. Chatterly followed him past two clerks seated at their desks and into a private office. Once they were inside the small room, he motioned for them to be seated in the two chairs opposite the desk.

As Mr. Rowe moved to take his seat, Ella took a quick peek around the chamber. It was a small space. The floor was rough planked wood, and centered on the white plaster wall behind the desk hung a large map of London. A table, cluttered with haphazard stacks of books and papers of all sizes, stood against the far wall, and above it hung a smaller map of England. A candle lamp sat on his desk, and two more occupied the chamber's opposite corners.

Determined to express her interest, Ella leaned forward. "I did receive your letter, Mr. Rowe, and I'm curious about what it is that you wanted to tell me."

"Ah yes. The letter. I did weigh the wisdom of contacting you. You may need a little background." He leaned back in his chair and rested his elbows casually on the carved arms. "I'm a solicitor, and a great deal of my work comes from what you would expect—wills, documents, purchase agreements, and the like. From time to time my clients require other services, such as assistance in locating an individual who defaulted on an agreement, that sort of thing.

"One of my regular clients is a bank that collaborates with a gentlemen's club here in London. They assist gentlemen who've amassed debt within the club's card rooms and require immediate funds to cover them. The money lent on the spot is a legally binding contract, just as it would be if the gentleman walked into a bank and signed for a loan.

"About two months ago my client extended a rather sizable loan to Mr. Bauer. The terms of these are rather short, you see, and when Bauer failed to repay the loan by the agreed-upon date, he informed my client that he'd have money by the end of the symposium, at which time he'd repay the debt. So the loan was extended."

She frowned. "But the experts who speak at the symposium receive no honorarium, so how would he get the money for the loan?"

Mr. Rowe shrugged. "That was my understanding as well, but he was quite clear that he would have the funds following the symposium. Either it was a lie to build false confidence, or he has a plan of some sort. Again, he's committed no crime against the Society, but his intentions are questionable. I thought you should be informed."

Ella exchanged a glance with Mrs. Chatterly. "What will happen if he doesn't pay his debts?"

"Debtors' prison, no doubt. It's a significant amount. Given that Mr. Bauer does not primarily reside on England's shores, my client fears that he might leave the country without satisfying the debt."

"Oh." Ella attempted to process what she'd just heard. It was not unheard of for ne'er-do-wells to approach the Society in search of funding. Or perhaps he was more interested in Phoebe? Her father was wealthy. Could Mr. Bauer be wooing Phoebe to gain access to her dowry?

His voice cut through her musings. "There is one more thing."

Ella flicked her eyes up toward him.

"Andrew Clancy is my friend, but he is also one of my clients. Last night before I left, Mr. Clancy informed me that Mr. Bauer's assistant approached one of the footmen before the phrenological assessments and offered to, for all intents and purposes, 'buy' information about the guests in the assembly rooms."

Ella winced. "What sort of information?"

"Personality traits, unique behaviors, reputations, and so on."

The meaning of what he'd said trickled through her. "Are you suggesting that the things that Mr. Bauer says in an assessment are curated?"

"That is the question at hand."

Ella bit her lower lip. What was she supposed to feel? Validation at having correct suspicions? Anger at the fact Mr. Bauer would attempt to trick her? Pity for those who had already fallen for his falsehoods?

Mr. Rowe's words recentered her. "I wanted to share this because I have great respect for the school and the Society. I don't want to see them taken advantage of."

"May I ask why you did not go directly to Mr. Hawthorne?"

Mr. Rowe leaned back in his chair and ran his palm over his freshly shaven jaw. "I considered it, but I understand that he, not to mention his family, has become very good friends with Mr. Bauer over the last several months. No one likes to think they have put their trust in the wrong people."

"Or my father?" she prodded.

"I thought of him as well, but given the tie between the school and the Society, your father and Mr. Hawthorne are known to be like-minded. I did not think your father would go against Mr. Hawthorne."

Ella wanted to argue and state her father would surely see reason, but given her own conversations with him, she knew that would most likely not be the case. Perhaps Mr. Rowe was right. Perhaps this was a better way to address the situation at hand.

She did not look toward Mrs. Chatterly before speaking. "I'm not sure if you recall this, but shortly after my mother died, a group of phrenologists published a pamphlet about her and the circumstances surrounding her death."

"I have heard of it."

"When she was alive and in Austria with those same phrenologists, she kept detailed journals of her observations. In the months prior to her death, she indicated that she was noticing faults in the theory. What was more, some of the colleagues, Mr. Bauer included, had begun to take money to skew the findings of their readings. She confronted them about it, but of course they denied any wrongdoing, and then she died shortly thereafter."

She watched him intently, waiting for him to poke holes in her explanation. He did not, and the strength of his attention and focus spurred her to continue. "My mother indicated that Mr. Bauer, more than the others, would do private parties and was handsomely paid. She questioned his integrity numerous times."

"You said this is written in her journals?"

Ella nodded.

Mr. Rowe stood, came around his desk, and leaned informally against the other table in the room. "My purpose here is to make sure my client recoups their money, but I also don't want to see the Society taken advantage of. Everything I know about Mr. Bauer points to the fact that he's desperate, and desperate men are unpredictable. I'd like to attend the symposium to keep an eye on things. If I'm mistaken and all is well, no harm is done. But if I'm right, well, we will both benefit."

Ella considered his suggestion. Mr. Rowe's attendance at the symposium would not be surprising, given that he was, at one time, a student and that his father had been a Society member, but Phoebe's warning about Mr. Rowe and his profession bellowed. Even without looking at Mrs. Chatterly, Ella sensed the censure oozing from her, but if Ella had this opportunity, why would she not take it?

"Very well, Mr. Rowe. I thank you for sharing your information with me. Please consider yourself officially invited to the symposium at Keatley Hall."

Mr. Rowe bowed and grinned. "I humbly accept."

Chapter 9

ELLA WANTED TO trust her father.

His brilliance and confidence inspired her, and for years they had been of one mind on numerous topics. He consistently challenged her to question the world around her—to seek new solutions and explore new ideas.

But in the two years since his first heart episode, small changes had chipped away at the man she'd known. He'd grown quieter. More guarded and cautious. She knew he wanted the best for her, but she no longer understood him in the way she once had.

Two weeks had passed since she returned from London. Her conversation with Mr. Rowe remained at the forefront of every thought, and up until then she'd believed her biggest problem was Mr. Bauer.

Now, as she sat across from Mr. Abernathy at the dinner table, it was clear: She faced a much larger quandary. She could only stare as Mr. Abernathy and her father spoke of the upcoming school session.

How could her father think this man was the best person for her?

Ella had never been a romantic at heart, and emotions were not a priority at Keatley Hall, but she could not ignore Mr. Abernathy's dull disposition. He was a very plain man. In fact, everything about him was ordinary. Ordinary height. Ordinary weight. He was neither handsome nor repulsive. Even the inflection of his voice was tediously monotone, and he never seemed to smile.

At least the Hawthorne family was scheduled to arrive the next day, and the symposium guests would arrive the day after that. She hoped that Phoebe could help her come to some acceptance of this, for she certainly could not do it herself.

As she forced herself to take another bite of the white soup before her, she could not help but compare Mr. Abernathy to the engaging Mr. Rowe. Just the thought of Mr. Rowe's alluring energy and his vibrant confidence boosted her sense of vitality, but she had to be practical. He would be here for one reason only—to help prevent Mr. Bauer from taking advantage of a situation.

When they were nearing the last course, Mr. Abernathy turned toward her, as if finally noticing her presence. "Miss Wilde, your father tells me that you have plans for improvements in the conservatory."

Surprised at the sudden turn of topic, Ella lowered her spoon to the table. "Yes. Well, I hope to in the coming year or so. There is a greenhouse in London where they installed pipes inside the walls, and they use steam to help heat the room during the colder months by warming the walls. I hope to do the same here."

Eager to engage in a topic that might help her develop some sort of common interest with Mr. Abernathy, she was keen to hear his response, but Mr. Abernathy turned back to her father with a question regarding the chemistry curriculum.

Ella wiped the corner of her mouth with the linen napkin, reminding herself of her promise to consider Mr. Abernathy. She did not possess an unrealistic expectation of marital bliss, but she would prefer to be able to hold a conversation with the gentleman. Time would tell if she and Mr. Abernathy could find congruity, but for now, her confidence in the plan was waning.

In a matter of hours Keatley Hall would be unrecognizable.

Ella clutched her ecru wool shawl tightly about her shoulders as the three Hawthorne carriages turned through Keatley Hall's timeworn stone arched entrance and rumbled up the long gravel drive.

Hoofbeats intensified as the conveyances drew closer and the carriages' ornate finishings came into focus. It would be another day before the rest of the guests would begin arriving for the symposium, but, as usual, the Hawthornes and their servants arrived early to prepare.

Fresh enthusiasm seized her as the first carriage rolled to a stop and one of the Keatley Hall footmen opened the door. She prepared to rush toward the carriage to embrace her friend, but she stopped short. It was not a Hawthorne family member who emerged. Instead, a striking, unusually tall older woman clad in an elaborate traveling gown of aubergine merino wool emerged. Glittering sapphire jewels—ostentatiously bright for the early hour—sparkled at her throat, and an ostrich feather plumed from her velvet-trimmed chip bonnet and fluttered in the afternoon's damp breeze. The newcomer paused long enough for her gaze to climb Keatley Hall, and then her painted lips curved in a slow, approving smile. She accepted the assistance of a footman to step down the carriage block and then turned as Mr. Hawthorne trailed her from the carriage and offered her his hand.

Confused at the unanticipated guest, Ella leaned toward her father. "Who is that?"

He shrugged. "I've no idea."

But then Phoebe, bright-eyed and pink-cheeked, poked her head from the carriage. Smile beaming on her thin lips and her periwinkle bonnet ribbons fluttering, she eagerly accepted the footman's assistance. Hands outstretched, she hurried toward Ella. "Dear Ella!" Phoebe embraced Ella and kissed her cheek.

Her father stepped forward to greet the Hawthornes, and Ella pulled Phoebe's hand closer. "Who is that lady?"

Phoebe giggled and glanced over her shoulder at the woman in question. "I have so much to tell you. It's all gossip and wicked to talk of such things, of course, but so much has changed. Come. I'll introduce you."

Once the group gathered, her father spoke first. "Ah, Hawthorne, you are full of surprises, I say. Will you introduce us to your lovely traveling companion?"

Mr. Richard Hawthorne, a hefty man with thick pewter hair and a round face, beamed as he extended his arm toward the distinguished woman accompanying them. "I didn't think you'd mind an additional guest, Wilde. May I introduce Miss Louisa Sutton."

Before any response could be made, Miss Sutton placed a gloved hand coyly on Ella's father's arm, and her dark gaze was unwaveringly direct. "I do hope I'm not intruding, Mr. Wilde. I've been so fascinated by phrenology for quite some time, and the moment Mr. Hawthorne told me of this symposium, I just knew I had to be a part of it."

Ella's father bowed. "Well, you are very welcome at Keatley Hall, Miss Sutton."

Miss Sutton pivoted and fixed her coffee-colored eyes on Ella. "And this must be Miss Wilde. Oh, my dear, how I've heard your praises sung! From how Miss Hawthorne has described you, I know we are going to be the best of friends. I can tell already."

Still unsure of what to make of the confident, unexpected guest, Ella suppressed her questions and returned a polite smile. "I sincerely hope so, Miss Sutton."

A flurry of activity ensued as the footmen and stable boys began unloading trunks, and the other servants scurried toward the house to prepare it for the onslaught of guests soon to arrive.

Ella looped her arm through Phoebe's, grateful for her friend, but her curiosity about the new lady tugged. During the next several days, as men dominated at Keatley Hall, any female might become a friend, and at the moment Ella would take all the friends she could get.

Chapter 10

PHOEBE PRESSED THE palm of her hand against the crown of her straw poke bonnet, looped her free arm through Ella's, closed her eyes, and drew a deep breath of the late-afternoon air. "I'm so glad to finally have a moment alone to talk!"

"Are you certain you're up for a walk?" Ella inquired as they stepped from Keatley Hall's east entrance toward a footpath that led to the rear gardens.

"Indeed! A walk is just what I need, especially after being confined to the carriage for so long this morning. La, what a drive!"

"Was it terrible?"

"No, not terrible, but the rain did plague us most of the way, which was unpleasant. Oh!" Phoebe exclaimed suddenly as the full garden came into view, and she reached out to touch a climbing rosebush as it arched over the walkway. "I've always loved these gardens. How beautiful."

Ella inhaled, allowing the floral scent of roses and late-blooming lavender to wash over her. "We do our best to keep it tidy, but it's quite a task. The gardens were always Mother's domain. She always kept them so immaculate, but there are so many of them! After the gardener left last autumn, we tried to have some of the students tend it, but over the summer I fear it's been left to grow wild."

"Well, I think it's charming. I could spend all day here."

They resumed their walk down the brick path, careful to avoid the puddles from the day's earlier rain. "Were your companions much company on the drive?"

"Father slept most of the way, but Miss Sutton was pleasant."

Interest surged through Ella. New men were common in the Society, but women were not. "Speaking of Miss Sutton, I can't wait to learn all about her. Who is she exactly? How are the two of you acquainted?"

"I can't believe I've never mentioned her before. Had you been in London more this summer, you would have undoubtedly met her. She's been positively everywhere! She and my father have become very friendly over the last several months. I was not aware that she intended to join us until just two days ago; otherwise I would have written to let you know. I hope her attendance is not an imposition for you or Mrs. Chatterly."

"Any friend of yours is welcome at Keatley Hall. That should never be in question, but where did they meet?"

"It was about seven months ago, just before the Season really began. They were introduced at a dinner at the Silvers' home. I did not attend it, so sadly I don't know many details, but they've been inseparable ever since."

Ella cast a sideways glance toward her friend. Over the years Ella had become adept at reading Phoebe's unique mannerisms. At the moment she seemed quite content and easy with the topic, but Ella acutely recalled Phoebe's distress two years prior when her mother had died. Any talk of Phoebe's father possibly remarrying would send her into hysterics. "Do you like her? As a friend for yourself, not as a match for your father?"

Phoebe's lip twitched before a full smile returned once again. "I do like her very much. She's been nothing but kind to me, and she really has brought a new sense of life to our family gatherings."

Sensing hesitation, Ella shifted the conversation away from Phoebe's feelings. "And did I hear her introduced correctly as Miss Sutton? Has she never married, then?"

Phoebe plucked a small cluster of white yarrow and tucked it in her bonnet's band. "No, she never did. Is that not a marvel? A woman of her beauty and wit. She's not shared a great deal about her past, at least not with me, but I've gathered from comments that her father was independently wealthy—a merchant of some sort—and she felt no pressure to marry."

The comment recalled Ella's own situation. What would it be like not to have to force a matrimonial union? Determined to keep the conversation light, Ella continued, "I'm so glad to hear your father is happy."

"He is. Very much so. In fact, I wouldn't be surprised if he were to make her an offer of marriage. Can you believe it? He was so devastated after Mother's death that I wondered if he would ever smile again. And now, here he is."

"I wish my father could find such a companion, but I fear he is far too set in his ways now."

"It would help if he would venture to London every so often," teased Phoebe. "How is he to meet anyone when he rarely leaves Keatley Hall?"

How often had Ella had the exact same thought? Many people filtered through the school, but mostly fathers and school-age boys. Never women her father's age. Given his current health, she lamented that he likely would never find that sort of happiness again.

A chaffinch swept down from the boughs above the dirt path they were walking, and Ella glanced up in time to see it disappear in the branches of an ash tree. She then noticed the gathering, quick-moving clouds overhead. According to legend the bird's song signaled a change of weather.

A sharp, decidedly cool breeze rushed in from a nearby meadow, thick with the scent of moisture. "I think we might get more rain. Shall we turn back?"

They turned to trace their steps back to Keatley Hall. After several silent steps, Phoebe tilted her head playfully toward Ella. "So we have recently discussed my impending romantic prospects and my father's, but we've not discussed yours. Mr. Rawlston behaved abominably and no doubt left you cautious, but surely you must have thought for your future."

It was Ella's turn to hesitate.

She'd have to apprise Phoebe of her father's plan regarding Mr. Abernathy sooner or later. The teacher's attention toward her would likely become obvious. Perhaps if Ella was forthright about it, she could avoid awkward conversations later.

"There's something you should probably know," Ella began slowly.

Phoebe squealed and tightened her arm still looped through Ella's. "I knew it!"

"I would save your excitement, Phoebe, for I'm not sure you'll be pleased with what I am about to tell you."

In the privacy of the garden, Ella told her friend all about the decline of her father's health and his plans regarding Mr. Abernathy.

"Oh, Ella." Phoebe paused to face her as they approached the garden's gate, her wide-set eyes brimming with sympathy. "Mr. Abernathy! Are you sure there is nothing to be done?"

Her friend's disheartening reaction dashed Ella's hope for encouragement. "I'm not sure. You'll see for yourself as you spend more time around my father. I really do fear for his health."

"I could cry for you."

Ella, however, straightened her shoulders. The entire situation with Mr. Rawlston had been embarrassing, but to Ella, it was far worse to be pitied. Humiliation she could handle. Pity she could not.

Ella forced a smile. "As I told you, that was my father's plan. Nothing is certain until all is said and done. Who knows? Maybe a handsome stranger will show up at the symposium and change all of our minds."

A misty rain began to drizzle as the women returned to Keatley Hall to dress for dinner, but even as talk of a handsome stranger crossed Ella's lips, the image of Mr. Rowe floated through her mind. He'd be joining them soon, but it would be imprudent to allow thoughts to flow unfettered.

No, practicality and truth were more reliable than fantastical thoughts that risked disappointment. She needed to focus on discovering the truth about Mr. Bauer and leave thoughts of romance to the others.

Chapter 11

THE NEXT MORNING, the unmistakable sound of wheels crunching on the gravel drive below Ella's south-facing window pulled her from slumber. As sleep's effect cleared and the day's significance dawned, Ella sat upright in bed, reached for her linen wrapper, and moved to peer from her window.

Already the Keatley Hall grounds buzzed with activity. The hour was early, yet two carriages conveying symposium guests stood in the drive. She'd been planning for this day ever since she'd spoken with Mr. Rowe in his office. Could this be the start of learning the truth about Mr. Bauer?

Ella had told her father that she'd encountered Mr. Rowe at the assembly rooms and he would be attending, and Mrs. Chatterly had assigned him a chamber, but Ella left every other aspect of his visit shrouded in secrecy. She'd omitted the fact that he'd be investigating the guest of honor. Each day her guilt intensified—she had, after all, lied to her father, and she'd be foolish to think Mr. Rowe's arrival would not incite more questions.

How could she continue down this duplicitous path?

She wanted her father to trust her, just as he wanted her to trust him, but they were both extending trust in pieces and parts. Her father refused to relinquish any control regarding Keatley Hall's future. She was keeping the entire topic of Mr. Rowe and Mr. Bauer close to her chest.

Ella's bedchamber door opened, and Mrs. Chatterly appeared with a gown flowing over her arm.

"Good. You're awake." Mrs. Chatterly draped the gown over a chair and propped her hands on her hips. "We must hurry. Your father will want you to help greet the guests."

The relationship between the two ladies, which had always been so positive and strong, had seemed strained ever since the visit to Mr. Rowe's office. It was an odd dichotomy—Mrs. Chatterly was the only person at Keatley Hall who knew the details of Ella's plans. Ella never doubted Mrs. Chatterly's loyalty, but the fact that her most trusted ally doubted those plans heightened her insecurity.

What if Ella was wrong?

What if she had jeopardized her entire future by following her own stubborn pursuits?

Mrs. Chatterly assisted Ella into her stays and into a blush muslin gown with small cream and pale green flowers embroidered on the bodice and the cuffs of the long sleeves. A filmy, milky-white fichu was tucked in the square neckline, making the gown more appropriate and modest for daytime hours, and once she was dressed, Mrs. Chatterly brushed her light hair and pinned it into a simple chignon at the base of her neck.

Before long, Ella was swept away into the day's activity. Concerns of trust and her future were replaced with the more practical tasks of ensuring the guests had appropriate chambers and that there were sufficient refreshments, but as the hours flew by, Ella kept one eye on the carriages arriving. Whereas Ella was acutely aware that Mr. Rowe had not yet arrived, Phoebe was devastated that Mr. Bauer had yet to make an appearance.

As the afternoon waned, Phoebe and Ella retreated to the White Parlor on Keatley Hall's ground floor, where the tall leaded windows overlooked the long gravel drive and grassy forecourt, allowing them to observe the arrivals without being seen.

In an abrupt lurch Phoebe jumped from where she was sitting near the window. "This might be him."

Drawn by curiosity, Ella joined Phoebe at the window. Sure enough, an unmarked black carriage turned from the main road and passed through Keatley Hall's open wrought-iron gates.

Phoebe whirled from the window and began to pace.

"You must calm down," suggested Ella, keeping her words slow. "You'll make yourself ill, and the last thing you want is to appear as a dithery, nervous thing when he arrives."

"You're right. I know you are." Phoebe fidgeted with the ruffled sleeve of her mauve sarcenet gown and returned to the window. "Do I look all right?"

Ella assessed her eager friend's flushed face and tense jaw. "You look lovely, but you look the most beautiful when you smile, yes?"

Phoebe blew out the air she'd been holding and turned her attention out the window. They waited as the carriage in question pulled around the drive. She did not brighten until Mr. Bauer's unmistakable silhouette became clear. "It's him. I might faint."

"You're not going to faint." But even as Ella said the words, she could not tear her eyes away from the broad-shouldered, stocky man in a black coat, black beaver hat, and jet hair who emerged from the carriage. He looked just as she remembered from the assembly room, except perhaps a bit older due to the harsh daytime light.

A second man, whom Ella recognized as his assistant from the demonstration, exited after him. The men shook hands with both of their fathers, who had been waiting at the entrance to greet guests as they arrived.

The pretty flush that had colored Phoebe's high cheeks just moments ago drained to a sickly pale. "I've not seen him since we spoke to him at Clancy's. What if his opinion of me has changed?"

Ella decided it best to keep her thoughts about Mr. Bauer's interest in Phoebe's dowry to herself and, instead, attempted to focus on something more positive. "If he cares for you as you have described, then nothing will change him. You'll see."

The men ambled toward the house, and within moments the boisterous roar of animated male voices reverberated from the great hall's paneled walls and stone floors just across the corridor from the White Parlor.

"Let's go greet him!" cried Phoebe, starting for the door. "I—"

"No, no. Restraint is needed," cautioned Ella. "Consider, he's just arrived and there are others in the great hall—the Nortons, the Parkers, maybe more. Do you want your reunion to be when he has just gotten out of a carriage and surrounded by people? Stay here. He'll come to you."

"You're right, of course," Phoebe lamented as she toyed anxiously with a ruby pendant on a gold chain that had previously been tucked into her fichu.

"That's pretty." Ella angled to see the bauble more clearly as she attempted to distract her friend. "I've not noticed it before."

Phoebe expression sobered, and she quickly tucked it back in her fichu. "It was a gift."

It was unlike Phoebe not to want to discuss anything related to fashion. "From whom?"

Phoebe bit her lower lip and turned toward the window. "If I tell you, you will think it wrong that I accepted it."

Dread trickled through her. It was inappropriate for a man to give a woman a gift unless the relationship was serious. "Mr. Bauer?"

Phoebe's voice was low. "He gave it to me about a month ago. Father has not seen it yet, and I don't think anyone else would notice, but I want Thomas to see me wearing it."

Ella stiffened. *Referring to him by his Christian name and accepting gifts?*

"You won't say anything, will you?" pleaded Phoebe, her light brown eyes wide.

Ella dropped her shoulders and sighed. "I won't, but I do wish you to be careful."

"I assure you, I am careful, Ella. I wish you could experience this feeling. It seems that after so many years of just drifting, waiting, and hoping, I might find the person I am meant to be with."

Ella understood that feeling of drifting—of merely existing while the rest of the world sped ahead. "Does anyone else besides me know of the attachment?"

"Miss Sutton knows, of course. She has been present so often during our encounters and figured it out. She is so observant."

Ella forced a smile. It would not do to make her friend uneasy when so many unanswered questions lingered. "I like seeing you this way. Happiness suits you."

Phoebe sniffed and shrugged. "I don't feel like I deserve such happiness."

"Why would you say that?"

"I have so little of significance to offer in comparison. He's such an impressive individual. Why would he choose me when any lady would be glad for his attention?"

Phoebe's low opinion of herself concerned Ella. "*You* are remarkable, dear Phoebe. Truly. I wish you could see it as clearly as I do."

Guilt descended. Phoebe was a good person, not to mention an extraordinary judge of character. How could her perception of Mr. Bauer contrast so with her own and Mr. Rowe's? Ella was confident in the details in her mother's journals, but a small seed of doubt vexed her. She and Mr. Rowe could be completely wrong in their assessment. What sort of friend would she be to cast shadows on Phoebe's beau?

Ella and Phoebe moved to the corridor just as the men were approaching the White Parlor. But then they paused. Mr. Bauer looked directly at them both, but he made no motion, gave no greeting, and continued down the corridor.

Ella froze. Given Phoebe's account and her own personal observation of their conversation at the assembly rooms, she'd expected a very different response.

The men continued talking quietly amongst themselves.

Phoebe's face drained of color. Moisture filled her red-rimmed eyes, and a fat tear skipped down her cheek. "He didn't greet me. Not even a smile!"

Ella gripped her hand. "Perhaps he didn't see you. They were all talking, and—"

"He saw me, Ella. And he said nothing. Nothing!"

Eager to avoid a scene, Ella wrapped her arm around Phoebe's and guided her from the parlor, down the same corridor the gentlemen had just traversed, and to the east staircase. Ella was not exactly sure what she had just witnessed, but his dismissive behavior toward the woman he was allegedly courting gave her a little more evidence to support her suspicion: Mr. Bauer was not to be trusted.

Chapter 12

AS THE HIRED carriage slowed along Keatley Hall's outer walls and turned through the arched entrance, Gabriel knew that he would no doubt encounter many acquaintances.

But he was not here to reunite with friends.

Gabriel was here for one reason only: to investigate Mr. Bauer.

He angled his head to look up at the majestic manor house with its red-brown stone, impressively symmetrical facade, and uniform steep gables that soared into the stormy pewter sky.

The sight transported him to the past and opened access to a bittersweet part of his mind that had been sealed for so long. He'd been seven years of age when he first made this drive. Over the course of the next several years, the people here became his family—including the Wildes. Returning to Keatley Hall felt, in many ways, more like a homecoming than if he were returning to his parents' house in Manchester.

As the carriage rounded the looped drive, energizing activity met him. Carriages and wagons lined the drive, servants bustled to and fro, and gentlemen—some of whom he instantly recognized—milled about the grounds, but it was the sight of Mr. Wilde standing at Keatley Hall's main entrance that really made Gabriel feel as if he were stepping back in time.

The wind sweeping down from the west gables flapped the folds of Mr. Wilde's fawn-colored frock coat. He was speaking with a servant, and he turned as Gabriel's carriage approached.

He recalled Philip Wilde as a robust man with broad shoulders and a barrel chest, but time had robbed him of those brawny features. His hair, which had been fair like his daughter's and had always needed a cut, was wispy and sparse. His once-ruddy oval face was pale and thin, his shoulders stooped.

The carriage stopped, and the servant opened the door and Gabriel stepped out.

When their eyes met, Mr. Wilde's bushy gray brows rose. He chuckled and placed his fists on his hips. "As I live and breathe! Dare I say young Gabriel Rowe?"

"Not so young anymore," Gabriel quipped and extended his hand.

Mr. Wilde laughed again and shook Gabriel's hand emphatically before he clapped his hand on Gabriel's shoulder. "Ella told me you'd be attending. I wasn't sure I believed her, but here you are, in the flesh."

"I'm grateful for the opportunity to return." Gabriel handed his satchel to the waiting footman.

"I'm sure you want to rest after the journey, so I'll not keep you. We'll speak later, but it is good to see you here, Rowe."

Gabriel followed the servant in through the main doors, through the screens passage, then to the great hall. The familiar scent of age, dust, and woodsmoke greeted him. A fire simmered in the broad hearth on the chamber's north end, and a faded, rectangular tapestry depicting an ancient pastoral scene hung over the mantel. Gray light filtered in through the bank of tall leaded windows on the opposite wall and reflected on life-size oil paintings in gilded frames. Flagstone slabs grounded the entire space beneath his boots, and in the center of the chamber stood a large table. Ornately carved chairs with faded-crimson velvet pads lined the oak-paneled wall.

He followed the footman through the crowd toward the east staircase, and they began the ascent to the third floor—the attic floor. Once there, he was engulfed by boyhood memories as he ducked beneath the low threshold and stepped onto the uneven floor. The floor creaked under his feet with each step, a sound so distinctly familiar it almost sent chills up his spine.

At some point the attic had been divided into small rooms for students, and it appeared that he was to lodge in one of those rooms during his stay. The footman stopped at a chamber near the end, and Gabriel peered inside. It was comforting in its plainness. Rough planked floors. Two low beds on each side of the narrow room. A small chest with three drawers, a washbasin, and a single wooden chair. Two hooks hung on the wall, but it was the window that drew his attention. He'd never been fortunate enough to be in one of the dormitories containing a window.

"Dinner will be in two hours, and the guests will gather in the great hall and ground-floor parlors an hour prior." The footman placed Gabriel's satchel on the nearest bed and extended the bedchamber key toward him. "Will there be anything else?"

"Yes." Gabriel tucked the key in his pocket. "Has Mr. Bauer arrived yet?"

"He has."

"Thank you."

The footman bowed and withdrew, leaving Gabriel alone in the bedchamber. He stepped to the room's north-facing window and looked down. The northern gardens stretched to where two large oaks marked the end of the property gardens and the beginning of the woods.

He turned back around and tossed his satchel and hat on top of the bed, then removed his portfolio with his notes. Using the water in a pitcher near the basin, he washed his face, combed water through his hair, and changed from his traveling clothes into dinner attire.

He paused in front of a small looking glass on the chest.

Every so often, he'd see his father in his reflection, and today was one of those instances. They shared so many physical attributes—light brown, almost hazel eyes fringed with thick black lashes and a straight nose with a slight aquiline shape.

It pained him that he could not think of his father fondly. As a boy he'd idolized his father. As a man he despised him.

If Gabriel was honest, his father was even more responsible for his decision to study law than Mary was. Gabriel would never understand how his father had remained silent while Mary endured such cruelty at the hands of her husband. His sister's agony combined with the shock of his father's inaction was what spurred Gabriel to fight for those who could not fight for themselves. His passion bordered on obsession, as if he could atone for past offenses by bringing those who wished to harm others to justice.

He reached for the cloth and dried his face.

He had to put thoughts of the past out of his mind, for he had a task to accomplish. He'd convinced Miss Wilde to allow him to attend. She had as much, if not more, to lose than he did if he failed.

Furthermore, another battle raged—one even more incessant than the other.

Gabriel had not stopped thinking about Miss Wilde since their meeting in his office. She was one of the most beautiful women he'd ever seen. Her spirit and zest were attractive to him—her passion for something bigger than herself matched his own. He related to it in a way that he hadn't related to anything in a very long time. It was a rare trait, and one that, if he was not careful, could make him forget his purpose for being here.

Gabriel tied the cravat around his neck and checked it in the looking glass.

Everything he had been investigating regarding Thomas Bauer was about to come to pass, and he had a very small window to find the truth. He owed it to himself and to Miss Wilde to accomplish the one thing he was here to do: protect them from Mr. Bauer.

After leaving a still-distraught Phoebe in Miss Sutton's consoling company and dressing for the evening, Ella descended the broad, intricately carved east staircase. She trailed her fingertips along the timeworn wooden railing, drawing energy and courage from the house itself.

Despite Ella's reservations about the symposium, the polite chatter and happy laughter resounding from the rooms below infused her with energy. The dinner hour was quickly approaching, and as Keatley Hall's hostess she would be expected to greet and entertain the three ladies who had accompanied their husbands: Mrs. Parker, Mrs. Norton, and Mrs. Shiveley.

In truth there was only one person she was seeking.

Taking advantage of the extra height of the steps, she looked over the top of the crowd gathered in the great hall and the corridor.

Almost immediately she spied Mr. Abernathy across the chamber, near the tall leaded windows at the front of the great hall, speaking with two other gentlemen. In the two days since their dinner, he'd barely spoken with her. She'd hoped that in time she would start to feel some sort of softening toward him, or at least find some commonalities with him, but she felt nothing when she looked at him. Not attraction. Not infatuation or intrigue. If anything, melancholy stole over her.

Ella shifted, but instead of seeing Mr. Rowe, as she'd hoped, she noticed Thomas Bauer talking with her father.

A double-breasted tailcoat of finely textured black superfine broadcloth hugged his full shoulders, and a sizable sapphire pin held his silk cravat firmly in place. His meticulously groomed silver-streaked jet hair and side-whiskers framed his angular face, but it was the intense—almost mesmerizing—shade of his dark eyes and how they contrasted with his fair skin that demanded attention.

He glanced toward her and stopped talking. Her father pivoted at Mr. Bauer's obvious distraction, and upon noticing her, he motioned for her to join them.

"Ah, Miss Wilde," Mr. Bauer declared as she drew closer. "We meet again."

"Good evening, sir. And welcome, at last, to Keatley Hall."

"A true honor." His bow was ostentatiously low, and if possible his grin was even broader when he straightened once again.

She forced herself to maintain eye contact. "You've been to Keatley Hall before, if I am not mistaken."

"I have been, but not since I was a very young man. Your grandfather invited me to visit before my first journey to Austria. It was he who initially piqued my interest in phrenology."

"That must have been before my time here," her father added, offering his arm to Ella and patting her hand as she took it. "I daresay it hasn't changed much."

Mr. Bauer lifted his eyes to the beamed ceiling and then around the chamber. "It was so long ago, but my most vivid memory of the entire visit was a conservatory. Am I mistaken? Is there one here?"

The mention of her precious conservatory on Mr. Bauer's lips irked her. "You are correct. It was a wedding gift from my grandfather to my grandmother."

"Well then." He smiled and rocked on his toes. "I do hope you will do me the honor of showing it to me again at some point in my stay here."

"Of course."

The crowd around them was ever shifting as the guests ambled around the space, and from the corner of her eye, movement distracted her.

Mr. Rowe stepped into the great hall.

Ella's heart jolted. How handsome he was. How exciting and intriguing.

Mr. Bauer stepped closer to be heard above the others, and the sharp scent of sandalwood almost overwhelmed her and snapped her focus back to him. "I've an unusual request, and I hope that you, as the mistress of the house, will grant it."

She raised a brow, fighting the protest already rising within her.

"It is more of a favor, actually," he continued. "It would be my great honor if you'd permit me to be seated at your side during dinner."

The odd request stunned her—one so impudent it could be

considered rude—yet she could not refuse. Phoebe's disappointment at Mr. Bauer's dismissive behavior flashed in her mind. Perhaps this would be the perfect opportunity to learn more. Plus, her father's eyes were upon her . . . expectantly.

Ella smiled her prettiest smile. "Of course, Mr. Bauer. I shall speak with Mrs. Chatterly and have her make the arrangements."

He clasped his hands heavily before him. "I am elated."

Mr. Bauer turned to her father, and Ella did not miss the pleased expression flushing her father's face. For Phoebe's sake and because her father had asked her, Ella would be civil toward Mr. Bauer, but her guard was raised.

Chapter 13

RARELY WAS KEATLEY Hall's Ivy Chamber so full of people. Over the centuries this room had traditionally been used as a music room, but because of its immense size and narrow rectangular dimensions, it was transformed, once a year, into a dining chamber. A single long table was pieced together to span the room's extraordinary length, making it large enough for all the guests to dine simultaneously in one room.

Elegant ivy-patterned relief work carved into the ceiling gave the chamber its name. Large tapestries and portraits covered the dark paneled walls, and two identical chests of drawers with dark walnut inlay flanked each side of the main door. Two-pronged sconces hung at regular intervals along the walls, and at the moment the room hummed with conversation and cutlery clinking against porcelain bowls. Under normal circumstances Ella would enjoy the activity, but Mr. Bauer's nearness put her on edge.

"I do hope I did not offend you with my request to be seated next to you." Mr. Bauer wiped his mouth with his napkin and lowered it. "I realize what a brazen request that was, but I had a very specific reason, you understand, and I was unsure if or when you and I might have a moment to talk privately." A more somber tone emerged. "I'll be blunt, Miss Wilde. My very good friends, the Hawthornes, who were instrumental in my participation at this symposium, shared that you believe I'm in part responsible for the pamphlet that circulated about your mother and, ultimately, you."

His bluntness was surprisingly refreshing—and it emboldened her. Her appetite for the meal's second course had faded, and she pivoted and pushed a bit of mutton across her plate with her fork. "But you did have a hand in writing it, did you not?"

He hesitated. "Several phrenologists contributed their thoughts to the report, but it was written in the very early days of phrenological study. The intention was to collectively comment on one case of familiarity. It was never intended for circulation."

"I see," she responded flatly. "Surely you understand my resistance then. Those accusations were damning."

"They were not accusations, my dear. The objective was simply to document how certain behaviors could be explained via phrenology, but I am older now and I daresay wiser, and I can see how such a publication might have led to unnecessary scrutiny."

Ella fumed. Unnecessary scrutiny? Perhaps more like a lifelong albatross she'd borne since the pamphlet had become available. "The purpose of the writing might have been a private study, but someone was responsible for its dissemination."

He lifted a piece of mackerel with his fork but did not eat it. "Not long after we collaborated on that study, the group fell out. I can only imagine one of the others published it." He shifted and rested his elbow on the table. "I can see I've upset you."

"No, sir, on the contrary," she said, doing little to mask her sarcasm.

He narrowed his eyes and studied her. "You do not support phrenology, do you, Miss Wilde?"

Her father had asked her not to contradict his teachings to others. But he'd said nothing about sharing her opinions with him.

"No, sir. I do not."

"My goodness, you are direct."

He no doubt intended his comment as a slight, but she refused to perceive it as such. She lifted her chin. "I am sure Mr. Hawthorne informed you that some of the Society members might not be all that receptive. That report, regardless of its intention, caused a great division in the Society. Some endorsed the study and others unequivocally denounced it. There is a mixture of those people here. It might be beneficial for you to keep that in mind during your presentations."

"Time has a way of softening attitudes, I've come to learn, and I hope that those who are against it—such as yourself—will at least consider the facts behind it. I've devoted my life to this study, and I'm confident it will one day, in the not-so-distant future, shape our entire understanding of human behavior. Whether we like it or not, there are those who will always bend knowledge to their benefit. I cannot explain why someone shared the pamphlet publicly, but I can say I am sorry for the repercussions for you and your family."

For the first time she turned to face him fully. "Will you defend her then?"

The first break in his domineering countenance flickered. "I-I'm not sure what you are asking me to do."

"You knew my mother, yes? So you knew the truth about her—that she was rational and in no way capable of the things they claimed."

A nervous, throaty chuckle emanated from him. His formerly confident eye contact faltered. "You are asking me to do something I ethically cannot do. I think the best thing I *can* do is to educate people and let them make their own decisions."

"That is a shame to hear, Mr. Bauer."

"Come now, Miss Wilde. Clearly we will not see eye to eye on this matter, but surely we can still find a common ground of friendship."

Ella could not help briefly lifting her gaze to Phoebe, who was seated at the other end of the table. Her friend's attempt at a cheery visage and conversation was overshadowed by her frequent glances in Ella's direction.

"Well then, Mr. Bauer, I believe true friendships are built on trust and time and shared experiences. But I do hope we can become friends over time."

His jaw twitched ever so slightly before he smiled broadly. "I couldn't agree more."

She returned her attention to her plate of mostly uneaten food to signal the topic's end, but even though she did not trust this man, she at least felt she had, somehow, gained the upper hand.

After dinner concluded and the women retreated from the dining room to leave the men to their port, Gabriel stood from his chair and took a moment to observe his surroundings. It had been a long time since he'd attended anything that resembled a refined event. He recalled a time when his family would host such events frequently. As a prominent textile producer and one of the most influential men in Manchester, his father had always been entertaining. Their home was a never-ending succession of elegant dinners and balls.

After he and his father parted ways over his sister's situation, such events faded from Gabriel's lifestyle and were replaced by whatever events his cases required. He still attended sophisticated events from time to time, but often his work required him to frequent dark village taverns and dockside inns. His ability to fit in anywhere and converse easily with others was his most valuable asset, but this particular case posed unique challenges.

Normally he enjoyed anonymity. People knew his name, but they didn't know about his family. His childhood. At Keatley Hall there was no hiding them.

"Rowe!"

The familiar voice interrupted Gabriel's musings, and he turned. Felix Templeton, a chum from his school days, approached from the other side of the table.

Gabriel could almost breathe a sigh of relief. Of all his former classmates to encounter in such a situation, Templeton might be the most accommodating—and the most amusing.

Templeton stretched out his hand once he was near, a lopsided grin on his ruddy, full face. "I couldn't have been more surprised to see you at the other end of that table tonight. Why did you not tell me you were going to attend?"

Gabriel matched Templeton's enthusiasm and shook his hand. "A last-minute decision."

"I'm glad for it, although I can't say why you would choose to come. Did you forget how dull these are? I'd have passed, but my father would disown me."

Gabriel chuckled. "Do I detect sarcasm?"

"I hope so." Templeton paused to accept two glasses from the footman's tray and then extended one to Gabriel.

Gabriel accepted the port. "Tell me, Templeton. What have I missed in this last decade?"

Templeton took a swig of the dark liquid, leaned his elbow against the chimneypiece, and motioned toward his own father, who was speaking with Mr. Bauer on the other side of the chamber. "You know that nothing ever changes with these men. Same discussions, same opinions. That's hardly a surprise, is it?"

"Oh, I don't know," countered Gabriel. "It seems to me that if *this* group is willing to discuss phrenology after the hullabaloo it caused all those years ago, I'd say that's significant change."

Templeton gave his russet head a shake. "Say what you will, Rowe, but you know the truth about this sort."

"And that is?" Gabriel raised his brows.

"Not a single thing is done, discussed, or considered unless there is something to be gained."

Gabriel paused to consider the statement and took a sip of his drink. He was about to ask Templeton to clarify, but then Mr. Wilde approached.

"Mr. Rowe. Mr. Templeton," Mr. Wilde said in greeting. "So good to see you both. It gives me hope for the future knowing young lads such as yourselves are interested in furthering the natural philosophies. Tell me, Mr. Rowe, arc you regaining your sea legs here at Keatley Hall?"

"I am."

"And my daughter tells me that you are a solicitor. The law!" Mr. Wilde's light eyes widened in perceived interest. "A diversion for you, then. I recall your main interest was in astronomy, I believe."

Gabriel could not resist a smile at the memory of his childhood interest and gave a slow nod. "I was indeed very fond of the study. I suppose time has a way of changing things."

"And don't forget the need for practicality." Mr. Wilde lifted his glass in a toast to the field. "The law is a noble profession. Our country desperately needs clever men with good heads on their shoulders."

"Practicality." Templeton snorted. "Where's the fun in that?"

"I'm interested to know." Mr. Wilde folded his arms over his chest and tilted his head to the side, just as he would when Gabriel was a student. "What interest does a solicitor have in phrenology?"

Gabriel shrugged. "More curiosity than anything, I suppose. I encounter criminals who engage in every manner of illegal activity. If there is any truth to the idea of phrenology, and if there was a way to predict behavior or even the propensity for it, think of how beneficial that could be in our line of work."

"*If* there is any truth?" challenged Mr. Wilde in a tone that made Gabriel feel as if he were ten years old again. "Do you not believe it, then?"

Gabriel chuckled to mask his discomfort. "Is that not what you taught us? To be curious? To examine evidence and rationale before coming to conclusions?"

"Ah, bright boy." Mr. Wilde grinned at the response and then clapped his hand on Gabriel's shoulder. "We will catch up later, yes?"

The two young men remained quiet until Mr. Wilde was out of earshot; then Templeton leaned close. "I'm sure you're aware that he isn't well."

Gabriel had heard as much, but any new information could be useful. "I've heard rumors that his health was failing, but nothing definite. What is the issue?"

Templeton took another drink. "His heart, I'm told. It's a shame too. Who knows what will happen to this school if he should die, especially given what happened to his daughter."

Gabriel's interest piqued afresh at the mention of Miss Wilde. "Do you mean the engagement to Rawlston?"

Templeton nodded. "It was all set, and then it just ended. My father said that if Miss Wilde is not married when her father dies, the school will pass to a relative, which would mean it would likely close. There is hope, though. I've heard through the gossips that there is another suitor afoot."

A flash of unexpected jealousy sparked. "Who might that be?"

"Prepare yourself." Templeton smirked. "None other than the illustrious Mr. Abraham Abernathy."

Gabriel winced at the absurd match. How could such a prosaic, sheepish man be considered a match for such a vibrant woman? "Surely not Mr. Milksop."

Templeton erupted in laughter at the nickname the students would whisper behind Mr. Abernathy's back. "Nothing is set in stone, or so I'm told. Say what you will, but not many rational men would be willing to take on a woman as erratic as Ella Wilde, not to mention the added burden of the school and all that comes with it. Would you tie yourself to a woman whose mother was rumored to be a lunatic? I daresay the gamble is greater for Mr. Abernathy, not the other way around."

Gabriel laughed along to mask his personal opinions about the ludicrous gossip about Miss Wilde. He found her immensely alluring, and not just for her beauty. It was that very strong-willed nature that some would consider erratic that he found so enticing. As charming as she was, he reminded himself that he was not here for personal pleasure. He'd been hired by Jameson & Company to keep track of Mr. Bauer. Even so, experience had taught him that every detail and snippet of information, no matter how small or seemingly unrelated, could lead to answers.

Gabriel was certain that he could connect all these details and discover the truth. And he would do just that.

Chapter 14

AS THE WOMEN were making their way to the White Parlor after leaving the men in the Ivy Chamber, Phoebe grabbed Ella's arm and whispered, "I'm dying to know what you and Mr. Bauer spoke about over dinner. He seemed very engaged with you."

Phoebe's question was hardly a surprise. Ella had lost count of the number of times she'd noticed her friend staring in their direction. Given Mr. Bauer's cool behavior toward Phoebe thus far, Ella couldn't blame her.

Sharing her disapproval of Mr. Bauer would only add to Phoebe's pain, so Ella lightened her tone. "He spent most of the dinner attempting to convince me of phrenology's merits."

"Did he succeed?"

Ella smiled at her friend and patted her hand. "Not yet. I will keep an open mind, for your sake."

Once in the White Parlor, the women spread out to the various sitting areas within. Whereas many of the walls in Keatley Hall's chambers featured dark oak paneling or were covered with faded tapestries, the White Parlor on the ground floor boasted cheery white plaster walls with intricately carved relief work on the ceiling.

During the morning hours, the bright eastern sunlight would flood this space with a lovely warm glow. A large emerald-and-cobalt Persian rug softened the otherwise hard flagstone floor, and two large oak cabinets displaying her grandfather's private library flanked the main window that overlooked the forecourt's circular drive. Her grandmother's collection of blue-and-white chinoiserie was displayed above the chimneypiece, and tall sky-blue curtains emphasized the chamber's impressive height.

"May I beg a seat next to you, Miss Wilde?"

Ella turned from her position on the sofa as Miss Sutton's genteel voice approached. Ella nodded, and Miss Sutton carefully adjusted the jonquil folds of her satin netted gown as she sat down. "Keatley Hall is such a lovely home. Mr. Hawthorne told me it has been in your family for centuries. Imagine!"

The memories that flooded Ella at the reference to her family warmed her. "Yes, my mother was raised here, and my grandfather before that, and so on. I assure you, though, when the students return in a matter of weeks, the grounds will be completely unrecognizable."

Her delicately arched brows drew together. "How do you mean?"

"There will be roughly fifty boys and young men in these halls," explained Ella. "I often remind myself to enjoy the silence while I can."

Miss Sutton seemed not to hear Ella's statement. Her pleasant countenance dissolved into one much more sober, and she fidgeted with her lace shawl as she leaned even closer to Ella. "I'm happy to have a moment alone to speak with you. Phoebe has simply sung your praises, and I know I'm going to adore you. If we are to truly be friends, however, I must be candid. I'm not sure if it is to my detriment or to my benefit, but I must speak my thoughts plainly, and I detest secrets."

Ella allowed herself to really look at Miss Sutton. There was an honesty, a sincerity, that radiated from her warm, dark, deep-set eyes. "You and I must be very much alike then. Feel free to say whatever you wish."

Miss Sutton drew a deep breath, and her emerald earbobs danced with the movement. "I've shared, quite unabashedly, that I'm an enthusiastic proponent of phrenology and enjoy Mr. Bauer's demonstrations immensely, but I think it only fair to tell you that I am fully aware of your family's history with phrenology. Mr. Hawthorne told me about the rumors surrounding your mother's death and the subsequent rift in the Society. He also shared there was a pamphlet circulated indicating your mother was responsible for the death of her maids. He asked that I not bring it up to you, but I do not wish to start our friendship with a deception."

Ella stiffened. The topic was a personal one, and yet Miss Sutton was refreshingly blunt. Most people would whisper about the rumors behind her back and eye her suspiciously.

Miss Sutton raced ahead. "And I wanted you to know that I did indeed read the pamphlet and what was implied about you. I'm sorry to hear such a thing. About a child! It must be horrifically difficult for you to have this topic forced upon you in your home. I hope you don't take my interest in phrenology as a sign that I accept all that is said about it at face value."

Ella was so used to defending herself and her mother that she barely knew how to respond. "I appreciate your thoughtfulness, Miss Sutton, but I've had ample time to come to terms with what was said. Besides, I know the truth of the situation."

Miss Sutton frowned. "Just so I am clear on the matter, am I to understand that you are a proponent of phrenology? I took it from Mr. Hawthorne that you were not and, as such, were against Mr. Bauer's role as the guest of honor."

Ella's father's request not to contradict Mr. Bauer echoed in her mind, but it was not a contradiction to tell the truth. "My mother documented her studies on phrenology in journals, and I've spent a great deal of time reading them. I've also read anything else on phrenology I've been able to find. I have to say, I do not agree with the discipline, but one never knows. Perhaps Mr. Bauer will change my mind."

"Your mother kept journals on the topic? How wonderful!" Miss Sutton laughed—a delighted, airy laugh that made Ella think of tinkling crystal. "Imagine having the discipline and presence of mind to document her observations in such a manner. Your mother must have been a fascinating woman."

"She was a force, to say the least."

"Oh, that more women should be as such!"

The next hour passed pleasantly—much more pleasantly than Ella had anticipated. She'd been so wrapped up in her opposition that she had forgotten that some of the women were indeed friends. Not another word about phrenology or natural philosophies passed their lips until the men joined them again.

Once all the women began milling about and mingling with the men, Ella did the same, but instead of lighthearted conversations, she had another thought in mind.

She had spied Mr. Rowe at various points throughout the evening. Even during the awkward conversations with Mr. Bauer, she had an eye on him. Speaking with Mr. Rowe before she retired for the night was imperative for the success of their plan.

As much as she wanted to deny it, Mr. Bauer's presence and all the conversations about him had taken a significant emotional toll. Under normal circumstances she prided herself on being level-headed and practical, but the stakes of this event were too high. The fear that the guests would be persuaded by Mr. Bauer's arguments rattled within her like a noisy bird. If they believed his arguments, would they revisit the pamphlet? If so, what did that mean for her mother's legacy? For their perception of her?

Ella told herself it should not matter, but it did. Her dream of running the girls school depended on the Society's support. She and her mother had both grown up in families that valued them as equals, and the fact that so many girls were never given such an opportunity pained her. Ella wanted nothing more than to offer young women a school where they could freely study and explore ideas that had been traditionally reserved for men. If the Society members thought her a lunatic, how would they continue to endorse her participation in the school?

Ella made her way to the great hall, where she found Mr. Rowe speaking with Mr. Templeton. The easiness of his expression and his relaxed mannerisms bolstered the optimism she felt slipping from her.

When he noticed her, he excused himself from Mr. Templeton and wound his way toward her through the somberly clad crowd.

Her heart gave an unusual thump as he approached. She told herself it was the anticipation of advancing their plan, but it was impossible not to notice how handsome he was—how his broad shoulders and height made him stand out from the other men, and how his tanned skin emphasized his light brown eyes and contrasted with the stark whiteness of his cravat.

He stopped a few feet in front of her and bowed. "Miss Wilde."

Ella curtsied. "Welcome back to Keatley Hall, Mr. Rowe."

"Thank you." He lifted his gaze to the ceiling and glanced around the room. "It is actually quite nostalgic to be back here."

"In a good way, I hope."

"Yes. Of course." Mr. Rowe took a step closer, bringing with him the subtle scent of leather, and lowered his voice. "And I want to thank you again for arranging my attendance. I can see you have a great deal to tend to, but I was hoping we could speak somewhere before the lectures begin tomorrow. Privately."

"I was thinking the same thing. The ladies will be retiring shortly. After they do, I will go to the conservatory. It is far enough out of the way that we won't be disturbed. Do you remember where it is?"

His grinned. "I do. Ironically, I remember it because it was the one place students were not allowed to go, which made it all the more interesting."

The glimpse into his memories gratified her. "Very well. I'll speak with you shortly then."

They parted ways, and Ella, energized by a subtle yet viable sense of solidarity, returned to where she'd last seen Phoebe. Her goal of exposing the faults of phrenology might be difficult, but at least for the time being she was not facing it alone.

Gabriel glanced at the oak case clock in the great hall. Evening had given way to night, and nearly twenty minutes had elapsed since the ladies retired. The men, many of whom were older, were beginning to follow suit and return to their chambers or had dispersed to the billiards room, another parlor, or the library.

Gabriel requested a chamberstick from one of the servants who was replacing spent candles, and when the opportunity presented itself, he stole away to the north end of the house. As he stepped through the shadowed ancient corridor with its uneven stone floors and plastered walls, he contemplated what Templeton had told him about Miss Wilde's failed engagement. Clancy had already apprised him of the gossip, but the news about Abernathy had struck him.

Gabriel remembered Abernathy and wondered if the teacher had changed any from the spindly wisp of a man who'd been frightened of his own shadow. He'd displayed no backbone in those days and hid behind Mr. Wilde's authority, using the threat of the headmaster's leadership to keep the gaggle of energetic boys in line instead of commanding any respect of his own.

How could Miss Wilde, a young woman with such a vivacious and sharp personality, possibly be content with someone so passive? Surely she would have no trouble attracting any number of men, but he could not forget that society was often vicious to a woman who was involved in any sort of scandal, whether it was warranted or not.

Relying on his memory, Gabriel traversed the ground floor's east corridor and proceeded through a smaller, less formal parlor to access the conservatory. Candlelight spilled from the open conservatory door, and Gabriel slowed his steps as he approached. Rustling and the sounds of movement echoed from the space, and he glimpsed the hem of Miss Wilde's gown pass by the door's opening. He smoothed his hair with his fingers and straightened his cravat before he stepped to the ajar conservatory door.

He tapped his knuckles against the doorframe. She turned at the sound.

This should be a simple, practical conversation between two

individuals sharing the same goal. They were suspicious of the same man, and it only made sense to combine their investigative efforts. It was not uncommon for him to work with other solicitors and even magistrates or constables to obtain information about a person of interest, but then again, he'd never spoken with any of them in a moonlit room and with candlelight catching the golden strands of their hair.

He cleared his throat as he stepped farther inside. "I'm sorry for the delay. I hope I haven't kept you waiting long."

She turned. Her expression and tilted chin exuded confidence. "Thank you for meeting me here."

Gabriel already knew her self-assurance was an attractive trait, but as the gentle candlelight reflected from her alabaster cheek and glistened in her light blue eyes, how could he possibly concentrate? The flax flower-blue fabric of her gown shimmered, highlighting her petite, feminine form and making her eyes appear even bluer than he knew they were.

He jerked himself from his thoughts and assessed the conservatory. Even in the darkness, earthy scents and the humid atmosphere hinted of the plant life around him. His sight continued to adjust to the faint light. Plants adorned every nook and cranny: Exotic fruit trees planted in large clay pots were dispersed around the room. Large bushes and flowering plants found a home in containers and in long raised beds along the walls. Plants even hung from the ceiling. "I don't recall ever being in here before. It's incredible."

"You should come to see it during the day when it's light. The colors are magnificent. And your chamber?" She shifted topics abruptly, adjusting her shawl around her narrow shoulders. "Is it suitable? Most had already been assigned after we decided you would be joining us."

"It is very suitable." He chuckled. "You know, all the years I was here, I never had a room with a window, so for me it's quite an improvement."

She laughed a charming little laugh—one that had the potential to disarm him if he wasn't careful.

He needed to stay focused on the task at hand and cleared his throat. "Regarding the conversation we had in my office. Are there any developments or changes of which I should be aware?"

Miss Wilde brushed a loose lock of hair from her face and folded her arms in front of her. "There is one thing. When we met I failed to mention that Phoebe Hawthorne, Mr. Hawthorne's daughter, is in a romantic relationship with Mr. Bauer."

Gabriel winced. "A relationship?"

"Yes. Phoebe told me of it in confidence, and she'd be mortified if Mrs. Chatterly knew, so I didn't say anything. It's a very great secret, you see. Her father doesn't even know. Apparently it has been going on for quite some time, and Phoebe fancies herself in love with him. He insisted that she tell no one of the relationship because he was concerned about being accused of using her to sway her father. He was quite attentive when I saw them together in the assembly rooms, but ever since his arrival today, he's ignored her completely. She's quite distraught."

Gabriel wished he could be surprised, but the account seemed all too familiar. Bauer was hardly the first man to feign affection for a woman for his own benefit. "What do you make of it?"

"It is just another reason I don't trust him. Inconsistency is always a reason for suspicion."

The perceptive nature of her words struck him. "I couldn't agree more."

"Have you any new information to share with me?" she asked.

"I spoke with my client just before I departed London. Bauer ensured them payment by the end of next week. Unless he's already accumulated the amount, I fear something will happen here. I've reached out to some colleagues in London and on the Continent to see if any other information on him is available, but I don't harbor much hope that those inquiries will be fruitful. I've also written to other natural philosophy societies in England and Scotland to see if anything can be found there."

"I didn't even think about that."

Laughter sounded from somewhere in the house. She was risking her reputation by being alone with him in the conservatory. Everything within him begged to remain in her presence even a few moments longer, but this was the first day, and the last thing he wanted to do was cause her trouble. "Tomorrow's lecture will be early, so I should let you go about your evening."

"Oh wait," she blurted out, "there's one more thing." She stepped over to the table and lifted a small stack of bound books. "If you recall, in your office I shared that my mother wrote about Mr. Bauer in her journals. I thought you might find it helpful to read her accounts for yourself."

He accepted the tomes and thumbed through the top one. Each page of scribbles, drawings, and writings filled him with optimism. "This is wonderful! Thank you. I'll take care of them and return them as soon as I am able."

After bidding Miss Wilde good night, Gabriel left her in the conservatory and retired to his attic chamber for the night, eager to learn everything the journals had to teach him. Even more than the journals, however, the realization that Miss Wilde was going to be a forceful partner in this endeavor infused him with new enthusiasm for the task ahead.

Chapter 15

Ella awoke the next morning to a sliver of tender light floating through her still-drawn curtains. A dewy breeze wandered through the open window, carrying with it the sound of male voices on the forecourt and disrupting the pages of the open journal next to her. She'd not been awake long when a knock on the door and a soft voice sounded from the corridor.

"It's me," whispered Phoebe. "May I come in?"

Ella jumped from bed, reached for her linen wrapper nearby, tossed it over her shoulders, and opened the door to see Phoebe. Her high cheekbones flushed pink, the color deepened even more by the rose hue of her gown.

"I've been so worried about you. You were nowhere to be found last night," stated Ella once the door closed firmly behind her.

"I'm so sorry for causing concern." Phoebe whirled to face her, her eyes bright. "After I left you and the ladies, I had the opportunity to converse privately with Mr. Bauer. Oh, Ella, what a goose I was to even consider that his feelings might have changed. He was every bit as attentive as I hoped he would be. There's no need to look so alarmed!"

Phoebe's laugh tinkled in the space. "It was all quite proper.

Several hours after the conclusion of dinner, Father sent a note to both Miss Sutton and me, requesting that we join him in the upstairs gallery. I'm so happy I did, for Mr. Bauer was with him, and it was as if we were back in the London parlor again."

Ella frowned, unwilling to overlook Mr. Bauer's dismissive behavior as quickly as Phoebe. "Did Mr. Bauer give any reason for his coolness earlier?"

Annoyance flashed in Phoebe's hazel eyes. "Why must you look so much into it? He was anxious and wanted to be perceived as professional. If anything, he was protecting me from the questions that might arise from any special attention."

Ella could hardly imagine the supercilious Mr. Bauer as anxious, but justifying her opinion was not worth furthering a disagreement. "I meant nothing by it. My concern was only for you. I don't like seeing you upset."

Phoebe's dismissive giggle sounded forced. "I do tend to jump to conclusions, and by doing so I'd convinced myself of the worst, but everything is perfectly fine. I must be realistic and supportive during this time. After all, I cannot be his sole priority while he is here. He is here to educate others. Let's think on something else, shall we? Besides, I've come to persuade you."

"Persuade me?" repeated Ella with a blink. "About what?"

"Please. Listen to what I have to say before you respond." Phoebe interlaced her fingers. Her expression grew sheepish. "I know you enjoy attending the symposium lectures, but I think it best, considering everything, that you forgo the lecture this morning and join me with the ladies."

"On the contrary," quipped Ella. "I think you should attend the lecture with me. The ladies who do not wish to participate can easily entertain themselves."

"Oh, don't be ridiculous." Phoebe turned away from Ella to assess her reflection in the looking glass and adjusted the Vandyke hem of her sleeve's cuff. "Father expects me to help entertain the ladies, you know that. Besides, no other ladies will be at the lecture besides you. There never are."

Ella felt a strange suspicion as a result of her friend's words, but she wasn't sure why. Ella always attended the lectures. Every year, without fail, as her mother had done. Why would Phoebe discourage it now? "Is there something I should know about?"

Phoebe sighed. "I know how important all of this is to you, but people are watching you and how you are handling everything that has happened with Mr. Rawlston. And people talk. And I—"

"Let me stop you." Ella lifted her hand. "I appreciate your concern, but I assure you that I've already been the subject of scrutiny and rumors more than I care to admit. Nothing that happens here will offend me. If anything, I wish to know what is being said. I know you mean nothing but the best, but this is important to me. Please understand."

Phoebe pressed her lips together and looked downward. "Very well. Maybe after the lecture, then, we can spend some time together." She turned to leave but then stopped. "Oh, and were you aware that Mr. Rowe was to attend? I thought it so odd to see him here."

It was a leading question . . . almost as if she suspected Ella had something to do with his presence. Not wanting to draw more attention to it, she shrugged. "We spoke of the symposium when I saw him at the assembly rooms. His father was once a member of the Society. Remember?"

"I do, but I still find it questionable. After all these years that his family has had nothing to do with the Society, why would he be interested now?" Her voice trailed away. "Just remember what I said about him."

Phoebe quit the room, leaving Ella alone and with an unsettled feeling. Determined to get on with her day and focus on more positive things, she loosened her hair from its plait and brushed it. She pulled her somber pale gray gown from the wardrobe and selected a necklace to put on once Mrs. Chatterly came to help her dress.

Try as she might, the conversation would not leave Ella's mind. Why would her dearest friend ask her to change her behavior and act in a manner that was not her own?

Ella reminded herself of what was at stake—she would never convince anyone of the truth if she did not know what was being discussed. She just had to keep her goal firmly in front of her.

Chapter 16

"Confidence, dear Ella. Even if you don't feel it, even if you don't think you possess one ounce of confidence in your whole body, lift your chin high, and whatever you do, never be the first to look away. You have as much intellectual prowess as any man does. Do not let them make you feel otherwise."

Ella drew confidence from the memory of her mother's words as she paused outside the long gallery on Keatley Hall's second floor.

The long gallery was the largest room in all of Keatley Hall and was used for formal gatherings. Today it was the lecture hall for Mr. Bauer's first talk.

With its white plaster walls, arched ceilings and antechambers, and light planked floor, it was by far one of the brightest rooms in the entire house. Chairs had been gathered, a platform had been constructed, and dozens of guests in somber wool coats milled about the room.

Ella straightened her shoulders, lifted her face, and stepped in.

All the members of the Society professed passion for advancing the natural sciences. They gathered monthly in London to engage in debates on topics such as medicine, astronomy, and geometry. These men were wealthy, and while they weren't directly involved in the research, they did decide which explorations to fund. They considered themselves seekers—looking for the next exciting development.

It was not uncommon for a specialist in one area of natural philosophy to propose an idea to the Society in hopes of gaining funding for his pursuit. Now that she knew Mr. Bauer was in debt, she wondered how that might play into the situation.

Ella scanned the room, and her attention fell on Mr. Rowe. At the sight of him—his strong jawline and straight nose—her energy soared. Phoebe's warning rang afresh. Gabriel Rowe had, as Phoebe had indicated, questionable behaviors.

Did not she as well?

Her father's request for her to marry flashed.

She normally considered marriage an act of duty—something that must be done to preserve her family's legacy. But what if the man she married was like Mr. Rowe—someone who cared what she had to say? One who looked at her when she was talking and asked her about her opinions? What would she think of marriage then?

From the corner of her eye Ella had not noticed Mr. Bauer approaching until he was next to her. "A very great surprise to see you here this morning, Miss Wilde. How kind of you to visit us."

"Oh, I intend to do more than just visit, Mr. Bauer," Ella offered cheerfully. "I'm eagerly anticipating your lecture."

Mr. Bauer laughed heartily.

Unnerved at his response, she pressed her lips together and waited for the laughter to subside.

When he stopped, the smile on his long face faded. "The lecture?"

"Oh yes." She raised her brows. "I'm eager to hear your presentation."

Mr. Bauer's countenance sobered. "I'm afraid my lectures, such as they are, are not suitable for women."

"Not suitable? I don't see how that could be," she countered. "I saw your demonstration at the assembly rooms."

He chuckled. "The demonstrations, yes, are suitable for ladies, but the lectures themselves, the insight into how and why phrenology works, are often considered uncomfortable for the more sensitive audiences. I'd prefer not to have any fainting or swooning."

"If there is to be any fainting or swooning, Mr. Bauer, I can assure you that it will not be by me. I have studied my mother's journals on the topic, and I consider myself quite informed."

"I understand why you may think that, Miss Wilde. I really do, but I've given many lectures to many sorts of audiences, and I find that these topics are generally distressing to the fairer sex. I insist that no ladies be present, but I'm happy to converse with you later, privately, to address any questions you might have."

Was this why Phoebe had suggested she not attend earlier that morning? She was about to protest yet again when a voice interrupted.

"Miss Wilde. Mr. Bauer."

Ella pivoted to see Mr. Abernathy approaching. When at her side, he said, "You two seem quite engrossed in conversation."

She stifled a groan. The sense that he'd been watching her—or worse, that he was attempting to intervene or even control the situation—irritated her.

"Mr. Abernathy." Mr. Bauer bowed. "Miss Wilde said she wanted to attend the lecture, and I was just telling her that I did not think this a suitable topic for ladies."

"I see."

She held her breath. What would this man—who, according to her father, was willing to marry her—say? Would he stand up for her? Or, better yet, support her as she stood up for herself?

Mr. Abernathy's face paled as if he was momentarily seized by panic. He forced a weak smile. "That does not sound unreasonable, does it?"

She could scarcely believe her ears. The disappointment at his insipid response vexed her nearly as much as Mr. Bauer's suggestion that she would be too sensitive for the lecture. Since any sign of frustration would only add to the rumors about her, she smiled her sweetest smile. "I do appreciate the concern, gentlemen, but I intend to stay, just as I have for every symposium since the age of twelve. If you'll excuse me, I will find a place to sit where I will be quite out of the way. You'll not even notice I am here."

Without a backward glance she made her way to the middle of one of the back rows. She knew exactly what she would see if she looked back: two men, who were likely shocked at her persistence, staring after her.

Perhaps she should be agreeable and sweet, as her father had requested. Perhaps she should have complied, but to comply would set a precedent. If Mr. Abernathy were to become her husband, she needed to establish firm boundaries and expectations.

Ella recalled her mother's constant struggle to be seen as an equal. Had so little changed in the years that separated them?

Once Ella was seated, she adjusted her position on the chair when a flash of Pomona-green cambric muslin with ecru lace trim and fichu caught her eye.

Miss Sutton.

Seeing another feminine form in the room relieved Ella, and

her interest in the guest intensified. Did Miss Sutton share the same types of hopes for the future—the idea that women should be considered far more equal than they were?

Curious, Ella abandoned her chair and approached Miss Sutton, who was speaking with Mr. Hawthorne and a handful of other guests. When she noticed Ella, she excused herself from the conversation.

"Miss Wilde! Isn't this thrilling?" Miss Sutton's dark eyes sparkled brightly with interest as she drew closer. "There is nothing I enjoy more than healthy banter."

Optimism—and perhaps relief—rushed through Ella. "I'm glad to hear you say so, Miss Sutton. If only more women were to feel the same way. It is a shame that the gentlemen should be the only ones encouraged to form such opinions."

"La, these men. They can be so stubborn and full of self-importance. They do not give us credit, do they?"

Ella had to ask. "Do you intend to stay for the lecture?"

"Oh no." She shook her head. "I've been told this is not a talk for ladies."

Ella couldn't help but be surprised, especially given Miss Sutton's outspoken nature. "But I thought you were an enthusiast of phrenology."

"I am, but I doubt I'd learn anything new at this point. Besides, I find that a feminine presence just upsets the men. They desire our presence at times, but it is always on their terms."

Ella pressed her lips together. Miss Sutton's opinion made her question her own.

And she hated that.

When Ella did not respond, Miss Sutton's brow furrowed. "Do you intend to stay?"

"I do."

"Well, then." Her singsong chuckle was almost condescending. "I wish you luck."

Was that sarcasm Ella heard in Miss Sutton's tone? Or disapproval?

Miss Sutton adjusted the reticule around her wrist. "I'm going to meet with Miss Hawthorne and the rest of the ladies for sewing. Since you intend to stay, I'll depend on you for a detailed account of what I missed."

Ella bid farewell to Miss Sutton, and her mother's words of confidence echoed in her mind. But what was the best way to be confident in such a situation? If she stayed, she'd likely be perceived as unruly and obstinate—fodder to support the information in the pamphlet. And if she left and joined the ladies, was she not cowering to their demands? How would that further secure any sense of authority or autonomy?

She returned to her chair in the back of the chamber, fully aware of the scrutinizing stares in her direction. Some seemed amused. Some were disapproving. In that moment it mattered only what she thought of herself, and she refused to give anyone else the power to discourage, for every measure counted.

As the men began to take their seats, Mr. Abernathy came and sat next to her. Ella resisted the urge to recoil. She'd promised her father she'd keep an open mind, but Mr. Abernathy's lack of support for her could not be forgiven . . . or forgotten.

"I'm sorry if Mr. Bauer upset you."

She attempted to ignore the insincerity in his tone. "He didn't upset me."

"I spoke with him further after you'd left us, and he expressed his concerns a little more completely."

She batted her eyes. "Concerns?"

Mr. Abernathy shifted stiffly. "He's uncomfortable using certain terminology with ladies present."

She could not help but scoff. "Then I am sorry for him if he cannot talk about his craft with more maturity and confidence."

"You don't understand." The pitch of his voice increased. "He—"

"Mr. Abernathy, I know you're trying to appease everyone, but I must stop you. You'll never succeed. I suggest that instead of placating those around you, you decide your truths and adhere to them. Mr. Bauer is entitled to his opinions, but given my family's history with phrenology, I'm convinced that not only do I have a right to be here, but I have a responsibility to be here. You may not agree, but for now I am going to sit right here and listen to the lecture."

Chapter 17

AS GABRIEL STOOD at the long gallery's west end and conversed with Roger Norton, one of the most long-standing members of the Society, he decided that Mr. Bauer's lecture could not start soon enough.

"And your father?" continued Mr. Norton, a plump, short man clad in an old-fashioned silk frock coat and breeches. "I've not spoken with him in quite some time. Is he in good health?"

The question would be an easy one for most sons to answer, but years had elapsed since Gabriel had spoken to either of his parents.

"I do hate to disappoint," responded Gabriel, "but I haven't spoken to my father in quite some time."

A flash of pale gray fabric shimmered at the heavy, carved door—a sharp contrast to the dark blue, black, and tan clothing in the chamber.

Miss Wilde.

Mr. Norton noticed her as well, narrowing his gray eyes in her direction. "Ah, there she is. Punctual as ever."

Gabriel tried to decipher his tone. Was it judgment? Criticism?

He saw the opportunity to shift the conversation from his family and took it. "What do you mean punctual as ever?"

"You've not been here the last several symposiums." Norton smirked as he retrieved his handkerchief from his coat and pressed it against the perspiration gathering on his brow. "For years Miss Wilde has been the only woman to attend the lectures, at least since her mother died. It's against our Society bylaws, and yet she's always here. An abuse of power, if you ask me."

Gabriel tilted his head to the side. "One could argue that it is her home."

"Yes, but this is a Society event, and Miss Wilde treats it as her own personal hobby. What's more, she's taking advantage of her family's reputation and plans to establish a girls school on the grounds. Absolutely wasteful, if you ask me. The Keatley family may have been instrumental to the Society's establishment, but all this feminine interest is detrimental to the organization. It will muddy our purpose and the quality of our ideas."

The animosity in the older man's voice was no surprise to Gabriel.

"You've no doubt heard about her engagement to young Rawlston. It's a shame for the Society. Rawlston has all the makings of a strong leader, with connections in Parliament that would be beneficial for all. But I suppose he can't be faulted."

At this Gabriel could not remain silent. "Faulted?"

"She might be a pretty thing, but just like I tell my own son, those sorts of women are the most dangerous. She's far too high and mighty, like her mother, and Wilde has given her far too much rein. If she were my daughter, I'd insist that she stop making a fool of herself. A daughter who does not know her place becomes an unruly, undisciplined wife. No, I can't fault Rawlston, and I'm sure he'll end up with a better situation."

Mr. Norton clarified why Miss Wilde was striving so hard to prove phrenology faulty. It did not matter what she said or how she said it—Miss Wilde had to work twice as hard to be recognized as sensible and steady. She could be loud, quiet, compliant, defiant, or display any other attribute, yet she would be discounted simply for being a woman.

It was not pity Gabriel felt for her, but more sympathy for the disrespect she was forced to endure. How difficult it would be to constantly be told to stand down. Mary had been in a similar situation. Very little she said was taken as fact. Men like Norton would never see a woman any other way.

After Mr. Norton moved on to another conversation, Gabriel looked back to Miss Wilde, who was speaking with Mr. Bauer just inside the entrance. He couldn't hear the words being said, but he recognized Bauer's tactic. His stance was wide, his chin was lifted, and his fists were propped on his hips—a tactic used by men, especially large men, to intimidate smaller persons by using their bodies in addition to their words to overpower others.

When the men began to take their seats, Gabriel sat next to Templeton at a far corner in the back where he could see the platform and still spy on Miss Wilde. Mr. Hawthorne took to the platform and called the meeting to order.

"Our Society has had its fair share of challenges over the years, and most of us here can recall the Society's first experiences with phrenology. Mr. William Keatley and his daughter, Mrs. Leonora Wilde, spent time in Austria at phrenology's birthplace, studying and testing the theory with like-minded individuals. I daresay we're all aware of the challenges that arose from the early days of that relationship, and I count it a dark shadow on the Society's past. It is my hope that we can move past previous prejudices, whatever they may be, and revisit this topic with open minds and an eagerness to discover truth and to separate fact from emotion."

A round of applause echoed, and Mr. Hawthorne invited Mr. Bauer to the platform.

Once the applause faded, Mr. Bauer's voice boomed. "As I stand before you as a phrenologist and a fellow natural philosopher, I'm well aware of how the topic of phrenology can incite division. As with many emerging theories, people will fall on both sides: those who understand and embrace the rationale behind it and those who are opposed. Many years ago I worked with Mr. William Keatley and Mrs. Leonora Wilde when they were in Austria, and in the decade since I've dedicated my professional life wholly to learning and understanding how phrenology could unlock our understanding of human behavior."

Gabriel crossed his arms over his chest and glanced at the somber faces of the men around him, noting how some nodded in agreement or glanced to the people next to them.

Mr. Bauer's resonating voice continued. "Mr. Hawthorne alluded to the discord caused when a pamphlet reporting Mrs. Wilde's phrenological assessment was circulated. I feel it only right to share publicly that, yes, I was involved in the writing of that report, but the study has changed since then. The last decade has seen many phrenological advances, and it is my solitary goal not only to bridge any broken gaps but to answer any questions you might have about this discipline."

His buckled shoes squeaked and the wood platform groaned as he began to pace the length of the stage. "What is phrenology?

It is not magic, nor is it sleight of hand. Phrenology, simply put, is the study of the shape of the head. Every bump, every indentation, every ridge tells us something about the personality or natural tendencies of the head's owner. Does he bend toward anger? Slothfulness? Will he be a doting father and husband? All of these and so many more traits can be determined. For you see, the brain is the organ of the mind. It is not just one organ; rather, it is a collection of twenty-seven regions or organs, if you will. Each region is indicative of a trait, such as concentrativeness, combativeness, secretiveness, and so on."

Mr. Bauer lifted a white porcelain model of a human head. The skull portion of the head was outlined with a thick black line, and the skull was divided into different sections, each of which was numbered. He pointed to the lines. "By studying the size and shape of each portion of the skull, we have a glimpse of the muscles and organs directly underneath it. Quite frankly, the size of that muscle or region is directly related to how much it is used. By correlating each region to a personality trait or characteristic, we can tell a great deal about an individual. When I feel for any bumps or indentations, note that I am looking for extremes. A neutral skull represents a neutral characteristic."

As the man talked about the different sections and the character traits to which they corresponded, Gabriel shifted his focus to Mr. Gutt, the assistant. As gregarious as Mr. Bauer was, Mr. Gutt was not. Gabriel had not heard the man say a single word, and he'd only witnessed him taking part in a handful of conversations. Men such as Thomas Bauer, who would attempt to manipulate a group this size, would rarely act on their own. They would need some sort of reinforcement. What role was Mr. Gutt playing?

Gabriel glanced over to Miss Wilde, watching for any sort of reaction. She remained stone-faced. He'd expected no less, for if she were to make any reaction at all, it would place her under scrutiny. Regardless, he was glad she was here so they could compare their thoughts on what they had experienced. And he, for one, was looking forward to it.

After the lecture Gabriel was certain of one thing: Mr. Bauer was indeed a persuasive speaker. He'd been engaging. Dynamic. Articulate.

Despite his impressive presentation, the audience's reaction was mixed. Some responded enthusiastically to what had been discussed. Some nodded occasionally. Others had no reaction. The phrenological theory that he explained was attractive—if it could be proven true.

A flash of shimmery gray drew Gabriel's attention to Miss Wilde as she stole along the back wall toward the west staircase. Curious, he angled his head to watch. The west staircase was reserved for servants and students. None of the guests would use the plain, narrow stairwell. She'd be alone.

Seizing the opportunity, Gabriel pushed against the crowd of slow-moving men and caught up enough to call to her. "Miss Wilde, a moment."

She had just descended a few stairs but stopped and turned at her name. Perhaps he was only imagining an expression of relief on her oval face, but even so, he took it as encouragement to join her.

She waited for him to catch up with her before continuing. Once he was sure they were out of earshot and no one was following, he said, "I am eager to hear your thoughts on what we just witnessed."

Her brows rose and she shook her head. "He said everything exactly as I expected him to say it, and he was incredibly eloquent. The sad thing is that there is no truth to it, and he presented the evidence as if the theory was conclusive."

"I've shared with you that I interact with individuals who might engage in dubious professions. How convenient it would be if I could place my hands on their heads and ascertain their integrity and morality. It would certainly make my life a great deal easier."

They reached the landing, and together they pivoted. Miss Wilde gathered her skirt in her hand and lifted her hem slightly to keep from tripping. "I can't help but wonder, what of education? What of free will? What of necessity? He will argue at some point that people are, at their core, incapable of true change because of the shape of their head and the organs therein. Does that absolve people of their bad behavior? What of those who are endeavoring to better themselves?"

He chuckled at her onslaught of questions. "That's a lot to consider. I can see you have certainly thought this through."

She stopped suddenly and gave a little laugh. "I must seem obsessed with the topic, but in my defense, I've had a great deal of time to consider all of this. Even though my mother is not with me, I feel as if her journals have been the best education on the matter—even as great as if I had been conducting the research myself."

"Speaking of the journals," he said as they traversed another flight of stairs, "I read the journals you gave me last night."

"You did?"

He nodded. "I agree with what you have said about them. She was incredibly meticulous in her records. I thought it particularly interesting that she shared her impressions of the person conducting the assessments. What a brilliant idea—to also consider any sort of prejudice or unrealized bias the person conducting the experiment might bring."

"She was so concerned with being invalidated because of her sex that she'd go above and beyond what was necessary. I think it was that attention to detail that made her such a good teacher."

They reached the landing to the ground floor, and she stopped. Gabriel didn't want this conversation to end. There were so many other things he wanted to ask her about. He reached for a topic he hoped would lengthen it. "I heard something interesting from one of the gentlemen at the lecture. Something about a girls school?"

A pretty spark twinkled in her wide eyes as if in a sudden burst of excitement. "Yes. Well, I—we—hope there will be. There is a cottage on the property—Keatley Cottage—it is currently being refitted, and after the Christmas holidays we hope to welcome the first of our female students."

"That's wonderful!" he exclaimed with genuine enthusiasm. "I imagine that would have made Mrs. Wilde extremely proud."

"It is a goal we shared. I want to expose young ladies to the same education my mother and I were fortunate enough to receive. Algebra, biology, botany . . . there is no reason why women cannot make contributions to those fields. I know it is not the most popular undertaking, but it is important. I'd be lying, though, if I said there aren't many, many things that must fall into place if it is to come to fruition."

"Such as?"

She opened her mouth to speak but closed it abruptly.

"My apologies if I am overstepping."

"No, no. It is not that at all. There are some personal matters, issues within the Wilde family, that must be sorted."

The information he'd learned about Rawlston resonated. *She must be married at the time of her father's death to remain at Keatley Hall.*

It was Gabriel's turn to hesitate. He had to remember that just because she was sharing several secrets with him about Mr. Bauer did not mean that she wanted to share her every personal thought.

He needed to stick to the plan.

Gabriel cleared his throat. "Mr. Bauer said he's to perform demonstrations after dinner. If I am not being too bold, perhaps we might meet tonight in the conservatory to compare any new information?"

She nodded. "Absolutely."

Laughter echoed from somewhere deep in the house, and she sobered. "I'd best be moving along. I am supposed to be meeting with the ladies as soon as the lecture is done."

He bowed. "By all means. Do not let me keep you."

Miss Wilde smiled, curtsied, and withdrew.

Gabriel stepped back as she exited the stairwell onto the ground floor, and then he began the climb back up to see if the men were still in the long gallery. The day would be over before he knew it, and there was still a great deal of work to do.

Chapter 18

THERE WAS NO way to avoid the interaction with the ladies in the White Parlor. Ella was, for all intents and purposes, Keatley Hall's hostess. Her absence was likely already noticed.

She knew what to expect when she stepped inside. Phoebe, Miss Sutton, and three of the wives would be present: Mrs. Norton, Mrs. Parker, and Mrs. Shiveley. Apart from Miss Sutton, Ella had known each of the ladies her entire life, yet she hesitated.

"I must say it." Ella overheard Mrs. Parker's raspy, booming voice say, "I do question the Society's decision to bring him here. I thought it tasteless, not to mention disrespectful, when Mr. Parker first told me of it."

"Disrespectful? Oh, I don't know," countered the petite Mrs. Norton in a pinched, singsong voice that always made her seem decades older than she was. "Leonora would have found humor in this, do you not think?"

"After the things that pamphlet said about her in the name of phrenology?" rebutted Mrs. Parker. "I think not! Mrs. Wilde may have been a proponent of phrenology, but after the vile suggestions of her in that ridiculous pamphlet, I think we can all agree that the whole idea is folly."

"Do not be so quick to jump to conclusions, ladies," Miss Sutton cautioned. "That debacle, albeit contentious, occurred nearly a decade ago, did it not? That is more than ample time for any discipline to be revised and modified. Since I never had the pleasure of being acquainted with Mrs. Wilde, I cannot speak to the pamphlet, but I can share what I know to be true. And I have seen outstanding revelations come from these phrenological readings."

Unable to bide more, Ella pinched her cheeks for color, straightened her posture, and then stepped in from the corridor. Mrs. Parker, Mrs. Shiveley, and Mrs. Norton were all seated on the long sofa perpendicular to the fire. Miss Sutton and Phoebe occupied the two wingback chairs.

The talking stopped. The women turned toward her.

"At last!" cried Phoebe, lowering her needlework to her lap. "We were beginning to wonder if you were going to join us at all."

"I envy your courage to join the men," stated Miss Sutton, who also lowered her embroidery hoop. "I've admittedly been curious. It must have been fascinating!"

Mrs. Norton patted the open space on the sofa next to her. "Do join us."

Ella accepted the invitation and moved to sit next to the woman, who, of the three of the members' wives, had always behaved the softest toward Ella.

Mrs. Norton's sparse brows drew together. "You've in my thoughts, my dear Miss Wilde. With all this talk of phrenology and the sort, I can't help but think of your mother. She was so passionate about this topic! Wasn't it just like her to be aware of it before everyone else? What would she think now of these conversations if she were here sitting with us?"

Ella sighed as she settled in the empty space to Mrs. Norton's left. "I'm not sure what she would think, to be honest. She was passionate about it, yes. You may not be aware, but she kept detailed journals of her research. In preparation for this symposium, I read them all. Toward the end of her life, she was beginning to doubt the theory and even spoke out against it."

"Really?" Mrs. Shiveley's gray eyes widened as she snipped an errant thread with her sewing scissors. "That's surprising. I'd always heard she was such a proponent."

Ella glanced over at Phoebe, whose pleading eyes and tightly pressed lips suggested that Ella remain silent on the matter. Yet she could not. "My mother was passionate, yes, but she was passionate about the truth and the advancement of knowledge. I would be happy to share her findings with you at any time you should like, but I fear you'd likely be disappointed if you expected her to share the same views as Mr. Bauer."

There. She'd said it. In one fell swoop, she had done what she had told her father she would not do. She'd contradicted Mr. Bauer.

The ensuing shocked silence was deafening.

"Do you believe that the Society's gathering is in vain then?" challenged Mrs. Parker.

"Not at all. I welcome the opportunity for everyone to learn as much as they can and come to their own conclusions. My mother's opinion was but one woman's opinion."

"And you?" continued Mrs. Parker. "We all know you are not short on opinions. Do you share your mother's view?"

"I am learning, just like everyone here, but I do hope that Mr. Bauer will convince me one way or the other."

An awkward silence fell over the group until Mrs. Norton, with renewed energy and her kind ability to make others comfortable, sprang to life. "Do you know what I find so surprising? Mr. Gabriel Rowe! What a delight to see him here."

A murmur circled the group, as if everyone welcomed a fresh topic.

"I spoke with him last night at dinner." Mrs. Shiveley's smile creased the lines around her mouth. "What an impressive young man. And so handsome! Such a pleasant conversationalist. If you ask me, that is what the Society requires for survival. Young blood."

"Normally I would agree with you"—Mrs. Parker's countenance darkened, and her graying head tilted to the side as if she was preparing to divulge a secret—"but we must be careful with what sorts of young men join the Society. You did hear about the scandal that befell his family a few years back, of course."

A rustle of gasps and whispers ensued.

"I've not heard a thing!" Mrs. Norton's ring-encrusted hand flew to her chest.

Mrs. Parker leaned forward and lowered her voice. "You all know how I hate to be the one to spread gossip, but by now this is common knowledge among many circles. Young Mr. Rowe's sister, Mary, was accused of murdering a man when she and her husband were abroad. I believe it was in Scotland. It eventually was proven that her husband was indeed at fault, but what a mess it all was!"

Mrs. Norton gasped. "That is abominable! No wonder the Rowe family has all but disappeared from society."

"Apparently the husband accused her of the act to avoid the consequence, and she was imprisoned. Can you imagine? A gentlewoman and a lady!"

Ella's ears rang with what she'd just heard.

"How have we not heard of it?" prodded Mrs. Norton.

"If you were the Rowes, would you not go to any length to prevent such news from spreading? The older Mr. Rowe completely disowned her, and I believe Gabriel Rowe sided with his sister and was disowned as well."

Ella picked up a basket of sewing and sorted through it for a project but tucked away in her mind what she'd just learned. If it was indeed true, she felt as if she understood him more. He, too, had been faced with an injustice to overcome.

Ella sat across from her father in his study.

The symposium—along with all the activity that accompanied it—was taking a toll on him, and everyone could see it. She'd overheard more than one conversation regarding the obvious decline in his health. Her instinct screamed to defend him, to tell everyone that he was perfectly fine, but such words would be a blatant lie. It was not just sickness from which her father suffered. It was concern—and maybe disappointment.

Over *her*.

Despite his frail appearance, his voice echoed strong and low. "Mr. Abernathy told me about what happened at the lecture, about how you defied Mr. Bauer's request and stayed to hear the presentation, even when he asked you to leave."

"Of course I stayed! It is what I've always done! Why would I not?"

Her father grunted as he shifted his position in the chair. "You're not grasping the gravity of this situation, Eleanor. Time is running out. Why would you push him away like that? Do you want to leave Keatley Hall? Your life is here. Your dreams are here.

I may not know much about young women, but I'm not so obtuse to think that Mr. Abernathy is your ideal match. Nevertheless, he's stable, secure, clever, and at his core is a good man, and you're practical enough to see that."

In this rare instance Ella was at a loss for words and unsure of how to respond. Her father so seldom spoke passionately. He was her only family, and she loved him with every ounce of her being, but even as the name Abraham Abernathy was being discussed, the name Gabriel Rowe haunted her. Dare she even allow the thought of defying her father to enter her mind?

Her confidence was cracking. The endless optimism she'd always harbored about her future was foundering. She'd always thought she'd be different from other women—that she'd be free to oversee her life and her decisions. Wasn't that what her mother had told her would happen?

Perhaps Ella was the one being unreasonable. Maybe the hope of Mr. Rowe having a romantic attraction toward her was her attempt to divert from the truth. Mr. Rowe was not interested in a school. He was passionate about law and justice. He might be a kind, handsome man, but had he not contacted her for one reason alone? To observe Mr. Bauer's behavior and report back to his client?

Mr. Rowe's presence here had everything to do with his career and nothing to do with her.

When she did not respond to the statement about Mr. Abernathy, her father's expression softened, and he even smiled. "I am not used to silence from you, daughter. I don't know how to interpret it. All I can say is that I wish this entire situation were different, Ella. I really do, but regardless, I believe this to be the best course. I'm going to tell Abernathy he has my blessing on the matter, and that is that."

Chapter 19

"ARE YOU GOING to tell me?"

Ella glanced up from the crimson ribbon she was absently winding between her fingers to see Mrs. Chatterly's reflection in the dressing table mirror. "Tell you what?"

Mrs. Chatterly spun from the dressing table to retrieve a gown. "You've got something on your mind. I can always tell. You get this look in your eyes and your brow furrows just so. If you're not careful, those wrinkles will be permanent."

Ella could feel the sting of tears burning the backs of her eyes. No doubt Mrs. Chatterly would faint away from shock if she were to display the emotion begging to be released.

But even if she wanted to share her feelings, how could Ella possibly describe them?

Truth and facts were the backbone of everything she did—not emotions and sentiment.

When Ella did not respond, Mrs. Chatterly sighed, put down the gown, pulled a chair closer to her young mistress, and sat. "I can almost see the thoughts running through that head of yours, each one faster and bigger than the last. You'd feel better if you got those thoughts out."

Ella stared down at her hands in her lap, unsure of what to say until the crushing, expectant silence wrestled the words from her and she could stand it no more. "Father just told me he will give Mr. Abernathy his blessing to propose to me. He's determined I should be married. Posthaste. I don't even think he cares about the man's identity so long as the bargain is struck."

Mrs. Chatterly's practical response was immediate. "And what do you think about that?"

Ella scoffed. "You know what I think about it. Mr. Abernathy is a dull, uninspired man. How could my father think it prudent or suitable that I should be shackled to such a person for the rest of my life? I do not think that fate would be worth it—not even for Keatley Hall."

Mrs. Chatterly waited until Ella's passionate tone faded before she settled against the chair, as if preparing to divulge a story. "I'm going to tell you something about your father, Ella. Your mother first met him at a lecture, very much like this one, and they were both immediately smitten. She was but seventeen years of age, and your father was a decade her senior, and her father—your grandfather Keatley—strongly opposed the match."

Curious, Ella sniffed. "I didn't know that. What reason did he have to oppose it?"

"Your father was from a good family, as you know, and he was financially stable and very, very intelligent. He was generally liked by all, but at times he was perceived as flighty or even absent-minded. Your grandfather knew that one day his daughter's husband would become the headmaster of this school. He did not think your father suited."

"How could that be? He has been such an excellent headmaster for so many years. Everyone thinks so."

"Mr. Keatley thought your father was too lighthearted and that he laughed too much. Your mother, oh so headstrong and stubborn, followed her heart, and it worked out just fine in the end." Mrs. Chatterly shifted and leaned forward, refusing to let Ella look away. "What I'm trying to say is that your father is acting out of fear. He's been in this situation for so long that he's forgotten what it's like to be young and excited about life. He was once carefree, but he learned how to be a headmaster. Just because Mr. Abernathy is a good fit practically doesn't mean he is the only one who can rise to the challenge."

Ella frowned as the words struck. "But Mother loved Father. I can barely abide Mr. Abernathy."

"You have more options than you know." She stood and moved back to the wardrobe. "Like your mother said, be curious about those around you and the different options that present themselves. Just because they aren't obvious doesn't make them wrong." Mrs. Chatterly paused her words to shake the wrinkles from the gown. "I had my doubts about Mr. Rowe attending the symposium, but I can admit when I'm wrong. I may be an old spinster, but I recognize the look of attraction between two people."

"I don't think—"

"Your eyes brighten when his name is mentioned," Mrs. Chatterly interrupted. "Normally I'd never encourage you to go against your father's wishes, but he's not himself at present. If your mother had one dream for you, it was that you should forge your own path. And that is exactly what I hope you will do."

As Mr. Bauer prepared to take the makeshift stage in the great hall for the evening demonstration, Ella and Phoebe selected two chairs near the front.

Ella thought she'd managed to avoid Mr. Abernathy since their uncomfortable interaction at the morning lecture, but just as the event was getting underway, he sat in the empty seat next to her. "Might I join you?"

She stiffened as he sat down without waiting for her response. Ella could sense Phoebe's surprise at the sudden interruption, but it would not do to cause a scene.

"I looked for you after the lecture this morning, but you were nowhere to be found," he said as he leaned uncomfortably close, his high-pitched voice barely above a whisper and the scent of freshly applied cologne overwhelming. "I thought that perhaps I upset you, and I wanted to apologize."

She inched away from him to the far edge of her chair. "No need to apologize, Mr. Abernathy. It is behind us."

To her dismay he continued, "I know you're not pleased that Mr. Bauer is here, but maybe seeing a demonstration will change your mind."

The more Mr. Abernathy talked, the less Ella heard, for she spied Mr. Rowe entering the great hall with Mr. Templeton.

The memory of her conversation with Mrs. Chatterly leapt to life. Could Mr. Rowe be the answer? He was energetic. Interesting. Confident. Incredibly attractive. Was he the sort of man she could find happiness with?

"Miss Wilde?"

Mr. Abernathy touched her arm to recapture her attention. She recoiled at the bold physical contact, but before she could respond, Mr. Bauer's voice filled the chamber.

"How pleased I am to have the ladies join us." Mr. Bauer stretched his arms out wide in a welcoming gesture, a broad smile on his face. The candlelight scattered around the chamber glistened from the jeweled ring on his finger and the gold pin in his cravat. "I had the immense pleasure of discussing the merits and hallmarks of phrenology with the men this morning, but now I'll demonstrate firsthand the power and accuracy of phrenology when it is practiced properly. What you are about to witness is not magic nor witchcraft but a calculated approach, tested and true. We've already had a volunteer for our first demonstration, and Mr. Norton will be our first guest."

A round of applause circled the room as Mr. Norton left his seat next to his wife and stepped up to Mr. Bauer.

"Now, Mr. Norton," Mr. Bauer continued as the older man sat in the chair next to him. "We've spoken about you being assessed today, but we have never met before, have we?"

"No, sir."

"I have never touched your head, and I know nothing about you."

"Correct."

"And you're aware I might ascertain character traits that might be considered unfavorable. Correct?"

"I am."

Mr. Bauer turned once again toward the audience. "It is far easier, even after all these years, to assess someone I've never encountered before. I can't begin to describe how many times I've assessed an individual whom I think I know well, only to find that they are nothing like I thought they were. Once I am armed with the phrenological truth of their character, the wool is removed from my eyes and I see them for who they truly are—with all their faults and virtues. Isn't that the reality of human existence? A blend of the positive and negative, the advantageous and the disadvantageous?"

A hush fell over the room as the man began to touch the volunteer's head. He measured Mr. Norton's great head from every angle. The circumference. The distance from the base of his ears to his crown. The distance from his eyes to the top of his head. The distance from his neck to his chin. And on and on.

After completing his measurements, Mr. Bauer placed his hands on Norton's head and moved them over it, methodically and symmetrically. Every so often he would pause his action and whisper to Mr. Gutt, who would then write something down. After about a quarter of an hour, Mr. Bauer turned to the crowd once again. Perspiration gathered on his brow as if he was under a great deal of duress, and he made a show of withdrawing his handkerchief and dragging it across his brow.

"Mr. Norton," boomed Mr. Bauer as he addressed his subject. "I've completed the assessment, and my findings, in my opinion, are quite conclusive. Your acquisitiveness organ is quite developed and prominent, which tells me that you are a frugal gentleman and very aware of where your money goes and how it is used. Not to the point of being miserly, for you do appreciate a luxurious life, but you recognize your limits. Your concentrative organ is also prominent, which tells me you are stubborn in your beliefs and are not easily swayed. You'll debate a topic and defend it until you have been decidedly disproven."

A chuckle sounded from the crowd.

"By examining your form organ, I can deduce that you have a definite gift for drawing or sculpting, meaning that you can replicate what you see before you. While you may forget a name, you will never forget a face. Once you have been to a location, you remember the details of the things around you. But, as with everyone, no head is completely balanced. I've yet to see a head with perfect dimensions. I can see that based on the indentation of the head at your time organ, you struggle with remembering dates and you often lose track of time. I daresay that your watch fob is not for fashion but rather a necessity, for your ability to estimate the passing of time is lacking."

Ella joined in with the ensuing applause, but doubts surfaced. Anyone who was around Mr. Norton for any length of time might know those things.

"Mrs. Norton, I will call upon you now," Mr. Bauer continued. "Have I said anything about your husband that rings true?"

She clasped her hands together as if amazed. "Remarkable. You have described him accurately. Not many people are aware of his painting skills, and yet you noticed it right away!"

Ella couldn't resist looking back toward Mr. Rowe. Surely he had the same feelings she did.

But he wasn't there.

She looked over her other shoulder. He was nowhere to be found.

Mr. Norton descended from the stage, and Mr. Bauer's booming voice echoed once again.

"It's important to note that the assessment of a woman is different than a man's. Men, by nature, have larger heads, and the general shape and dimensions also differ. Women generally tend to have larger organs in areas of domestic importance. But I digress. If possible, is there a lady present who would like to join me so I may demonstrate this difference?"

Phoebe's hand flew into the air.

Alarmed, Ella grabbed her other hand.

Phoebe shook it off.

Mr. Bauer smiled. "Ah, Miss Hawthorne! A charming subject. Please, please, join me."

He turned to the guests. "I do have the honor of being acquainted with the Hawthorne family, and I have had the pleasure of spending time in Miss Hawthorne's company. I mentioned that I prefer performing assessments on subjects I'm not familiar with, but I think in this case I'll happily make an exception."

Beaming, Phoebe sat in the chair, and when asked to do so, she removed the pins from her hair. Her light brown hair fell over her shoulders, and he began.

Mr. Bauer's assessment process was similar to that with Mr. Norton. He measured her head, and then he placed his hands atop her head. He whispered to Mr. Gutt. When he was done, he addressed Phoebe directly.

"Aw, Miss Hawthorne, a delight. When I see an assessment like this, I have hope in the future and the good in the world. As with many women, your philoprogenitiveness organ is prominent. You are fond of children and animals, almost to the point of indulgence. Your conscientiousness organ is also one to note. You are honest and faithful, nearly to a fault. Yet I also do try to share some of the areas that I note are lacking. When studying your head, I found a deficiency in your locality organ. Do not be alarmed, it is a common deficiency among the fairer sex, but it tells me you have very little navigational sense. That your ability to remember directions and locations is not great."

A chill traversed Ella's spine. She was watching a deception play out right in front of her. Her friend was being played for a fool. Anger burned in her chest. She determined to appear calm, but in her heart fresh determination flared: She would expose the truth about phrenology no matter the cost.

Chapter 20

GABRIEL HAD TO act fast.

At this very moment Mr. Bauer was beginning his phrenological assessment of Mr. Norton, and Mr. Gutt was assisting him. Every guest was engaged, so the bedchambers should be quiet and still. The perfect time to investigate.

After ensuring that no servants lingered in the shadowed corridors, Gabriel made his way to the Blue Room where he'd learned Bauer was staying. After glancing to his right and then to his left, he retrieved a pin from his pocket and quickly popped the door's iron lock. He pushed the door open, stepped in, and closed it behind him.

The thick damask curtains on the west wall were pulled tight against the night, leaving just the orange glow of the simmering fire to work by. He blinked to adjust his vision and took inventory of his surroundings. A canopy bed. A corner wardrobe. A chest at the foot of the bed. A small writing desk to the right of the chimneypiece.

He approached the desk first and riffled through a handful of books and letters. After finding nothing of significance, he pivoted to the chest, knelt next to it, and pushed up the lid. Nothing but linens. Methodically he made his way around the chamber, searching in drawers, under the bed, and in cupboards. Everything was just as it should be.

Eager to take advantage of the time he had, Gabriel left the Blue Room as he had found it and made his way to the west staircase. He wanted to check Mr. Gutt's chamber, which was in the servants' quarters on the basement level. So far Mr. Gutt had been a quiet, unassuming man, but Gabriel suspected that Mr. Bauer was not working alone.

As Gabriel descended the west staircase, Mr. Bauer's distant voice reverberated from the plaster walls, signaling that he still had time. Once in the basement, Gabriel lifted a candle lamp that hung from a hook on the wall and made his way to the male quarters and found Mr. Gutt's room.

It was unlocked. Gabriel hurried in and closed the door. His candle lamp illuminated a room far less opulent than Mr. Bauer's. The oblong, windowless chamber was barely large enough for the narrow bed, an old wardrobe chest, and a washbasin, and Gabriel nearly tripped on the uneven stones that comprised the floor.

Determined to make quick work of his search, he placed his candle lamp atop the washbasin and opened the wardrobe. Several items of clothing hung inside, and a few books were stacked at the bottom. He lifted one of the books, and as he did, several pieces of paper slid out.

He gathered them and angled them toward the light.

Mr. Chelten: Aloof, lives alone and has never married. An avid horseman and enjoys outdoor pursuits. Mr. Chamberlain: Is proud of the time he spent in the military and speaks of it often. He believes in order and rules. He is punctual and is outspoken.

Gabriel flipped through the names—all of whom were attendees. This was it. This was how Mr. Bauer knew so much about the guests. And it matched what Clancy had told him about Gutt approaching the footman to buy information about Mrs. Whetham.

Even though this was not an official crime, it was further evidence that these two men were frauds. But how did Mr. Gutt get this information? Were they his own observations? Did someone provide them?

Gabriel could contemplate the details later. He tucked three of the papers in his waistcoat and returned the rest to the book where he found them. He finished looking around the small space, and after finding nothing new, he exited and made his way back upstairs.

He never felt right about searching someone's private space, but in this case the end just might justify the means. He only hoped that all this work was not in vain.

Excited chatter ensued, but despite the festive atmosphere, Ella felt sick.

A fresh round of applause circled the group as Mr. Bauer completed Mr. Shiveley's phrenological assessment.

The stifling air in the great hall made it difficult to catch a full breath.

Mr. Abernathy was too close. The overwhelming scent of soap and sandalwood made her head ache, and the fine wool of his coat sleeve kept brushing irritatingly against her bare arm.

All around her the other guests whispered and waited, seemingly convinced they'd witnessed nothing short of a miracle. Ella did have to admit that Mr. Bauer was a persuasive speaker, and of the three guests he'd assessed, he accurately described their characters—including Phoebe's.

As soon as the demonstration concluded and she freed herself from Mr. Abernathy's possessive presence, she joined Phoebe and Miss Sutton in the corridor just outside the White Parlor.

Phoebe pivoted as Ella approached, her eyes bright. "Oh, wasn't that wonderful!"

Ella's face ached from forced smiles. "Very much so. I had no idea that you were going to volunteer."

A shadow crossed over her friend's countenance. Her tone darkened. "Do you not approve of it?"

Phoebe's sudden defensiveness caught Ella off guard. She blinked and looked to Miss Sutton before responding. "Of course I approve. I wasn't expecting it, that's all."

Phoebe's lips pursed and her round chin lifted. She cast a fleeting glance toward Miss Sutton before speaking. "Mr. Bauer asked me if I would be willing to participate earlier today, but I didn't tell you. I didn't think you'd consider it prudent."

Ella found herself at a loss for words. Never had she felt even a twinge of animosity from Phoebe. Now with her friend's hard glare and tense expression, it almost seemed that she considered Ella the enemy.

"I know you don't like him," snipped Phoebe, "but can you not just be happy for me?"

Ella felt as if she'd been slapped. The words were simple, but the delivery stung. "I want nothing more for you than happiness—you know that."

Phoebe tossed her head, sending the nutmeg curls around her face bouncing. "I daresay if you were in my situation, you'd be the same way."

The subtle accusation of jealousy smacked.

Ella looked to Miss Sutton, as if to gauge another person's reaction to this conversation, but her normally observant eyes were fixed on the ground. And then frustration soared. Phoebe never would have said anything like this to Ella before. Could it be Miss Sutton's influence? "Phoebe, dearest. I meant nothing by it. I just—"

"Oh, never mind," Phoebe blurted. "It isn't worth arguing about, is it?"

Coolness met Ella's further attempts at conversation, so she excused herself. She sought another conversation to join but found none. Mr. Rowe was nowhere to be seen. Her father was speaking with a group of men, and the other ladies were with their husbands. She was in a crowded room, and yet she was completely alone.

Chapter 21

IN THE YEARS that Gabriel had been tracking down criminals, he'd witnessed every manner of behavior and tactics. But the handwritten notes—and the fact he'd found them in Gutt's bedchamber—surprised him.

Bauer was the force behind this ruse, of that Gabriel was certain, but Gutt's participation seemed a critical piece of the puzzle. He needed answers.

Gabriel returned to the great hall on the ground floor as the demonstration was ending. An air of animated excitement hovered over the guests as they milled about the space, but Gabriel knew what he needed to do: He needed to speak with Gutt.

Gabriel found Gutt talking with Bauer at the platform's far end. Bauer's gestures and expressions seemed sharp, as if he was irritated. Gutt's face reddened and his jaw clenched.

They were arguing.

As nonchalantly as possible, Gabriel made his way around the great hall's outer edge and the small clusters of noisy conversations to observe the interaction more closely.

Gutt—quiet and unassuming—was always present yet easily

overlooked. He was a rather nondescript man with light hair, light eyes, and fair skin, and he blended into the background. He never engaged with the guests unless it was at dinner or in conjunction with Bauer.

The argument appeared to end, and Bauer motioned to the supplies they had used—the head model, measuring tools, and notebooks—as if ordering him to clear them away, and then he stomped off. Gabriel knew angry men were more likely to rant, and if Gutt was angry, he might let something slip.

He picked two glasses of wine from the footman and, once Bauer was out of sight, made his way toward Gutt.

"Name's Rowe." Gabriel extended the glass toward him as he approached.

Gutt looked up from the notebooks and items he was organizing and accepted the glass. "Thanks."

"So the first demonstration is done," exclaimed Gabriel. "Seems a tedious process."

"Does it?" Gutt responded flatly after he took a drink.

Several moments passed before Gabriel spoke again. "How exactly does one become an assistant phrenologist?"

Gutt exhaled a noisy rush of air, and the muscle just above his cravat twitched. "Years ago I attended one of Bauer's lectures. I then became a student. And now . . ."

Gabriel let the man's words fade completely before speaking. "Surely after years you must be able to practice as a phrenologist yourself."

He scoffed. "You'd think so, wouldn't you?"

"Do you always agree with him? Bauer's assessments?"

Irritation contorted the young man's features, and perspiration dotted his brow. Whatever they had been discussing had quite an effect. "As with most behavioral theories, techniques can vary from assessor to assessor."

Gabriel needed to tread lightly. Gutt seemed willing to talk, but Gabriel needed to establish some sort of relationship before he could expect Gutt to trust him with information. "Will you go on the hunt tomorrow?"

Gutt propped his hands akimbo and looked out at the other guests. "I'm no horseman. I'll stay here."

"You needn't be a horseman; you just need to keep your seat."

But the young man seemed in no humor.

Gabriel continued to chat with Gutt until the guests began to disperse. He was on the right track. He would simply need to be patient.

Ella clipped a spent bloom from the plant before her. Then another.

Night had fully fallen. Slivers of silver moonlight filtered through the glass panels in the ceiling and fell on the plants and trees growing within.

For the first time since she'd awoken that morning, the tension in her shoulders eased. Perhaps it was the conservatory's solitude or the simple diversion of a task, but in here she could close her eyes and imagine the sun's warmth on a peaceful afternoon and forget the worries plaguing her.

She lifted the potted milky-white gardenia from her worktable, moved it to where it belonged, and picked up another plant with fragrant purple flowers. As she did, footsteps tapped against the plank floor of the parlor just outside the conservatory. She glanced up to see Mr. Rowe standing in the doorway. The candlelight caught his strong features as he entered, highlighting the straight bridge of his nose and the curve of his lips. "What's that you're working on?"

She wiped her hands on her apron and looked to the plant in question. "Pruning. I fear I've neglected some of them since the guests started arriving."

He drew closer and nodded to the pot before her. "It's a pretty flower. What is it? I don't know if I've seen it before."

"*Matthiola longipetala*," she stated confidently. "Otherwise known as night-scented stock. It only blooms in the evening."

He smoothed his fingertip over the delicate lilac-hued petals. "Beautiful."

"The flower closes during the day," she explained. "Its fragrance is strongest in the evening to attract nocturnal insects."

"And those big white flowers?" He pointed to an indoor arbor on the far wall. "Over there?"

She smiled, happy to talk about something other than phrenology—and happy to have someone to talk to about it. "That is *Ipomoea alba*. The moonflower. Isn't it magnificent?"

"There are so many of them!" He propped his hands on his hips as he looked to the ceiling where the vines were wrapping around the support beams.

"Those only open at night and close during the day as well. If I'm not careful, this plant would readily engulf every inch of this conservatory."

Ella would have been content to continue discussing the flowers, but Mr. Rowe's expression sobered, and she prepared for a shift in the topic.

He cleared his throat. "I was trying to read your expression tonight at the reading."

"And what did you think of my expression?"

"I can't say you looked comfortable."

"Was it that obvious?" she quipped, returning to her task of pruning to avoid eye contact. "I really did try to be objective."

He rounded the table to stand at its edge. "Oh, objectivity. Isn't it clear the entire purpose of the evening was mere entertainment? From where I sat everyone was happy. People heard what they wanted to hear, and Bauer played to the vanity of the masses."

His bluntness was refreshing and gave new voice to her thoughts. "My goodness. How succinctly you read the situation."

She clipped a bloom, and it fell to the stone floor. He bent to retrieve it and then handed it to her.

The simple action, and the nearness of his hand to her, distracted her.

Needing to refocus her thoughts, she set the bloom aside and returned to the conversation. "I couldn't help but notice you were absent during some of the assessment."

"A pity. But necessary."

"Why?"

The boyish twinkle in his eye reappeared. "In the interest of sharing information, I must confess something."

Why should her heart race at this moment? Was it knowing she was in his confidence? That he was about to share a secret that only the two of them knew?

"I told you why I'm here, and I've been very up front about my intentions." He pulled a slip of paper from the welt pocket of his waistcoat. "I found this."

She accepted it and read the information about Mr. Chelten. Confused at what she was reading, she tilted her head to the side. "What is this?"

"Do you recall how I told you that Mr. Gutt was buying information about the assembly room guests to aid Bauer's assessments? During the demonstration upstairs I searched both Bauer's and Gutt's chambers. I found these in Gutt's room."

Confusion was quickly followed by shock. Had he really gone into their chambers, uninvited and without consent? "You did what?"

"I searched their chambers."

The nonchalance with which he said the words stunned her. His actions were an invasion of privacy. As the hostess she was unsure how to react. "Why would you do that? We did not discuss it."

He relaxed his stance and leaned against her worktable. "If we *had* discussed it beforehand, would you have permitted it?"

"No. Of course not. I—"

"It needed to be done."

Did he approach everything with such assumed authority? She faltered for words as she organized her thoughts. "How did you even get in the chambers? Weren't they locked?"

"Mr. Gutt's was not, but—" He fished in his pocket and retrieved a pin and held it up.

"You picked a lock?" Ella wasn't sure if she was impressed or appalled. "I suppose there's a great deal about what you do that I don't understand."

"You'll catch on," he teased. "This was not the only slip of paper. There was information on almost everyone here. I'm not sure how this is all going to come together yet, but this evidence is damning."

"So what now?"

"We watch. We listen. Bauer's behavior should tell us what we need to know."

We. The word—the sense of belonging and togetherness, and

the idea of working together on something—warmed her. But she wasn't sure she understood completely, so to mask her discomfort, she lifted the potted night-scented stock to return it to its usual spot.

"Allow me." He reached to lift the pot from her hands. "Where shall I put it?"

She stepped aside to give him more room. "Here, I'll show you."

"May I ask you something?" he queried as he fell into step next to her.

"Of course."

"When we've talked, you've seemed very concerned about what the members think about phrenology. Why?"

The question should be easy to answer. She'd answered it hundreds of times in her own head, but no one had ever asked her directly. "You've read the pamphlet and know what is in it, Mr. Rowe. When I was younger, all I wanted was to prove to everyone that the vile claims were false, but now that everyone is discussing the theory, I feel differently than I anticipated."

"How so?"

"I thought I'd be spending the entire symposium searching for opportunities to prove Mr. Bauer wrong, but like you said, I'm not sure others are interested in the truth. They are here to be amused. If they're not here for truth, then why bother? Now I'm focused on my family and what comes next for us. This school is so dependent upon the Society, and if Mr. Bauer makes the Society look foolish, then it reflects poorly on the school. It's a vicious dilemma, and I'm not sure how to navigate it."

Mr. Rowe lowered the pot to where she indicated and brushed his palms together. "I don't have a legacy to protect like Keatley

Hall, but I understand having something to prove. I won't say I know how you feel, but I do know what it's like to endure a scandal. You can't change opinions, but you also can't permit them to hold you captive."

"You speak of scandal," she began, emboldened by the sense of connection that surged through her. "Last night you said you were in law because of your sister. And I know it is not my business, but the ladies in the parlor were speaking about your family."

He exhaled heavily and raked his fingers through his hair.

Had she upset him? "If you'd rather not discuss it, then I—"

"No, no. I'm actually surprised you aren't already aware of it. It's a sad tale, really. My father arranged a marriage for my sister, Mary, to a much older man. He was wealthy and influential, but the situation was horrible. She often told my mother of his cruelty, but what could be done? They were man and wife.

"After a few years of marriage, they were traveling, and her husband, while heavily intoxicated, became angry with an innkeeper in Scotland, and in a fit of rage he shot him. To clear his own name, he claimed Mary shot the man in a fit of delirium. He paid the witnesses to back up his story, and my sister was institutionalized."

"That's terrible! I had no idea."

"Even worse, our own father sided with her husband. I was infuriated. This happened when I was at university, so I began to go daily to the professors to learn what could be done. Initially they ignored me, of course, so I started to gather information. I visited the place where it occurred and spoke with the supposed witnesses, and after a period my professor, either through interest or annoyance, began to pay me heed. Eventually we located a witness who was willing to speak the truth and ultimately changed the course of justice. Mary was released, and her husband—because of his power and influence—managed to avoid the noose. He was sent to Australia and will never return."

"He's still alive?" Ella's mouth fell agape.

"Yes, he's alive. Mary resides with me now. She's my daily inspiration to help those who have no one else to fight for them or protect them."

"And how is your sister now?"

"She's as well as can be expected, I think, but there are aspects of it that she'll never fully overcome."

Remembering her mother's journals, Ella turned to a small table behind her and retrieved another one. "This is for you if you are still interested. This one has to do with my mother's first interactions with phrenology and meeting some of the others interested in it as well."

He reached to accept it, and then sounds of movement reached her ear. She turned just as a shadow fell across the door.

Abraham Abernathy.

Never had she seen his long face so severe, his eyes so narrowed. A frown tugged downward on his thin lips, emphasizing the hard lines etched in his face. His chin tilted upward in presumed authority. "Miss Wilde. Mr. Rowe."

Her stomach dropped. How would she explain this?

Mr. Rowe's response was calm. "Mr. Abernathy."

Mr. Abernathy ignored Mr. Rowe and fixed his eyes on her. "Your father was looking for you. I thought I might find you here, but I can see I'm interrupting."

"You're not interrupting anything," she said lightly. "Mr. Rowe asked to read some of my mother's journals."

"Is that so?" Mr. Abernathy responded flatly and looked toward the other man. "I had no idea your interest in phrenology extended so far, Mr. Rowe."

If Mr. Rowe was the least bit uncomfortable, his manner gave no indication of it. He tapped the journal against his hand and smiled broadly.

"It's an intriguing study, isn't it?" Ella asked.

Mr. Rowe's ability to stay cool and unreadable under any situation was uncanny—and a bit unnerving. "It is. Thank you. I'll return this when I'm done."

She nodded and turned back toward Mr. Abernathy. "And where is my father?"

"In the great hall. I'll escort you if you like."

Embarrassment flared. She had no choice but to accept. She bid farewell to Mr. Rowe, but even as she did, Mrs. Chatterly's words about forging her own path echoed. At some point Ella would need to start taking the first steps. She might as well start those steps now.

Chapter 22

THE NEXT MORNING, as Ella joined the guests already gathered on the forecourt to prepare for the hunt, cautious optimism flared. The clear blue sky welcomed her, and the goldfinch's song entranced her. Despite the turmoil of the last few days, a renewed sense of purpose infused her.

Perhaps her interaction with Mr. Rowe the previous night—and the encouraging sense of solidarity she felt with him—had something to do with it.

As she made her way through guests and servants, Ella set her sights on Phoebe and Miss Sutton, who were standing at the east edge of the drive.

"How charming you look this morning!" called Miss Sutton as Ella drew nearer.

Eager to put the perceived disharmony from the previous evening behind them, Ella smiled. "Thank you. As do you both."

"'Tis the fresh air." Miss Sutton lifted her face to the sky, closed her eyes, and inhaled deeply. "What wonders it does for the soul." When she opened her eyes, she used her hand to shield them from the sunlight and turned to the forecourt. "And how handsome the gentlemen look in their hunting attire!"

Ella turned as more of the men filtered through the stable yard gate, leading their horses, their riding boots shiny from the morning dew. Hunting dogs raced about them, barking and weaving amongst the horses. The refreshing breeze flapped their riding coats and carried their boisterous laughter, making them seem more like schoolboys than grown men on the verge of a hunt.

"I suppose there could be only one man drawing your attention, Miss Wilde."

Shocked at Miss Sutton's odd—and personal—statement, Ella winced. "I'm not sure what you mean."

"Oh, don't you?" Miss Sutton's giggle seemed harmless. "I am, of course, referring to Mr. Abernathy. One could not help but notice his amorous attention toward you last night during the demonstration."

Fire coursed through Ella. The nerve to comment on something so intimate. To someone she barely knew!

"There, do you not see him?" Miss Sutton nodded in Mr. Abernathy's direction.

"I fear you've misinterpreted the situation, Miss Sutton," blurted Ella, refusing even to glance at the man in question. "I've no interest in anyone."

"La, isn't that what we all say?" teased Miss Sutton. "But look."

Ella's stomach knotted, and she steeled herself as she turned to see Mr. Abernathy approaching.

Mr. Abernathy was not dressed for a hunt. Instead of breeches, ill-fitting trousers hugged his long legs, and leather pumps, each boasting a bright brass buckle, enclosed his narrow feet. As he drew closer, he lifted his seemingly too-tall beaver hat, and the morning sun highlighted the silver glint of his otherwise brown hair. His bow was ostentatiously low. "Ladies."

"Do you not intend to hunt today, Mr. Abernathy?" inquired Miss Sutton.

"Indeed, no. I believe the other gentlemen have that task all but covered, and I hope to spend my day in much more pleasant ways."

"I don't blame you, sir," corroborated Miss Sutton. "I agree—it is such a vile way to spend the day when there are such lovely grounds to be explored."

Ella blinked, astounded. What was happening? Miss Sutton was acting as hostess, and Phoebe's silence was unprecedented.

When did Ella lose control?

In a sudden change of topic, Mr. Abernathy shifted to face Ella and fully extended his arm toward her. "I was hoping, Miss Wilde, that you would do me the honor of showing me the formal garden. Your father claims that no one is better acquainted with it than you, and I'm exceedingly fond of such things."

Panic clutched her as she stared at his offered arm. He clearly intended her to take it. From the corner of her eye, she spied Mr. Rowe crossing the yard to the main gate, chatting intently with Mr. Templeton. She wanted to run. She wanted to gather her skirts and race through the meadows to the woodlands and hide among the oaks, just as she had when she was a girl.

But there was no running away from this.

Regardless of her own personal desires, the realities of life were happening all around her. The best she could do in this moment—in any moment—was to try to keep the promises she made to her father and do her duty. Her cheeks ached at the forced smile as she placed her hand atop his arm. "Of course, Mr. Abernathy. I'd be delighted."

Under normal circumstances, Ella could think of no lovelier way to pass the early morning hours. The dew still clung to the grasses, like diamonds scattered in every direction. Purple-hued aster and delicate rose hydrangeas bent and swayed in the gentle breeze, and bees hummed above them. As much as she tried, however, not even the loveliest thought could negate the fact that she was here alone with Mr. Abernathy.

Compared to Mr. Rowe, Mr. Abernathy seemed lackluster in every way. His words. His appearance. Mr. Rowe made her feel alive in every sense of the word, and Mr. Abernathy's presence, whether he intended it or not, made her feel like a child, as if she were incapable of forming her own thoughts and opinions.

But she had promised her father that she would try. And try she would.

She'd employ one of the only bits of social advice that her mother had given her, which was simply to ask questions when she didn't know what to say. "Are you fond of gardening, Mr. Abernathy?"

"Immensely."

His response gave her very little to respond to, so she proceeded to the next question in her queue. "Have you visited the Vauxhall Gardens in London?"

"I was there not even a fortnight ago. Brilliant layout."

It had been months since she'd last been to the beautiful garden with Mr. Rawlston when the spring tulips and daffodils dotted the space. She forced the memory to subside so she could focus on the task at hand. "Are you fond of the formal layout of such gardens, or do you prefer a more natural layout?"

"Certainly a more manicured design." He paused on their path and turned to a clump of delicate white oxeye daisies. "Take those, for instance."

"*Leucanthemum vulgare*," she muttered.

"What?"

"*Leucanthemum vulgare*," she repeated. "It's the botanical name for the oxeye daisy."

"How clever of you to know that! Now, if it were me, I would not plant the daisies here at all. I would put them there, along that stone fence. Wouldn't that be lovely?"

It dawned on her that this was the first time they'd had a conversation. A real conversation about something they both seemed interested in. Perhaps, if she tried hard enough, she could find some common ground with him.

They walked farther into the north garden until the sounds of horses, men, and dogs had completely faded, and after several moments of strolling, he stopped abruptly. "Do you see your future here at Keatley Hall, Miss Wilde?"

"My future?"

"Yes. Your future. I'm sure you have a strong attachment to this place."

"I do."

"It is a lovely thought, is it not, to think of your children growing up in the same house as their ancestors? Such a sense of continuity." He bent down and snapped a small white rose from its stem. The rose did not tear away completely, as he had likely intended, and instead the delicate stem splintered. He chuckled at the failed action and then, as if quite pleased with himself, handed her the rose. She accepted the damaged flower and offered him a weak smile.

"Your father shared with me that he informed you of the conversations we have had about the future of the Keatley Hall School for Boys and all that would entail."

All that would entail.

He was talking about her. About marriage.

She looked around, hoping for a diversion to save her from this conversation. Suddenly the sun that had been so lovely seemed harsh, the gardens seemed so isolated.

She remained silent.

"I know such a future may not be the one you had envisioned, but we should probably, at some point, discuss it. Your father is anxious for closure and security."

The disapproval she'd felt from him the previous night weighed heavily on her mind, and the current tone of his voice was practical and transactional. Was this the moment? Was Mr. Abernathy going to propose?

The thought incited a panic within her, and Ella's ears rang with such intensity that she felt almost faint.

"What are your thoughts on the matter?" he prompted.

"I-I'm afraid I've not had time to come to a conclusion on it."

His tone neither persuasive nor emotional, he said, "It is your father's desire that we should marry, and the Society members are already speaking of it. Even though you might not consider me the most fitting man for a husband, I am a fitting man for the school. I've dedicated my life to it, and I hope that we can, in time, figure out a way to make this plan viable for us both. But I must add, if this is something that would even be considered a possibility, I would suggest you employ a little more decorum."

She stopped abruptly at the accusation. "Decorum?"

He clicked his tongue disparagingly. "Arguing with the guest speaker in a public forum. Talking alone with a young man in the conservatory. It does not paint you—or the school—in the best light. And tomorrow is the visit to the site where you want to open a girls school, am I right?"

At his criticism of her behavior, her panic gave way to anger. She refused to be reprimanded and steadied her voice. "You're right, Mr. Abernathy. I intend to teach young ladies to think for themselves and to question the norms around them. They should embrace their abilities and contribute to the intellectual community. I was fortunate enough to have my mother to guide me in such matters. I hope to continue her passions."

Satisfied that she had made her point, she continued walking beside Mr. Abernathy along the curved path in silence until he paraded a lengthy list of neutral topics, from the new species of turtles discovered off the Italian coast to the plans to build a new dovecote on his property. She listened politely, responded when needed, and kept her expression engaged.

If it weren't for her father's request, she'd find a way to break free from Mr. Abernathy and his oppressive views. In the meantime she had to be true to herself—and her mother's memory.

Chapter 23

GABRIEL HANDED HIS horse's reins to a waiting footman and made his way to the tent that had been set up for refreshments. He removed his top hat, wiped the perspiration from his brow with the sleeve of his wool riding coat, and then pushed his damp hair away from his face. Even with all the energy exerted, the day's hunt had been relatively uneventful. Most of the men abandoned the task early on in favor of port and leisurely conversation, and Bauer was one of them.

Knowing that Bauer would be immersed in conversation for most of the morning, Gabriel kept to his unfruitful task of tracking a hare, but all the while he watched and waited for his opportunity to finally engage the man one-on-one. When he saw his chance to speak to Bauer as the man stood alone near one of the tables beneath a canopy of trees, Gabriel took it.

"We've not been formally introduced," Gabriel said as he approached.

Mr. Bauer turned, his normally fair complexion ruddy with heat, and beads of perspiration dotting his upper lip. "No, but I know who you are. You're Mr. Gabriel Rowe."

"I am. I'm surprised—and flattered—that you know who I am."

Bauer inhaled noisily, and the corners of his broad mouth lifted in a smug grin. "I make it a point to be aware of who is attending these events. Although I believe I've seen you somewhere before. In London, perhaps?"

"It's quite possible. I currently reside in London."

"Ah, that is why you look so familiar then." Bauer motioned for Gabriel to be seated at the table. "No doubt we've encountered each other at some point. Let's sit. Devilishly hot today."

Gabriel did as bid. "Perhaps at the Clancy Assembly Rooms. I believe I saw you there."

Mr. Bauer's brows lifted, as if he was pleased to have been recognized. "Ah yes. I've enjoyed a pleasant following there for most of the summer." Bauer paused to accept a pewter tankard of beer from one of the footmen before returning his attention to Gabriel. "So, Mr. Rowe, my good friend Mr. Hawthorne informed me that you are in law."

"I am. I work as a solicitor."

"Fascinating. I've long been a proponent of utilizing the power of phrenology to deter or possibly detect crime. I'm glad you're open to learning about how it might help you. But as a solicitor, do you not deal mostly in documents and paperwork? Or am I mistaken?"

Gabriel followed suit and accepted a tankard from the footman. "You'll find a great deal is changing in law. I do oversee a significant amount of paperwork, but I also find that just because paperwork is in place, compliance is not guaranteed."

"I see. So tell me, young man. What do you think so far? Do you find value in what I'm sharing?"

Gabriel chuckled. "I'm a skeptic, Mr. Bauer. Do not hold it against me."

Mr. Bauer's guttural laugh echoed from the canopy of tree branches overhead. "You're hardly the first I've encountered, and I daresay you're not the only one here. If anything, I consider it a challenge to change your mind. But if I may be so bold, I sense you don't like me very much, or at least what I am teaching."

"I don't know you, Mr. Bauer," Gabriel responded bluntly, "and if we all blindly accepted everything we heard, where would we be? Isn't that the whole point of the symposium? To challenge new ideas?"

Bauer pointed a thick finger in Gabriel's direction. "I've met men like you, Rowe. You've convinced yourself that you are aware of things that others aren't. I've seen you watching, waiting. My suspicion is that you came here with your skepticism so firmly in place that you are waiting for the exact moment that will prove everything about phrenology to be false."

Gabriel let the words simmer in the late-morning stillness.

Bauer's deflection—an attempt to make Gabriel think he was wrong or irrational—would not gain purchase over him.

"Do you know what phrenology has taught me?" continued Bauer. "It's taught me that people will be who they will be. We are all predisposed to a certain behavior pattern. It is fixed at the time of our birth. I suspect you are skeptical by nature, and unable to change it, you claim that skepticism is a positive trait. But I would challenge that the opposite is true. It keeps us from learning. Growing."

Gabriel wanted to laugh. Bauer was trying to manipulate him. He'd not allow it. "I am interested in truth, Mr. Bauer. If there is truth to phrenology, then I'm happy to hear it. But there is something I must confess. I'm friends with Andrew Clancy, and he has expressed concerns on this topic. His footmen have shared reports of certain phrenologists attempting to buy information about his patrons."

The crimson color of Bauer's face deepened. "I have neither the time nor the inclination for riddles. If there's something you have to say, then let's have it."

Gabriel straightened and folded his arms over his chest. "I'm aware very wealthy people are in attendance here, and I'd hate to think that someone was attempting to take advantage of them."

Bauer's words seethed. "If I were you, Mr. Rowe, I'd be very careful about making assumptions, especially when you yourself are such an object of scrutiny. So if we are asking questions—nay, making accusations—would you like to hear the accusations about you? Why would a man such as yourself, of questionable employ and the member of a scandal-ridden family, return to such a place as Keatley Hall? You can pretend all you want that this weak argument is why you are here. But your real intent is clear as day to everyone. And it is pitiful."

"Is it now?"

"A little friendly advice. You'll make no friends by pretending to be here for phrenology when it's clear you're here to woo Miss Wilde and make Keatley Hall your own."

"Ah, there you are!" Miss Sutton exclaimed as she swept into the White Parlor. "I've been looking high and low for you."

Ella looked up from her reading, surprised by the interruption. "You've been looking for me?"

Miss Sutton stepped farther into the room, and as she did, the sunlight filtered through the windows and caught the folds of her cranberry-hued gown, the deepness of which emphasized the chestnut color of her eyes. "Mrs. Chatterly told me that you'd returned from your walk with Mr. Abernathy, and I wanted to speak with you."

Ella angled her head to peer into the corridor, uncomfortable with the idea of speaking alone with her after their awkward exchange earlier that morning. "Where is Phoebe? Is she not with you?"

"She had a headache and wanted to rest. Which is just as well." Miss Sutton's expression sobered and the fabric of her taffeta gown rustled as she sat next to Ella on the sofa. "I was hoping to speak with you privately, for I fear I owe you an apology."

Ella bristled, unsure of what to expect. With the exception of Miss Sutton's cheeky observations on her romantic attachments, Ella had no tangible reason to dislike Miss Sutton. The newcomer had been kind and enthusiastic and had brought fresh life to a group of people who could be quite sedate and set in their ways. Even so, Ella felt cautious.

Miss Sutton's dulcet tone filled the space. "In the days I've been here, I've been so impressed with you, Miss Wilde. You've had some unique challenges before you, yet I've never seen you without a smile on your face or a pleasant thing to say. That very much speaks to your credit."

Ella looked down to her hands, unsure of how to respond to such praise.

Miss Sutton continued, "I fear I spoke out of turn this morning when I mentioned Mr. Abernathy. You see, I consider myself to be quite a matchmaker—I fancy that I have a unique instinct and can recognize when two people are well suited. I meant nothing more than encouragement, and I apologize if I overstepped a boundary."

Ella smiled as she attempted to gauge the woman's sincerity. "That is very kind, but an apology is not needed. I'm sure that Phoebe apprised you of my father's plan regarding Mr. Abernathy."

Miss Sutton shifted, but she did not break eye contact. "Yes, Phoebe did tell me of it, but only out of concern for you. She asked my advice on how she could best support you. While on this topic, I feel compelled to speak with you on a related matter. It's hardly my business, by any means, to intervene in the friendships of others, but my heart is aching."

Ella would not be pulled into theatrics. "Are you referring to Phoebe?"

Miss Sutton's lips formed a pretty pout, and she fussed with the lace cuff of her sleeve. "She adores you, you know. Dear Phoebe sings your praises and holds your opinion in the highest regard."

Ella nodded. "And anyone may know of my fondness for Phoebe. She has been my dearest friend for as long as I can remember."

"Then I feel I must tell you something. Last night Phoebe came to my chamber. She was quite distraught. About you."

Ella refused to allow any emotion to cross her face.

"I know that as her friend you understand how she's longed for a happy marriage, and how fate, cruel as it is at times, has kept such happiness from her. I'm also aware she shared with you her growing attachment to Mr. Bauer."

"Yes, she did mention it to me."

Miss Sutton's elegant brows arched. "When she was in tears, she shared that you did not approve of Mr. Bauer—that you thought him too old for her. Too different from her."

Ella's defenses rose. "I did not say those things exactly, but I gave her my honest advice, which was simply to be cautious until she has known him longer."

"I've no doubt that your intentions are pure, Miss Wilde, but I feel you need to know the entire story. Her father very much approves of this attachment. In fact, he is eager to make it an official one. There are other things he would like to do with his life, but he cannot move on until he sees his only daughter settled in marriage."

Ella shook her head. "Phoebe said her father was not aware of their relationship."

"Oh, dear Miss Wilde, she *thinks* he is not aware, but would a father really not notice such a change in his only daughter? Mr. Hawthorne and I have discussed it at length. As for the difference in their ages, I understand your concern. He is, indeed, nearly twenty-two years her senior, but many, many marriages flourish despite the years between them. After all, an older husband is stable and secure, settled in his dealings, and knows his goals. Phoebe is young, strong, and ready for the demands of motherhood and married life. I wouldn't dare to tell you how to communicate with your friend. I only wish for you to have all the facts at your disposal."

Ella's ears burned with what she'd just heard. Elements of it made sense, but something about the way the woman spoke to her—with a presumed authority—was intended, no doubt, to make Ella question her knowledge of Phoebe.

But had they not years' worth of time and shared experiences together? Had she not seen every major milestone and witnessed every major loss?

Ella considered each word carefully before allowing them to pass her lips. "I'm sure that everything you say is true, and that you also want what is best for Phoebe. If she were to tell me that this is her ultimate choice, then I would be happy for her, but until then, if she asks me for my opinion, I will give it to her."

Miss Sutton's smile did little to hide the tension tightening the skin around her eyes. "I wonder, if your situations were reversed, what you would think of receiving advice from her. Perhaps you should ask Phoebe's advice on matters . . . of the heart."

Ella's blood boiled within her. Miss Sutton was crossing the lines of propriety. "If there is something you wish to tell me, then I urge you to do it plainly."

"You have a perfectly viable suitor in Mr. Abernathy. I know nothing has been announced, but it is whispered in the corridors and almost accepted as fact, but those around you are not blind to what is happening. If you are thinking of shifting your matrimonial sights toward Mr. Rowe, I would caution you."

Ella lifted a brow.

"His reputation is . . . dubious. His family is questionable—scandalous, even—and his occupation, well, he keeps company with those with ambiguous reputations. You might consider him an exciting match now, but many a woman has followed her heart only to find she would have been wiser to trust her mind. Keatley Hall would be a prize for any man, and if it should fall into the hands of the wrong individual, everything your family has worked for would be in vain."

Miss Sutton's voice lowered. "I know you're a sophisticated woman, Miss Wilde, but do not allow your enlightened way of thinking to overshadow the truths of the society in which we live."

When Miss Sutton had ceased talking and the chamber was silent once again, Ella straightened her shoulders. "You needn't concern yourself for me, Miss Sutton. I'm very aware of Mr. Rowe's profession and personal attributes. I'm also far from naive."

Miss Sutton stood, the smile of her face sickly sweet. "I am glad to hear it. I would hate to think of a woman being taken advantage of. Now, if you'll excuse me, I'm going to rest before the men return. It should be an exciting evening, correct? I believe there will be another demonstration tonight."

Ella maintained her composure until she was certain Miss Sutton was nowhere near the White Parlor. Then she sighed and leaned back against the sofa. The fleeting thought had crossed her mind that Mr. Rowe might be here to woo her under false pretenses, but she had immediately dismissed it. It was such a far-fetched idea. But could Miss Sutton be right?

Ella's other concern followed—was Mr. Rowe being kind and attentive to her simply to gain access to Mr. Bauer? Did he really care about Mr. Bauer's impact on the Society, or did he just want to watch him? He'd investigated Mr. Bauer's and Mr. Gutt's bedchambers without asking her. If Mr. Rowe thought of her as a partner in this endeavor, he would have informed her. Wouldn't he? She didn't want to think that Mr. Rowe might be less genuine than he seemed.

The thought of it hurt her heart in such an unexpected way.

And then the question came back to her—what was she willing to risk for Keatley Hall?

Chapter 24

ELLA STOOD JUST outside the conservatory in the north garden, observing the guests as they milled about and basked in the unusually cool breezes coming off the meadow. With abundant laughter and animated chatter, everyone appeared happy and content. The ladies sat in the shade of the sprawling ash trees, and the men engaged in lively games of croquet.

She wished she could share their carefree sentiment, but the uncomfortable walk with Mr. Abernathy earlier and the odd conversation with Miss Sutton weighed on her.

Ella tried to focus on the people around her and engage in conversations, but memories of different times flooded her. Her father, who would normally join the men for croquet, sat on the side conversing with Mr. Abernathy. Even his laugh was only half the strength it used to be. Phoebe, her dearest friend, was ignoring her. And the future, which at one point had seemed so promising, loomed dark and uncertain.

Feeling weary, Ella decided to go to her chamber and rest before dinner. She prepared to walk back toward the house, but the sight of Mr. Rowe at the iron gate stopped her.

He saw her and lifted his hand in greeting.

How could one single action change the trajectory of her emotions? The afternoon, which had moments before been lonely and forlorn, roared to life.

"Miss Wilde!" he exclaimed enthusiastically as he approached. "Just the lady I was seeking."

Refusing to behave like a giddy schoolgirl, she tucked a wayward lock of hair behind her ear. "You've returned from the hunt, I see. Any luck?"

"Not a single animal was harmed by my hand." Humor danced in his expression. "You must help me keep this day from being a total loss. Will you walk with me?"

Mr. Abernathy's and Miss Sutton's warnings flashed, but her stubborn streak refused to heed them.

Ella *did* deserve happiness.

And maybe, just maybe, Mr. Rowe felt the same way.

She pushed her doubts from her mind. "Where would you like to walk?"

As he looked out toward the garden, the breeze lifted his dark hair from his brow. Everything within her wanted to reach out and smooth it into place. "How about down to the oak tree?"

Ella didn't have to ask which tree he meant. It was the largest and unquestionably oldest tree on the grounds, and students had congregated under its branches for as long as she could remember.

They began to traverse the path, and she noticed some of the ladies in the rose garden watching them from beneath their parasols and from behind their fans. She lowered her voice. "We are being watched."

"Of course we are." He shrugged without looking back. "Does that bother you?"

"I'm very used to being the topic of conversation."

"That's not what I asked," he challenged as they walked, casting her a sideways glance. "Does that bother you that they're watching you? Watching *us*?"

The question cut through her defenses. No one had ever asked her how she felt about being an object of gossip. How did he do it? How did he seem so unfeigned, so sincere?

Unsure of how much to share, she kept her voice light. "It doesn't matter if it bothers me or not. I'm destined to be the topic of conversation here, as was my mother before me."

"Ah yes. I believe you're right." He smirked. "I did hear a rumor about you."

"You did?" She laughed, grateful for his ability to make any conversation seem easy and effortless. "Which rumor was it, I wonder?"

The teasing nature of his tone softened. "I've heard—all gossip, mind you—that you and Mr. Abernathy have an understanding. That a wedding is imminent."

The statement shocked her. It was direct—and improper for a man to discuss such a personal topic.

"I would not mention it," he hastened to add, "but if that were the case, it would explain why he was so upset when he encountered us in the conservatory last night."

How was she to respond? Her heart wanted to emphatically deny an attachment to Mr. Abernathy, but her head urged caution. Her father's plan was clear, and Miss Sutton's recent words came to mind. "There is no understanding between Mr. Abernathy and me."

"Good."

Was he truly happy about it, as he seemed, or was he being polite? "I understand why everyone is saying so, though. My father is not well, and the Society is concerned about the school's future. We all have a duty to fulfill. Mine is to preserve Keatley Hall."

His response was soft. Almost tender. "I witnessed firsthand what happened to my sister when she did as expected. Things do not always end up the way we hope they will. You've not asked my advice, but I'll share it anyway. Don't give away your future happiness to fulfill another's expectations. One day you'll be faced with the consequences of your decisions, and no one wants to live with regrets."

How did he do it? How did he say the words that touched the part of her soul that needed soothing and the part of her heart that needed care? Mr. Rowe's sincerity stood in sharp contrast to Mr. Abernathy's censure and warnings.

As they made their way to the quieter parts of the garden, she was reminded of what she loved about it—the scent of the late-blooming wisteria on the gate that separated the kitchen garden and the wood pigeon's song. The path led them past the box gardens and hedgerows to, at last, the oak tree. Once under the boughs of the magnificent tree, Mr. Rowe propped his hands on his hips and stared up at the canopy above them. The sun streaming through the branches dappled his face and shoulders.

He then stepped toward the trunk and placed his hand on it, as if reliving a memory, and grinned. "I learned the fine art of gambling in this very spot. I owe all my success to John Woods, you know. He always had licorice, and we would gamble for that instead of money."

He stepped away from the trunk, looked at the ground, and nudged a rock away with the toe of his boot.

"What are you doing?" she asked, confused by his odd action.

He lifted his head. "Every year the students would bury a box around here. I was just looking for the signs."

"Ah yes"—Ella smiled at the memory—"the boxes. On the last full moon before the winter solstice."

"What?" He jerked up his head. "How do you know that?"

"This area is not so isolated as you think. Just look at the house. We could see every gathering, just like anyone can see us now. I watched every year from the window. Do you really think my father would let a bunch of boys sneak out at night without him knowing?"

"It was meant to be a secret ceremony." Mr. Rowe chuckled. "We thought we were so clever."

"That's the point, I suppose. There is something important to be said for traditions."

"There?" He suddenly changed positions and pointed to Keatley Cottage—a distant small brownstone house that mimicked Keatley Hall in its design. "Is that where the girls school will be?"

She followed his gaze across the meadow, and her heart ached at the sight and for all that it symbolized. "Yes. That's it."

"That's marvelous. You must be excited."

She nodded. "Tomorrow we'll be leading an excursion there. We hope that if the members see the school grounds and learn more about the plans, enthusiasm will grow. A great deal depends upon the Society members buying into the idea."

"I've no doubt they'll see your passion for it. I know it was your mother's dream, but if you are to lead it, then I also hope it is yours."

His words resonated. Yes. That was what she wanted.

Wasn't it?

She looked back to Keatley Hall. Even from this distance, she spied Phoebe staring at her, and the reality of her situation rushed her. "We should probably return."

"Yes. I think Mr. Abernathy is jealous."

At this she laughed—a genuine laugh.

How good it felt.

As their laughter faded and they turned back toward the house, his countenance sobered. "Before we return, please allow me to say one thing. It's not the house or the school. It is what your mother instilled in you. If you take away Keatley Hall, you will lose something important to you, but you would not lose who you are."

His words challenged one of her deepest fears: that she was nothing without Keatley Hall and without her family's legacy. They walked back through the garden in silence—mostly because Ella did not trust herself to speak.

Chapter 25

ELLA COULD NOT tear her eyes from the stage as Mr. Bauer placed his hands on Abraham Abernathy's head.

She wanted to melt into the floor.

Fearful of making eye contact with anyone, she kept her gaze straight ahead. She dared not look at Phoebe, who sat at her side, or, heaven forbid, Mr. Rowe.

Were Mr. Abernathy and Mr. Bauer doing this to persuade her? Or to prove a point?

Fixed to her seat by utter humiliation, Ella willed her breathing to stay slow and watched the scene play out before her.

On the platform in the great hall, Mr. Bauer ran his fingers over Mr. Abernathy's head, observed his head from several different angles, and occasionally paused to whisper to Mr. Gutt. Every time Mr. Abernathy snuck a glance in her direction, she wanted to slink back into her chair.

After the assessment concluded, Mr. Bauer turned to the audience. "I attest that I've never met Mr. Abernathy prior to this event. I've examined hundreds of heads, and I must say, I'm quite impressed with this one. This man has a strongly developed sense of domestic propensities—organs that reside in the occipital region. This tells me his priorities are with family. He possesses a strong paternal tendency—his children will be a driving force in his life, as will his wife. He has strong and loyal friendships.

"Along the frontal lobe we learn that he has a strong sense for things of beauty, and here, on this part of the forehead, I see that he is witty and lighthearted. As always, no head is perfectly fashioned, and I can tell by this indentation here that he has little fondness for music, and he will, sadly, probably never master a musical instrument."

At this, satisfied murmurs rose from the guests, and a round of applause rang out from the group.

Ella could only stare. What was wrong with everyone? Did they not see the fault in this? All of Mr. Bauer's assessments had been directed toward matters of marriage and the heart. Clearly this farce was intended to feed the rumors of an impending union between her and Mr. Abernathy.

Mr. Bauer conducted two more assessments, but it was not enough time to calm her racing thoughts, and by the end of the evening's demonstration, her frustrations soared to new heights. She had tried to see Mr. Abernathy as a viable option, but her suspicion that he had somehow influenced Mr. Bauer to sway his findings was too much. When her father was alone, she asked to speak with him.

Once they were in the privacy of his study, her father's brows drew together in concern. "What is it?"

Her words erupted. "Father, you must discourage Mr. Abernathy. Did you not hear that assessment? Did you not think that intentional? That it was directed to me? Everything Mr. Bauer said about him is a lie."

"Eleanor," he soothed, placing his unsteady hands on her shoulders. "You're getting riled for nothing."

Emboldened by her conversation with Gabriel, she could not stay quiet. She did not want to end up like his sister—in a situation where she had no voice. No freedom. No future. "I understand what all is at stake, Father, but he is not a match for me."

"You must calm down. I agree, this reading did seem a bit . . . provoked . . . but do not be too quick to judge."

A thousand retorts sailed through her mind. She did not want to argue with her father, but how could he be this calm?

"We've discussed this ad nauseam." His steady voice was barely above a whisper, and his pale eyes locked on hers. "I need to know you're settled."

"And I need to know that I'm not going to be trapped in a marriage where I'm reduced to—"

"Your future is here, at Keatley Hall," he interrupted more forcefully. "It's your legacy. You must protect it. For when I am gone, who will protect you?"

She wanted to scream. How could he not see the error of his judgment?

His voice remained unnervingly low. "I've heard rumors about you and Gabriel Rowe being friendly. He's a nice young man, but he's hardly the sort who could lead a school like this."

"Father, I—"

"Hear me out. He might seem attractive, more exciting, but stability, tradition, staying true to our family values—this is what's important."

A wave of defeat threatened. Her father had always been so open-minded and encouraged her to blaze new trails.

He cleared his throat and straightened. "Mr. Abernathy and

I had a conversation just this afternoon, and despite his concerns about your lack of enthusiasm, I told him again that he had my total blessing. You can expect a proposal from him."

"Father!"

"It's for the best."

"And if I refuse?" she fired back.

He stared at her. The softness in his expression hardened, and his jaw clenched. "I've always been very easygoing with you. I have let you have your way—to your detriment, I fear. This must happen, Eleanor. Do you understand? I know you are angry with me, but in time you'll see the wisdom. This is already settled. He will lead the school moving forward, and you will accept it."

Gabriel should not be irritated with Bauer's assessment of Abernathy. But he was.

The hour was late, and he had gathered with some of the men in the billiards room. At the moment, Templeton and Abernathy were engaged in a game, and he stood against the wall, watching.

He was here to observe Bauer to make sure he paid his debt. So why did it bother him that Bauer painted Abernathy as a wholesome, doting husband-to-be? Everyone present had to know that Mr. Milksop's ability to relate to children was laughable.

Gabriel knew why it bothered him, even though he did not want to admit it.

He liked Ella Wilde.

He liked everything about her.

It angered him that those around her were coercing her into a future he could clearly see was not best for her. It was infuriating.

Abernathy retrieved his jeweled snuffbox from his pocket as he waited for Templeton to take his shot. "So, gentlemen, tell me about the hunt. It had to be more interesting than my day."

Templeton leaned his lanky frame against the table. "Our conquests, such as they were, are nothing compared to yours, for I believe you had a hunt of your own, did you not? Tell us, how was your walk with Miss Wilde this morning?"

Abernathy opened the box, pinched the snuff between his fingers, inhaled it deeply, and then put the box away. "A dismal failure, I'm sorry to report."

Templeton smirked. "Hate to hear it but not surprised."

Abernathy lined up his billiards shot. "She was not interested in a single thing I said. I brought up every topic I could think of that might be of interest to a woman like her—the new species of turtles, Prussian history—and I found nothing."

"Give it time," encouraged Templeton. "She'll come around, especially with the right encouragement."

"Speaking of encouragement," said Abernathy, grinning as he stepped away from the table, "Mr. Wilde and I have spoken extensively on the matter. He's certain she will come around and see the benefit for all involved."

Templeton guffawed. "Very romantic of you, Abernathy. I'm surprised she's not falling at your feet."

Chuckles rounded the room.

"Make all the jokes you will, Templeton, but her father would like to see her settled as soon as possible, given his current state. I'd be lying, though, if I said I didn't have a few concerns."

At this Gabriel had to interject. "Concerns? Such as?"

"Oh, you know. What is said about her mother. About Miss Wilde herself. She does have different interests than most ladies and is far more outspoken. What if her oddities only increase over the years?"

Gabriel's defenses rose, and yet he kept his comment jocular. "Perhaps she just does not prefer you."

Templeton burst out with laughter, but Abernathy's expression grew taut. "Not all of us can wink and have the ladies fall at our feet, Rowe."

Gabriel shrugged. "I assure you that's never happened to me. A word of advice, though. If I wanted to win a lady's affection, the last thing I'd do is talk of turtles and Prussian conquests."

Templeton snorted again.

Abernathy forced his long, white fingers through his thinning brown hair. "I do wonder if I might have competition for Miss Wilde's affections. You seemed quite eager to speak with her after the hunt. A private walk? Private conversations? Considering that you are a skeptic of phrenology, not to mention that your family has not been a part of the Society for years, people might question your motives for being here."

The tension in the room grew, and the other men began looking in their direction.

Gabriel had to defuse it.

He laughed nonchalantly. "What are anyone's motives for being here, I wonder? Your personal life is not my business, nor is mine yours."

The conversation shifted from Miss Wilde, but even as the topic returned to the hunt, Gabriel reprimanded himself. He almost let his emotions affect the work he was doing. The last thing he wanted to do was draw more censure to Ella. He was walking a very fine line, and he knew one thing for certain: He needed to be more careful moving forward.

Chapter 26

IT WAS ALL too much. Day by day, even hour by hour, Ella's life was changing.

She started this symposium with the goal of discrediting phrenology and proving herself worthy of leading a girls school. How had everything become so convoluted? Now her best friend would barely look in her direction. She had a suitor she did not want. Even more concerning was that her heart yearned for a man whom she was not entirely sure she could trust.

She needed peace.

Clarity.

Ella made her way to the conservatory. On her way, she decided to gather more of her mother's journals, which were stored in her mother's old study in the basement.

With a candle lamp in her hand and a shawl about her shoulders, Ella made her way down an ancient stone staircase just off the conservatory. The candlelight flickered off the rough stone walls and cast long, odd shadows on the uneven steps. As she moved from the last stair to the basement's stone floor, a noise caught her attention.

Was that a giggle?

Curious, she inched toward the cellar—the source of the sound. She drew closer and rounded a corner, stopping just in front of the cellar door.

Whoever was in there should not be there at this hour. With so many additional servants in the house, she was concerned that something inappropriate might be afoot. But as Ella pushed the door open with her fingertips, she gasped.

Phoebe and Mr. Bauer were locked in an embrace, engaged in a passionate kiss.

"Phoebe!" Ella cried.

Phoebe jumped back and covered her mouth with her hands. "Ella! I—I—"

Ella's glare shot to the unaffected Mr. Bauer, whose smug expression derailed her. She stomped toward her friend. "You shouldn't be here. What are you thinking!"

"W-we were just talking," blurted Phoebe, unblinking.

Mr. Bauer stepped between them, his towering posture intimidating. "This is not your concern, Miss Wilde."

Ella forced all her attention on Mr. Bauer. "It certainly *is* my concern. This is my house! Phoebe, you need to go upstairs. At once."

Phoebe made no argument. She sniffed, angled her shoulders to brush past Ella, and disappeared down the corridor.

Ella whirled back to Mr. Bauer, aware that she was, for the moment, alone with him. Her father's plea for her to keep her composure raced through her mind, but what did that matter now?

She stepped toward him and said through gritted teeth, "You will consider her reputation."

"Or what?" he snipped dismissively. "You'll tell your father? Her father?"

Ella's hands shook with the fiery indignation coursing through her. "You may think I don't have a lot of influence, but do *not* underestimate me."

"Trust me, Miss Wilde. I don't underestimate you. I don't overestimate you. In fact, I don't think of you at all. What you think of me—or what you say of me—is of little consequence. The only thing I want is for you to simply stay out of my way, or believe me, I have ways to make things very difficult for you and for this little school of yours. After all, who is Miss Wilde?" His domineering words hung arrogantly in the thick cellar air. "Now, if you'll excuse me—" He brushed past her, and his elbow clipped her arm and knocked her back against the cellar's stone wall.

She steadied herself, but when she spun to address him, he was gone. Heat flamed in her cheeks, and tears of pure frustration gathered.

How dare he speak to her that way?

How dare he endanger Phoebe's reputation so recklessly?

But he was right on one count. Who was she to do anything? As much as Ella admired her mother, she was not Leonora Wilde. She was Ella Wilde. Small, relatively unimportant Ella Wilde.

She brushed off a bit of dirt that had clung to her sleeve when she'd fallen against the wall and adjusted her grip on her candle. She could not give in to self-pity. Not now. Not when everything was tilting and so many life changes loomed before her.

Suddenly aware of the darkness and silence around her, she drew a shuddery breath. What did one do after such an exchange? Should she go find Phoebe? But Ella's heart was racing. What counsel would she give? She certainly could not condone the behavior, and Phoebe would likely be embarrassed.

No, Ella needed to gain control of her own composure before attempting any sort of conversation.

Remembering her original intent to gather more journals, she brushed her hair from her face, gripped her candle tighter, and made her way down the narrow corridor before arriving at the study. During the daylight hours the northern light flooded the space from the small, high windows, or a fire lit the grate, but now it was completely dark. She lifted her candle, and the light illuminated the full shelves of journals, shells and rocks, small statues and sculptures.

After her mother died Ella had attempted to organize this room, but it was so like her mother had been—wild and unpredictable. Bits and pieces of thoughts and ideas scribbled on paper and tucked in books and journals.

With fingers still trembling Ella sifted through the journals, grabbed a year that would be appropriate, tucked it under her arm, and readjusted her focus. If she was going to expose Mr. Bauer as a fraud, she needed to do so quickly—and now she had more motivation than ever.

With tears of anger and disbelief still burning in her eyes, the journals under one arm and her candle in her other hand, Ella climbed the narrow staircase and turned into the conservatory.

Had Mr. Bauer really said those things to her?

Humiliation fueled each unsteady step as she hurried inside her place of peace. The soles of her kid slippers tapping against the flagstone floor was the only sound that broke the silence until a male voice stopped her in her tracks.

"Miss Wilde."

She jumped at Mr. Rowe's voice.

In her disgust over what had happened, she'd nearly forgotten about her hope of meeting him here, but now her emotions jumbled chaotically within her. She didn't know what to say. What to do.

His easy smile faded as their eyes met. He jerked in apparent concern. "What's wrong? What has happened?"

Unable to find the words, she shook her head and took a step away from him.

"You're trembling! Here, let me help you with—"

He reached out to take the journals from her, but she held them tighter. "Thank you, but I'm quite all right."

He pressed his lips together and studied her for several seconds.

Surely he must be confused by her behavior, but how could she explain what had just happened?

The glow from her candle glinted in his warm, dark eyes. If she wasn't careful, she could get lost in them. Forget what had just happened. Forget so many things.

His gentle words recentered her. "At least permit me to take the candle so you don't drop it. It's dripping."

She looked down. The candle had indeed tilted in the candlestick, and wax slid off the side. With a shaky breath she loosened her fingers around the handle. He took it, placed it on a nearby table, and then returned to her.

She forced her breathing to slow. Perhaps she was imagining it, but she could sense his concern. How she wanted to tell him everything—every detail of what had happened and every thought swirling through her head. It was the perfect opportunity, for they were completely alone.

He reached out a hand to her and placed it gently on her shoulder.

She should pull away. Abernathy's judgmental warning of being alone with Mr. Rowe simmered. But his hand was so warm, and the longer it lingered on her shoulder, the more a calm enveloped her—a sense of connectedness that she had been longing for, for such a long time.

"Tell me what is wrong." His whisper was soft.

Summoning bravery, she looked up to his entrancing eyes, which somehow were not that far away. The sincerity that met her there threatened to break her.

She had to be smart. Practical. Methodical.

In all her planning, nothing she'd ever experienced had prepared her for this weakening of her carefully constructed defenses. This realization that she needed someone's support, and not just anyone's support but that of a man who really cared for her despite her flaws, disarmed her.

She needed confirmation that she was interpreting his actions correctly. She had to hear him say it. "Can I trust you?"

Could she trust him?

Her straightforward question resonated within Gabriel. It was painfully honest and real. Miss Wilde had presented herself as strong, and considering her past and the rumors circulating about her, she had to be, but judging by her alert expression and trembling lip, something had frightened her. Something, he would guess, that was more impactful than a staged phrenological assessment. Now she was seeking reassurance. From him.

"Miss Wilde. Ella." A lock of golden hair clung to the tear that streaked down her flushed cheek. He slowly smoothed it back into place before he returned his hand to her shoulder. "This might not seem significant to you, but I've told you things about my family that I've told no one else. Ever. And what's more, I have shared my thoughts on my work with you, which is entirely new to me."

Gabriel slid his palm down her arm until his hand grazed her fingers. "All this is to say that *I* trust *you*. I hope I've proven myself worthy enough for that trust to be reciprocated."

With a shuddery sigh Ella glanced down at their joined hands. She did not pull away. Instead, she looked back up at him. Her brilliant, lovely blue eyes met his with such directness and confidence. Her breathing slowed. Her trembling ceased. "I trust you, Gabriel. You may be the only person I trust right now, but I do."

His Christian name on her lips bolstered him—this verbal confirmation of closeness affected him almost as much as any physical touch could.

Her words were slow. "I was just in the basement to retrieve more journals, and I encountered Mr. Bauer and Phoebe in a compromising moment. He threatened that if I said something, he'd make things difficult for me. I'm not scared of him, and I'm not intimidated. I'm just furious at his arrogance."

Gabriel tensed. This entire situation would get out of hand soon. He'd shown part of his hand to Bauer at the hunt, and now it sounded like Bauer was increasing his tactics. Everything within him wanted to find Bauer, demand answers, and take care of the situation himself, but he doubted Ella was the sort of woman who would be happy having someone else solve her problems. It would be far more prudent to tackle this together. "I think it's time to take this to your father."

"No," she blurted.

"Mr. Hawthorne, then," he offered gently. "I've no problem at all exposing Bauer for what he is."

She drew a quivery sigh and, after several seconds, nodded. "Perhaps you're right."

He looked from the golden strands of her hair to the sincerity in her eyes to the fullness of her lips. Gabriel had always known he'd never be satisfied with a woman who lacked fortitude, and in a society that told women to be quiet and meek, such a lady was rare. Ella's convictions, wit, and determination were unlike any he'd encountered. Her unique, vibrant energy captivated him every bit as much as her beauty did.

He ached to kiss her—to feel the softness of her lips against his and the warmth of her in his arms, but for now he refrained and stroked his thumb over the top of her hand instead. "I know that you will not rest until everyone knows the truth about Thomas Bauer. I promise you, Ella, that I will be by your side until we see that he answers for his actions, one way or another."

Chapter 27

AFTER LEAVING GABRIEL in the conservatory, Ella walked back to her bedchamber with her heart alive with what she'd just experienced.

Gabriel cared for her. She felt it in his touch. She saw it in his eyes and heard it in his voice.

Her mind hardly knew where to land. A strange, almost dizzy sensation overtook her. She worried for her friend, but at the same time, an enticing vision of a new future for herself formed.

She arrived at her chamber door and opened it, expecting that Mrs. Chatterly had prepared her room for bed. Instead, she was stunned to find Phoebe frantically pacing the space.

The moment Phoebe saw Ella at the door, she rushed toward her. Tears stained her pale cheeks. Her red-rimmed eyes were swollen. "I know what you must be thinking."

Ella's nerves tightened at the impending conversation, and she closed the door behind her. Her shock at what she'd encountered and how vilely she'd been treated was still fresh. She wanted to be sympathetic and understanding, but Mr. Bauer's coldness erased any ounce of compassion she could muster for them as a couple.

Garnering her patience, Ella placed the journals she'd brought with her on the small table next to the bed and turned to face her friend. "I assure you, there is no way you could possibly know what I'm thinking. I don't even know what I am thinking anymore, Phoebe."

"He's so kind to me, Ella," Phoebe exclaimed in a transparent, desperate attempt to sway her. "He loves me! I know you don't believe me, but it is true."

A dozen cynical retorts filled Ella's mind. Why then did he ignore her in group settings? If he really loved Phoebe, why would he be so harsh to her best friend?

"Please say something." Phoebe faltered, her voice shaky as she laced her fingers together before her. "Your silence is making me nervous."

Ella rubbed her forehead as she considered her response and sank onto the chair next to the fire. "I can't say I understand what you are doing. You know that I desire nothing more than for you to be happy, but I must ask: Have you two had a real conversation about the future? Alone? Has he asked about your opinions? Has he asked about you—what you like? Dislike? Does he listen to you, or has he only told you things you want to hear?"

"I-it isn't like that," Phoebe stammered, fidgeting with her fingers. "It isn't."

"Isn't it? Oh, Phoebe." Ella motioned for her friend to join her in the opposite chair. "I beg you. Do not let your admiration or infatuation blind you to truths."

"Truths?" Phoebe shot back, as if suddenly spurred, before she perched on the edge of the indicated chair. "I'm not blinded. Give me a little credit. I'm fully aware of Mr. Bauer's virtues and his shortcomings. I'm trusting my intuition. Isn't that what you always say?"

Ella twitched at how Phoebe misconstrued her past words.

Tears pooled afresh in Phoebe's eyes. "My time is running out, Ella. Father very well might marry Miss Sutton. The last thing he will want is a grown daughter living under his roof when he's trying to start a new life. And then what of me?"

At this Ella's heart softened, for she did understand the fear that came with this transition. To be without security was the greatest concern of any woman she knew, for how could they survive without someone to provide for them? "All I ask is that you do not let fear rule you. You're far too intelligent for that. Just don't act . . . rashly."

"Rashly?" Phoebe's tone sharpened. "That seems rich coming from you. You—who speaks of intuition. You—who justifies every statement and action by claiming intuition, yet you do not respect it in your friends."

The hurtful words burned. Not wishing to add fuel to Phoebe's ire, Ella steadied her tone. "I'm not in an ideal situation either, Phoebe. We all face uncertainty at some point."

Phoebe crossed her arms over her chest. The sorrow she'd displayed just moments prior had morphed into something darker, something more defensive. "You say that, but your actions say something different. You're doing everything you can to avoid change, not to mention you're the only person present who seems intent upon finding fault with Thomas. You are supposed to be my friend, but you feel like an enemy."

Ella stood from the chair. She would not argue with Phoebe. Not over Mr. Bauer. "I think the best thing for both of us is to get a good night's sleep. Perhaps we should talk about this in the morning."

Phoebe stood and, without another word, stomped from the chamber.

With an exhausted sigh Ella dropped atop her bed and stared at the deep blue canopy above her. Even though she was now alone, Phoebe's harsh words still echoed in the silence.

And they hurt.

Ella loved Phoebe, but her friend was unrecognizable.

A few minutes later Mrs. Chatterly appeared in the doorway with her round face drawn in confusion. "I just passed Miss Hawthorne in the corridor. Was she crying?"

She nodded, and as Mrs. Chatterly stepped farther into the room and closed the door behind her, Ella's words poured out. She could not have stopped them if she wanted to. She shared everything that she knew about Phoebe's romance, from when Phoebe told her about their attachment, to seeing them in an embrace, to Mr. Bauer's threat, to Gabriel's suggestion to inform Mr. Hawthorne of their suspicions. "Maybe I'm wrong. Maybe everything she is saying is right about me, but this entire situation is not right."

After listening silently, Mrs. Chatterly sat next to Ella, just like she had dozens of times over the last decade. She smoothed a piece of hair away from Ella's face in a maternal sort of affection. "People fall in love all the time, don't they? Maybe what Miss Hawthorne feels for Mr. Bauer is genuine, but I do find it odd that she would have affections for a person capable of speaking to someone the way he spoke to you."

"Phoebe has always been trusting and naive, but how can she not see the truth about him? It's so obvious."

"People see what they want to see. Phoebe is telling herself that his perceived attributes outweigh anything negative."

With a sigh Ella lay back against the bed and propped her head on her hand. "Did you ever meet Mr. Bauer when you traveled with my mother?"

Mrs. Chatterly moved to draw the curtains over one of the windows. "It's possible I encountered him at one point or another, but I can't remember for certain. Your mother was always so fascinated by those sorts of people, but they were a strange lot."

It was odd to hear Mrs. Chatterly speak any criticism whatsoever of her mother. "Strange? How so?"

Mrs. Chatterly shook her head. "They just thought and spoke differently than other people—as if in a world all their own."

"So what do *you* think of Mr. Bauer? You've seen him several times now. Do you agree with me?"

Mrs. Chatterly drew the curtains over the second window. "I haven't interacted with him at all, but I know you, and I trust your judgment. Your father is a good man, but he can be blind to certain details when his mind is fixed on a particular outcome. But here we are spending all this time speaking of Miss Hawthorne and Mr. Bauer when you are the one I'm concerned about."

"Me?" Ella blinked, straightening. "Whatever for?"

"You speak of the matters of Phoebe's heart, yet I don't want you to neglect your own." Mrs. Chatterly smiled softly and returned to sit again with Ella on the bed. "I saw you and Mr. Rowe out walking today. You looked happy."

At the memory of her hand in his while they were in the conservatory, warmth suffused her face. Her practical side wanted to conceal the giddiness bubbling within her at the mere mention of his name. But why should she hide it from Mrs. Chatterly?

"How did I never know that someone like him could exist? It seems like all of a sudden everyone is trying to tell me what to think and do, but he is different. He asks what I think. He's only been at Keatley Hall for a few days, yet I already feel a closeness with him unlike I have ever felt before. It defies logic, but I am more like myself around him than any other person here. Is that absurd? Perhaps I am the one misreading a situation and only seeing attributes that I want to see, not Phoebe."

"Oh, my darling." Mrs. Chatterly chuckled and patted Ella's hand. "That is the great mystery of romantic love, is it not? That is the unexplainable element that no amount of reasoning or research or practicality can prepare you for. It is elusive, and so many spend their entire lives searching for it. Or worse yet, some encounter it and are unwilling to embrace it. If Mr. Rowe is as supportive as you say, if he captures your imagination and makes you feel alive, then do not resist it. There is no greater respect a man can give a woman than to encourage her to be the person she truly is, not what society tells her she should be. Come now. Let's get you to bed."

After the bed was prepared, the fire was stoked, and Mrs. Chatterly departed for the night, Ella retrieved one of the journals and leaned closer to the candles on the side of her bed to read. She could almost hear her mother's steady, measured voice reading aloud.

Until something caught her eye.

The name Thomas Bauer.

Ella sat up straight at the discovery. Had she never read this volume? She double-checked the dates. It was from an earlier year, from before her mother's opinions on phrenology began to change.

> *Mr. Bauer is the most unusual man, with a strange propensity to smack his lips when he is anxious or drum his fingers on the table. But it is his eyes that make him seem the most intense—they are the most unique shade of blue.*

Ella froze.

Blue.

How had she not noticed this detail before?

Thomas Bauer—Phoebe's suitor and the current phrenological expert—had dark, coffee-hued eyes and dark hair.

Her heart thudded as her thoughts dashed to draw conclusions.

Could it be possible that her mother got it wrong?

It seemed highly unlikely. Her mother noticed everything. About everyone. Eye color certainly would not be something she would mistake.

But what did it mean? Her mind mapped the possible outcomes.

Was it possible that Mr. Bauer was not who he claimed to be? Surely not, for he was a phrenological expert. There weren't many people who understood the art.

The discovery did not make sense and left her with more questions than answers, but even so, a fresh fervor surged through her. Ella did not know what would come of this newfound revelation, but she knew exactly who she needed to talk to.

Chapter 28

A NEW ENERGY radiated through Gabriel as he woke up on his third morning at Keatley Hall.

He swung his legs over the side of the high bed to stand, stretched his arms over the top of his head to shake off the effects of sleep, and moved to the window. After pulling back the curtain, he determined the hour was much earlier than he'd thought. Gray light backlit the low-hanging clouds and cast the faintest bit of morning light on the north garden, where he and Ella had walked the previous afternoon. A neutral gray covered all, giving the trees and ground a sense of darkness and foreshadowing the impending autumn.

His sights fell on the oak tree that he and Ella had visited the previous day, and his thoughts turned to her.

Beautiful Ella.

Getting to know her was opening his eyes to what might be possible for his future. How in such a short time had she captured his every thought? Gabriel's logical side wanted to fight the idea that two souls could be predestined to find each other. Poets wrote of it, but it had always been an abstract idea to him. It certainly was not practical. Whatever this feeling was—this sensation that his life would never be complete unless she was in it—was new, exciting, and intoxicating. Could he, with all his faults, be fortunate enough to earn her favor? Maybe even her love?

For years now, bringing criminals to justice had been his singular goal, as if by doing so he could undo the wrongs done by others—as if he could atone for their own father's cruelty toward his sister. It was gratifying work, but now it seemed Ella was exposing another purpose for him—a part that he had kept guarded away.

Feeling slightly uncomfortable with lingering on his emotions for too long, he refocused on the task at hand: Thomas Bauer. Ella had been softening toward Gabriel, but when the full scope of what needed to be done came to light, would she still feel the same way?

He retrieved the satchel where he'd been storing his evidence. He reread the slips of paper he'd found in Gutt's chamber, and he browsed the notes he'd written about Bauer's activities in London. The more he observed Bauer, the more he was confident the man was not as he seemed. What was he missing?

Determined to get on with the day, Gabriel pulled on his trousers, tucked in his linen shirt, tied his cravat, and donned his maroon silk waistcoat and then his cobalt wool coat. He brushed his fingers through his hair and smoothed it across his forehead, and once he was completely dressed, he quit his room and made his way to the breakfast chamber.

He always strove to be the first person present, hoping for a moment to investigate, and today he planned to speak with Gutt. The man knew details, Gabriel was sure of it—and today he would find out what they were.

A few of the older men had already gathered in the east-facing breakfast room, and two footmen stood on either side of a long table laden with meats, cheeses, and breads. He set his eye on the coffee at the end of the table, but Mrs. Chatterly entered behind him and motioned to him.

A bit surprised, Gabriel turned toward her and bowed. He'd always liked Mrs. Chatterly, but she'd not been overly friendly with him since his arrival.

She cast a glance toward the other men present before refocusing her dark eyes on him and extending a note. "I've a message for you."

He thanked her, and after she exited, he flipped open the note.

Please meet me in the conservatory.—E

The notion of breakfast completely abandoned, Gabriel grabbed a roll, popped it in his mouth, and made his way back toward the staircase. He followed the mazelike path toward the ground-floor drawing room, and when he turned from the drawing room into the conservatory, the sight of her struck him.

She was beautiful.

Ella was clipping blooms from a large plant. The early morning light emphasized her willowy form's femininity. The hue of her pale peach gown accentuated her skin's alluring softness, and her brows, slightly darker than her hair, framed her face so elegantly.

His footsteps echoed on the stone floor, and she turned from the plant she was trimming. Her blue eyes brightened, and she lowered the scissors in her hand. "You got my note."

"I did." He lifted it between his fingers and, knowing it could be incriminating and make someone question her character if it was ever discovered, extended it to her.

She accepted it, tucked it in the pocket of the apron that was protecting her gown, and retrieved a journal sitting next to the potted plant. "I need to show you something."

"Is that one of the journals?"

"It is. It was written nearly two full years before my mother died. And look what I found in it." She flipped through the pages and then stopped. With a slender, elegant finger she pointed out the text. "Read here."

He learned closer, squinted to make out the tiny, sharply angled handwriting, and read silently.

> *Mr. Bauer is the most unusual man, with a strange propensity to smack his lips when he is anxious or drum his fingers on the table. But it is his eyes that make him seem the most intense—they are the most unique shade of blue.*

Surprised, he read it again.

"Blue," he mused aloud.

She shifted with her eyes pinned on him, as if watching for his reaction. "I know. *Blue.* What do you think?"

"Did you read the rest of it? Is there anything else like that in here?"

"No. I've read the entire thing and the journal she wrote immediately after this one. I don't believe my mother would err on something so obvious. She was far too particular."

Ella was right. Anyone who knew Leonora Wilde knew she saw everything. Noticed everything.

"Well?" she prompted eagerly, beaming with pride. "What do you make of it?"

It was definitely a promising development, but he knew better than to get ahead of himself. "Is there anyone else here who would have met Bauer before?"

"No. Not that I'm aware of. My father never traveled to Austria with my mother. Mrs. Chatterly did, but she doesn't recall him. The only other person who would have encountered him was my grandfather, and he did not keep journals."

Gabriel paced slowly as he contemplated what he knew. A piece of information like this should infuse him with motivation and breathe fresh life into the search. Such a discovery would bring him one step closer to the truth, but how could he be happy when exposing the man as an impostor would bring the reputation of everyone associated with Keatley Hall into question?

Based on her enthusiasm, he doubted she'd considered the situation from that angle . . . yet. "Does anyone else know of this?" he asked.

"No."

"What about Miss Hawthorne?"

"Definitely not," Ella huffed. "She'd be crushed at the very thought. Everything in me wants to confront him and demand an explanation for every inconsistency."

He chuckled at her impatience. How he could relate. "I wouldn't recommend that."

"Then I really would look insane, wouldn't I?"

Her words stopped him. This was not the first time she'd made such a comment. Surely she did not believe any of those rumors. Did she? It pained him that she'd been so affected by the opinions of others. He could never change what had happened to her or what was said about her, but he could expose the truth.

He handed the journal back to her. "I knew from the moment we talked in that assembly room that you were exceedingly clever, but this level of insight will put me out of business."

She blushed under his praise and accepted the tome. "I've told you, I'll not rest until my mother's reputation has been vindicated."

"Don't worry. We're getting close."

The sounds of morning were awakening around them. Voices wafted from the corridors, and a groundsman passed the conservatory window. Their time alone was coming to an end.

Reluctantly, he bid her farewell, and as he made his way back to the breakfast room, a bittersweet battle was brewing within him. He reminded himself that his sole purpose for attending this symposium was to recover the money for his client. It was a straightforward responsibility. But he had broken his one cardinal rule—he had gotten personally involved in the investigation. What was more, he was emotionally involved. He was not sure of the best way to navigate this unusual situation, but he did know one thing for certain: It was far too late to turn back now.

Now that he was armed with the information he'd received from Ella, any doubt that Gabriel had about Mr. Bauer's fraudulent intentions was eradicated. Regardless of his obligation to his client, Gabriel was now honor bound to formally inform Mr. Hawthorne of his investigation. He did not need to share all the details, just his suspicions, for if something were to happen and the entire Society were to be the victim of Bauer's deception, Gabriel wanted to ensure that he had given those in charge ample warning.

He'd never spoken to Mr. Hawthorne prior to his symposium arrival, but he'd certainly heard about him. As the leader of the Natural Philosophers Society of London, he was a powerful and influential man.

Gabriel would have to tread lightly. Hawthorne's reputation for anger was well known. If he was going to point out a flaw in the man whom Hawthorne had handpicked as a symposium speaker, then he needed to be prepared for retaliation.

Gabriel spied Hawthorne immediately once he returned to the breakfast room. After the man broke away from his conversation, Gabriel seized his chance. He approached Hawthorne and intercepted him near the guest hall entrance. "Hawthorne. A moment, please."

"Ah, Rowe. Have you enjoyed your return to Keatley Hall?"

"Very much. It hasn't changed much over the years, has it?"

Hawthorne made a great display of looking around the chamber. "No, I suppose not. These grand old country houses are like that, though. Frozen in time, eh? And now that you have returned, what do you think of the symposium?"

"Actually, the symposium is what I want to talk with you about. More specifically, Mr. Bauer."

"Ah, I see." Hawthorne lifted his chin, almost as if amused, and looked down his bulbous nose toward Gabriel. "My daughter told me that you do not appreciate Mr. Bauer."

"This has nothing to do with appreciation, sir," he countered matter-of-factly. "That's not why I'm here."

"Then why *are* you here if not to learn?"

Gabriel ignored Hawthorne's conspicuous condescension. "Mr. Bauer is not what he seems to be."

Mr. Hawthorne threw his head back in laughter and clapped a hand patronizingly on his shoulder. "Ah yes. She also told me you are a thieftaker, correct? So if you are looking for an opportunity to—"

"Mr. Bauer owes my client a great deal of money," Gabriel interrupted more intently, refusing to allow Hawthorne's conceited air of superiority to affect him. "He informed them that he will pay his debt after this symposium."

A brief shadow of confusion flitted over Hawthorne's expression, and Gabriel commenced to share pieces of what he knew about Bauer's actions. With each additional bit of information, Hawthorne's expression of disgust intensified.

"Additionally, I've received verified reports that Bauer and his associate are buying personal information so they can make accurate assessments. If this news were to be made public or if Bauer takes advantage of the guests here at the symposium, you could have a significant problem on your hands."

Hawthorne's glare narrowed. "Where are you getting this so-called information?"

Gabriel widened his stance. "I'm sharing this with you out of an abundance of caution. I hope my concern never comes to fruition. I urge you to remain vigilant."

"Very well, Mr. Rowe. You've warned me, and if you've nothing else to say, then I'll be on my way. I will leave you with a warning of my own: If you spread your assumptions about our honored guest to the others without any real proof, I will ruin you."

Chapter 29

ELLA HAD THOUGHT—NAY, dreamt—about this day since the workmen began renovating Keatley Cottage. She stood just in front of the small structure, soon to be known as the Keatley Hall School for Young Ladies, and surveyed the rust-hued stone and slate roof, the symmetrical windows, and the large wooden door.

In a matter of minutes she and her father would stand before this building and announce that the Keatley Hall School for Young Ladies would officially open after the Christmas holiday. In a few short months, four young ladies would embark on their education, but if the school was to sustain itself as a separate entity from the Keatley Hall School for Boys, they needed to enroll more students.

What had started as an overcast morning had given way to a day of both brilliant sunshine and late-summer warmth. A group of goldfinches flitted past her toward the east meadows, and several warblers had collected close to a small grove of blackberry bushes near the cottage garden.

White tents and chairs dotted the landscape around the school. The Society members had gathered and milled about, and even some of the local villagers and the vicar, drawn by the novelty of a girls school, had made their way to observe the festivities.

As she ascended the steps of the platform to join her father and Mr. Hawthorne, she spied Gabriel Rowe under the branches of a nearby ash tree, speaking with Mr. Templeton. Sunlight filtered through the fading leaves, dappling his broad shoulders and highlighting his features.

She knew what she was up against. Several members were adamantly opposed to educating women—especially in natural philosophies—but she'd not be deterred. They had already come so far.

The audience continued to gather, and as it did, Phoebe, in a gown of pale daffodil, stood at the edge of the activity with Miss Sutton. The distance was too great to make out Phoebe's expression, but it didn't matter. Ella did not like the unsettled air between them, but how could this situation be made right? Neither one of them was willing to change their opinion of Mr. Bauer.

When the crowd grew quiet, her father stepped forward. His voice, which had seemed so thin and feeble, echoed with a timbre that harkened to the voice she remembered. "My dear friends, many of you knew my wife, Mrs. Leonora Wilde, and her father, Mr. William Keatley. Referring to Mr. Keatley as a visionary is an understatement. We have his determination to thank for the founding of our beloved Society half a century ago, and due to his resolute steadfastness, Keatley School is a beacon of educational excellence. He was emphatic that young men should be inquisitive about the natural world—to study not only the classics but also the patterns of life around them.

"Mr. Keatley's only child, Leonora, shared that God-given passion. He educated her as he would have a son—to appreciate the wonders of our natural world. Her life ended early, but before she died, she had one goal: to open a school for young ladies that offered opportunities equal to those offered to their male counterparts.

"Inspired by her memory, the Keatley School for Young Ladies will open at the new year. Our daughter, Miss Ella Wilde, shares her mother's passions and will preside over the school as its headmistress. She will tell you more."

Butterflies darted through her belly as Ella stepped next to her father. Not even the current uncertainties could stifle her optimism. She turned to the faces watching her. Every one of them had an opinion of her—some positive, some negative. None of that mattered now, for if she could affect another young woman positively, her efforts would not be in vain.

The wind swept in and rustled the leaves in the trees, sprinkling down the first of autumn's color. She cleared her throat and spoke loudly. "My mother wanted all students to see the world as she did: as a marvel to be studied and a treasure to be discovered. Young women are often steered away from such endeavors in favor of more traditional feminine pursuits, and I count it a shame. I challenge this Society to question that norm. What contributions can your daughters and granddaughters make to the fields we study? As of now, four young women from Society families will be attending Keatley Cottage for their formal education. Our goal is to increase that number to twelve. These young ladies will be taught the classics, including areas of natural philosophies: biology, chemistry, anatomy, to name but a few subjects."

Ella continued the rest of her speech, and when she had completed it, Mr. Hawthorne and her father entertained questions.

Ella held her breath as she waited for the crowd's reactions. Would they go inside? Would there be more questions? Would they laugh and return to Keatley Hall and ignore her completely? Would she be mocked for her unusual behavior? Time would tell, and until then she would keep her goal firmly in front of her.

Chapter 30

ELLA COULD NOT look at Mr. Abernathy for a second more.

As she sat next to him at dinner that night, she couldn't figure out what he was doing. Ever since they'd returned from the gathering on the cottage grounds, his attentions—and praise for her efforts—had been extreme. His flattery had been, at best, ostentatious, and his normally sedate demeanor bordered on obnoxious.

She suspected he was attempting to make her feel supported, but the spectacle of his behavior made her feel more like an animal on display instead of a woman serious about the education of others.

Ella glimpsed Gabriel at the table's far end and found him engaged in lively conversation with two of the older Society members. She could only imagine what his thoughts on this display would be. They'd not spoken privately since the morning, but how many times had he caught her eye throughout the day? How many times had she glanced up to see him looking her direction?

Mr. Abernathy's uncomfortably near voice interrupted her musings as he bounced his animated attention back from Mrs. Shiveley to her. "You must be very pleased with yourself, Ella. Today was a resounding success."

She winced at his use of her Christian name, alarmed and hoping no one else heard the intimate exchange. How could it be so charming when Gabriel said it but on Mr. Abernathy's tongue sound so offensive?

Her appetite, which was already waning, fled completely. She lowered her soup spoon back to the table. "Do you think so?"

He wiped his mouth with his linen napkin and reached for his glass. "I overheard Mr. Parker say that he would like his granddaughter to attend your girls school. That should please you."

Was she imagining the patronizing edge to his tone? "It does please me. I'll be happier, though, when all twelve spots are spoken for."

He chuckled, sipped his wine, and placed it back on the table. "It will be a lovely hobby for you."

Her spine stiffened. A hobby? Did he deem her commitment to a girls school a hobby?

"I assure you, Mr. Abernathy," she responded firmly, "my participation in this endeavor is much more than a mere hobby."

He laughed heartily, his face reddening in amusement.

She shifted to face him fully. "I don't see why that is humorous."

He raised his hands and widened his eyes, as if innocent. "It's not humorous. It's that I admire your passion. It's quite a charming quality, and not many women possess it. But I do wonder: Do you feel that the natural order of things will happen? That one day you will be a mother and your interests will be more . . . domestic?"

She clamped her teeth over her lower lip until she was certain she could control the words coming out of her mouth. "I don't see why there couldn't be a mix of them."

He leaned back in his chair comfortably, as if oblivious to her mounting ire and reliving a great memory. "I remember your father commenting on that very thing. Your mother, if I recall, had difficulty balancing them. Your father spoke of it—the challenges it brought between them."

Heat rose up her neck. No doubt her cheeks had grown pink. He'd crossed a line. "I do not appreciate you speaking of my mother. In fact, I insist you refrain from it."

"I meant nothing by it, my dear," he countered, "only that I know your father had some, well, *regrets*."

Ella's retort was silenced when a footman entered and interrupted the dinner, approaching Gabriel and whispering something to him. Gabriel placed his napkin on the table, said something to the lady sitting next to him, and stepped out into the corridor.

Mr. Abernathy sniffed at the interruption. "I wonder what that was all about."

"I dare not speculate."

Mr. Abernathy gave his head a shake and retrieved his fork. "He's one to watch, that's for certain. Mr. Hawthorne said they had quite the interesting conversation."

Ella begrudged having to engage in more conversation than necessary, but curiosity prevailed. "How so?"

Mr. Abernathy smirked. "I know you're fond of the gentleman, and I would never presume to tell you what to do, but if I were you, I'd stay as far away from him as possible. I think his interest in Keatley Hall has less to do with phrenology and more to do with what he can gain."

Throughout dinner Gabriel was keenly aware of the conversation at the end of the table. He couldn't hear what was being said between Ella and Abernathy, but he didn't need to. Ella's face was pinched, her cheeks vibrant red.

Gabriel had been so proud of her earlier when she shared her vision for the school, when she spoke freely and confidently. Now she was shrinking away from whatever it was Abernathy was saying. Gabriel knew she would handle any conversation deftly, but he still desired to put a stop to it.

He was so focused on it that he didn't notice the footman approaching until he was at his elbow. "A visitor is here for you, sir."

Surprised at the unexpected interruption, Gabriel excused himself from his dinner partners and followed the footman to the corridor.

"A gentleman is waiting in the forecourt," the footman explained. "He would not give his name, nor would he come in. He said he preferred to wait for you outside."

With his mind reeling, Gabriel thanked him and made his way through Keatley Hall and into the evening air. He tensed as he spied his clerk, Edmund Clark, dressed in an oilskin coat and wide-brimmed hat, standing with his bay horse next to the east garden's gates.

Clark would never travel to him unless absolutely necessary.

Gabriel jogged toward him, and once he was close enough, Clark retrieved a missive from his coat. "This arrived earlier today in response to the inquiries we sent out. I knew you'd want it as soon as possible."

Gabriel eagerly accepted the outstretched paper. He unfolded it to see the line drawing of a skinny male face framed with thin hair. The accompanying text was in German, but the printed name *Thomas Bauer* glared. Gabriel knew just enough of the language to piece together the rest, and his blood grew cold. "Is this an obituary?"

"Yes. For Thomas Bauer, phrenologist. According to this clipping he died two years ago."

Miss Wilde's words about her mother's journal entry flashed in his mind.

Mr. Bauer has blue eyes, not brown.

The man they'd been interacting with was not Thomas Bauer. The real Mr. Bauer had blue eyes and, according to this piece, was dead. The man entertaining the Society guests, whatever his name, was not just a fraud. He was an impostor.

Chapter 31

ELLA HAD TO calm down. If there had ever been a doubt, their conversation at dinner confirmed it: She would never ever marry Abraham Abernathy.

The heels of her satin slippers clipped the wooden floor as she fled the White Parlor to the great hall, where the guests were already gathering for the fourth night of phrenological demonstrations.

My passions are not hobbies. My goals are important.

Her pace increased. If her father would not put an end to this monstrosity and tell Abraham Abernathy that she would not marry him, then she would.

And she would do it tonight.

Silently practicing the words she'd employ, Ella turned the corner into the great hall. Guests filled the space, and chatter, happier and livelier than she'd noticed the entire event, surrounded her, yet even with all the people present, she had never felt lonelier in her own home.

She scanned the hall, unsure of where to go and what to do.

Phoebe and Miss Sutton sat up near the front in their usual seats, but they'd not saved one for her. Gabriel had not returned since he disappeared during dinner. The other ladies were happily engaged with their husbands. Determined to avoid Mr. Abernathy at any cost, she moved to the back row of chairs and sat down.

Dozens of candles were scattered around the room for light, and a fire blazed in the long hearth. The windows were open to combat the heat of so many people gathered, and a damp breeze flowed in.

When Mr. Bauer took the stage to start the demonstration, perspiration beaded his forehead. His face flushed, and he swiped his handkerchief over his brow. "I have so enjoyed getting to spend these days with you, my friends. I'm sorry to say that my colleague, Mr. Gutt, is not feeling well today, so I am working alone now, but never fear. This is my passion, my joy, my zest! It might take a few moments longer than normal to organize my thoughts, but rest assured, I am at my best.

"Tomorrow morning I will lecture on phrenology and the effects on education, but I'm painfully aware that our time together will soon come to an end. I hope I've enlightened you to the wonders of the human body and the mind. All ventures into new and unknown territories, be they physical or philosophical, require a certain amount of energy, imagination, and capital to ensure they are fully explored and responsibly executed. I appeal to each of you members, as philosophers, as lovers of this human race, to contribute your support to the research I conduct."

Ella winced. He was asking for money. Was this it? Was this how he was going to obtain the money he owed his debtors? She looked around the great hall for Gabriel once again. He needed to know about this.

A hum of whispers circulated. Holding her breath, she watched for reactions.

Mr. Bauer procured a wooden box and started it around the audience. To her surprise, the group, accustomed to such appeals, took his petition in stride. The box passed from member to member, and each person, refusing to be outdone by his neighbor, contributed.

And she was helpless to stop it.

Mr. Bauer moved on to the demonstration, calling first on Mr. Hawthorne and then Mr. Templeton. When nothing new or insignificant occurred, Ella thought the evening would pass without further fanfare, but then Mr. Bauer shifted.

"Two men so far!" he exclaimed, dragging his handkerchief over his brow once more. "What interesting men they were. So now have I a lady volunteer?"

Mr. Bauer turned his attention toward Ella.

Their eyes locked. She suddenly felt ill.

He's going to call on me.

"As our gracious hostess, Miss Wilde, would you not like to come and sit for an assessment? I know you have a specific interest in the topic."

All eyes turned to her.

Her heart seemed to stop. He intended to intimidate—or humiliate—her. What else could he be doing?

His volume increased. "You impressed me when you spoke earlier today. Your distinctive interests and motivations would provide a fascinating phrenological assessment. So what say you?"

She froze.

This was a challenge, pure and simple. They'd not spoken since the intimidating interaction the previous night. No doubt he planned to ridicule her or make her appear unstable.

Ella's tongue felt thick in her mouth, yet she had no choice but to feign complete composure. She smiled sweetly and straightened her seated posture. "While I appreciate the offer, sir, I respectfully decline. Several other guests here have not had the benefit of one of your readings. I defer to them."

"Oh, come now!" Mr. Bauer's boisterous laugh boomed from the great hall's paneled wall, and he extended his arm toward her. "I know that your family had concerns about discussing phrenology at Keatley Hall, but I do think I've managed to share the truths of phrenology. Can we not celebrate it? Together?"

She glanced at her father. His face paled.

She was not ignorant. The biting memory of how Mr. Bauer had spoken to her burned. She'd never allow him to touch her—to place his hands on her head. Even more alarming, she knew that the members who opposed the girls school would take Mr. Bauer's fraudulent assessment as truth and use it against her.

She needed to respond. "Mr. Bauer, I assure you, I—"

"I'll do it."

Ella knew who spoke the words even before she saw him.

Gabriel Rowe.

Gabriel stepped farther into the great hall. "I'd appreciate an assessment."

Gabriel had just returned from speaking with Clark, and even though he was not entirely sure what he'd walked in on, it was obvious Bauer was singling out Ella, and he'd not allow it.

Without waiting for a response, he made his way toward the stage. Gabriel rubbed his hands together as he wove through the crowd, exuding enthusiasm and noting the flash of pained annoyance on Bauer's face.

He sensed the eyes of the other guests following him. He forced brightness to his tone, determined to take Bauer's calculated attention from Ella. "The symposium is almost over! What better way to convince me of phrenology's merit than to assess me and let me judge for myself."

Satisfaction soared as Bauer fumbled for a response.

"Where should I sit?" Gabriel forged ahead, refusing to give Bauer the opportunity to protest. "There?"

Bauer chuckled and recovered from the shock. "Why, yes! You've been one of our outspoken skeptics over the last few days. I look forward to changing your mind on this topic."

Gabriel ran his fingers through his own hair, preparing for the odd sensation of a man touching his head. Ever so briefly, he snuck a glance toward Ella.

She stared at him, unblinking, her mouth slightly agape.

"Just to reassure those watching us," Bauer said as he rounded the chair. "I've become vaguely acquainted with you during our time here, but can you confirm for the guests that you and I do not know each other? That you and I have never interacted before this symposium?"

"I can."

"Very well. Let's begin." Mr. Bauer began measuring his head with a set of tools and ribbons—the circumference of his head. The distance between his eyebrows and hairline. The distance from the crown of his head to the base of his skull. Bauer then dragged his heavy fingers over Gabriel's skull and shifted his body to observe it from different angles.

After completing his assessment, Bauer straightened. "As always, I can ascertain a great deal about your personality. You're a humorous man. You enjoy lighthearted conversation and will joke when the situation grows uncomfortable or serious. The width between your eyebrows indicates a strong sense of individuality. You crave new information, and your power of perception is enviable. There is another side to your personality, however. One that I fear will be seen as problematic."

Gabriel was not surprised at the negative finding. "Please continue, Mr. Bauer. Say what you must."

Bauer looked out to the crowd. "Based on my assessment, Mr. Rowe has a tendency toward deception. Now, remember, all these traits I mention are on a spectrum, from nonexistent to dominant. It's not unusual for men especially to exhibit this trait, but I find that Mr. Rowe might struggle with it greatly."

A murmur resounded in the crowd.

Gabriel, however, could only see humor in the supposed finding. Was this Bauer's best shot at him?

After Bauer finished speaking, the guests applauded and Gabriel shook Bauer's hand. The reading had communicated everything Gabriel needed to know.

It was time to act.

Chapter 32

AFTER THE DEMONSTRATION, Gabriel was determined not to let Bauer out of his sight.

The obituary blazed brightly in his mind. With this missing piece of information, the larger puzzle was taking shape. Gabriel could admit that Bauer was clever, but he'd made too many mistakes.

Gabriel stood in the shadowed corridor just outside the great hall, waiting for the crowd to disperse. He even avoided Ella, fearing he might miss his opportunity with Bauer. When only a few guests remained, Bauer exited the chamber, and once he was in the corridor, Gabriel stepped forward, blocking his way.

"Mr. Rowe," said Bauer, his tone flat, his eyes hard. "I thought you'd left us."

"That was quite an assessment you gave me."

Bauer raised his thick black brows. "The head's shape tells what the mouth will not admit. Now, if you'll excuse me."

Gabriel shifted to prevent Bauer from taking another step, and his gaze fell to the collection box under his arm. He would not allow this man to take advantage of the members, whether the money would be used to repay his client or not. The need for justice burned through him, and he knew what he needed to do. If he made Bauer uncomfortable or angry enough, he'd slip up.

Bauer attempted to step around Gabriel, but Gabriel stood firm. "Before you go, I want to show you something."

Once Bauer realized he was not likely to pass, irritation flashed in his eyes. "Be quick about it."

Gabriel retrieved the obituary from his pocket and held it before him.

Bauer's gaze narrowed onto the paper. "Where did you get that?"

Gabriel tucked the paper back away in the safety of his waistcoat and out of Bauer's reach. "I wonder if Hawthorne knows that the man he invited to come speak to the Society, or the man he *thought* he invited, died two years ago."

"I don't know where you got that, but I—"

Gabriel stepped closer and lowered his voice further. "I don't know who you are, but I don't really care. You may have already deceived these people, but I'll not allow you to steal from them."

Bauer's face shook. "The audacity to suggest I am stealing from the very people I am attempting to educate. You are overstepping your bounds."

"Thomas Bauer is dead. Your assistant possesses written descriptions of the attributions of everyone present here. You owe a great deal of money to Jameson & Company. I'm giving you this option out of respect for the Wildes: Either you tell these people the truth about who you are and return the money you collected, or I'll share everything I know."

In a sudden burst of action, Bauer spun on his heel and huffed back into the great hall.

Gabriel grinned in spite of himself. He had Bauer where he wanted him. It was not time to celebrate quite yet, but he'd won this battle. Now he needed to win the war.

The conservatory, for all the peace and tranquility it afforded, seemed oddly confining. Ella paced the flagstone floor. She wanted—needed—to speak with Gabriel. She had to thank him for his intervention with Mr. Bauer's request. He sacrificed his own reputation to preserve hers. Never had anyone done anything like that for her.

Normally Ella prided herself on her independence. She rarely accepted assistance from others. Why was accepting help from Gabriel different?

It dawned on her: She trusted him. His attention, his considerations were not motivated by the desire to dominate or prove her wrong.

He cares about me.

She expected that Gabriel would enter the conservatory with his customary grin and lighthearted disposition, but when he arrived, his brow was furrowed, his expression tense.

"What is it?" she asked as he stepped closer. "What's wrong?"

"I need to show you something." He pulled a piece of paper from his pocket and extended it to her.

She opened it, but the words were foreign. "Is this German? I don't—" Ella snapped her mouth shut. She saw the name.

Thomas Bauer.

Gabriel stepped closer to look over her shoulder. His breath rustled the hair by her ear. "It's an obituary. Thomas Bauer—the actual Thomas Bauer—died two years ago."

Gabriel's words—and all subsequent ramifications—took several moments to sink in. "So we were correct," she breathed. "That's not him."

"No. And he gathered a massive collection tonight. I confronted him about this obituary a little while ago, so he knows I'm aware of what he's up to."

"Where is he now?"

"He's still in the great hall, but if he intends some sort of move, it will be sooner rather than later. I did share my—our—concerns with Hawthorne this morning, but he was less than receptive. I think it's best we take—"

Suddenly, a distant muffled cry echoed.

They both jerked and looked at each other.

Then the sound reverberated again, sounding more like muted feminine words. Ella spun and pointed to the staircase that led from the conservatory to the basement. "It's coming from there."

They stood still for several more seconds, waiting for another sound. But none came.

"Stay here." Gabriel rested his hand on her shoulder. "I'll go see what that was."

She shook her head and grabbed his arm as he began to move past her. "I'm going with you."

He stopped and stared at her.

She fully expected him to deny her and make her stay in the conservatory, but to her surprise, he gripped her hand in his much larger one. "Very well. Let's go."

Chapter 33

"WHY ARE YOU doing this?" cried an indistinct female voice.

With Ella's hand still in his, Gabriel stopped abruptly at the top of the small stone staircase leading to the basement.

The woman's stifled, pleading voice returned. "This is a mistake, surely you see it."

Ella squeezed his hand and whispered, "It's Phoebe!"

A weak light flickered from somewhere below, casting erratic moving shadows against the stone walls.

Gabriel considered his options. He wished Ella would have stayed in the conservatory, for he had no idea what they were up against. Whatever was going on down here could be dangerous, and he'd never forgive himself if she was injured because of a decision he made.

Phoebe cried again, "You must stop!"

"You'll say nothing, do you understand me?" responded a male voice.

Gabriel could not stand by anymore—he needed to intervene on Miss Hawthorne's behalf, but without a weapon on his person, he had to be careful. He looked back to Ella. "Stay here. I'll be right back."

This time, to his relief, she did not protest.

Gabriel took cautious steps down the timeworn stairs, careful to make no sound or cast a shadow. Once he reached the foot of the stairs, Gabriel stepped into the corridor and quickly figured out the layout. The light and sounds were coming from the first door down from the stairwell. To his right was an east-facing exterior door that led to the stables. He returned his attention to the room from which the voices came. The door stood slightly ajar, and he angled his head to see inside. From his vantage point he clearly identified Bauer and Miss Hawthorne standing next to a small stack of wooden boxes and an open trunk.

Was Bauer . . . leaving?

Gabriel could not let him leave. He might not have a weapon, but he did have the element of surprise on his side. With his attention fixed firmly on Bauer, Gabriel shoved open the door and lunged inside.

The next seconds slowed . . . then sped.

Miss Hawthorne screamed.

Bauer whirled.

Gabriel pushed forward, but Bauer snatched Miss Hawthorne by the waist and yanked her in front of him. With his other hand he pulled a pistol from his waist and pointed it at Gabriel.

Gabriel stopped midstride.

Perspiration trickled down Bauer's scarlet face. He blinked rapidly, and his breaths were shallow gasps.

"If you discharge that weapon, you'll wake every single person under this roof," Gabriel challenged. "Release Miss Hawthorne. She has nothing to do with any of this."

"You." Bauer ignored Gabriel's words and jerked his head to the chamber's far corner. "There."

Normally Gabriel would take his chances with the man. He'd rush him and physically force the weapon from him. He knew he'd be fast and could get his hand on the weapon before Bauer could effectively react, but he couldn't risk Miss Hawthorne getting injured.

Without breaking eye contact and with his hands raised, Gabriel did as bid. He watched as Bauer, with Miss Hawthorne still trapped in his arm, inched his way closer to the door.

Then, in a sudden burst of energy, Bauer shoved Miss Hawthorne away from himself, grabbed one of the larger wooden boxes, spun through the door, and jerked it closed behind him.

Instantly a lock clicked.

Gabriel sped toward the door. The knob would not budge—it was locked from the outside. He stepped back and rammed it with his shoulder, and when that was unsuccessful, he stepped back, steadied himself, and kicked the heel of his boot into the middle of the door. Still, the heavy wooden door would not give way.

Heaving from the exertion, he turned.

Miss Hawthorne was lying on the floor. She was not moving.

He hurried to her, dropped to his knee next to her, and gently rolled her over. Blood trickled from a wound on her brow. He quickly located her pulse, and once he did, he tugged his cravat from his neck and gingerly pressed the linen fabric against the wound.

The lock jostled and then flew open. Gabriel prepared himself in case Bauer was returning, but it was Ella, wide-eyed and open-mouthed, with a key ring in one hand and a candle in the other. She scurried toward them and fell to her knees next to her friend. "Is she—she—?"

"She'll be all right." Gabriel fixed his attention on the door once more. "Come over here and hold this on the wound. Gentle pressure, like this." Once Ella had taken over the task, he sprinted from the chamber to the exterior door that opened to the stable yard.

He scanned the empty grounds. There was no moon, making it impossible to see even the edge of the gardens. He assessed the dirt outside the door for footprints, but nothing stood out as significant.

The smartest action Bauer could have taken was to get away on horseback, so Gabriel raced to the stables to see if anything was disturbed, but a padlock secured the stable door with the animals safely inside.

He needed help.

Refusing to waste energy being angry with himself for letting Bauer get away, he determined to return to Miss Hawthorne and assess her injury.

When he arrived back in the basement chamber, Ella was sitting at Miss Hawthorne's side. Her blue eyes were wide, her face pale. Alarm heightened her tone. "She's breathing, but she's not moving, Gabriel. And there's blood everywhere!"

"Move the light closer."

Ella lifted the candle from the stone floor next to her, and he once again pressed his fingers against Miss Hawthorne's neck. After finding a pulse, he lifted her eyelid to see the pupil.

Gabriel lifted the linen from the wound and turned to Ella. "Go get your father and Mrs. Chatterly as quickly as you can."

Chapter 34

WRAPPED IN A blanket, Ella sat next to Phoebe's bed. Try as she might, she could not cease the trembling that seemed to come from her very soul.

The events following her discovery of Phoebe were a blur. After Ella had left the basement chamber to fetch her father and Mrs. Chatterly, Gabriel had carried Phoebe up the stairs to Ella's bedchamber, which was far enough away from the other guests to avoid suspicion. Ella and Mrs. Chatterly began to dress the wounds immediately, and her father informed Mr. Hawthorne of the incident. Gabriel and two footmen rode out, attempting to locate Mr. Bauer. Another footman set out for the magistrate, and Mr. Parker, who'd been a physician in his younger days, was summoned to assess Phoebe's condition.

For now, the frantic activity had subsided. The men had gathered below to discuss the course of action, and Mrs. Chatterly had dozed off in a chair in the corner.

Ella pushed a piece of Phoebe's nutmeg hair away from the fresh bandage around her head, which had already soaked through with blood.

Her dear friend had been so blinded by Mr. Bauer—or whoever he really was.

Ella chided herself. She should have done more to convince Phoebe of Mr. Bauer's danger. She should have told her exactly what she knew. If she had, perhaps her friend would be sleeping peacefully instead of lying in a state of unconsciousness.

After about half an hour, her father entered the chamber, pulled a chair next to Ella, and sat down. How tired he looked. His disheveled, thinning hair hung in strands across his forehead. Dark circles emphasized the light hue of his rheumy eyes. He wore a waistcoat but no coat, and the stoop of his shoulders alarmed her.

He placed a hand on her arm but said nothing for several seconds. She could feel the concern, the worry, the heaviness he was carrying—all from that simple touch.

When he finally spoke, his voice was raspy. "I'm trying to understand how this came to pass, Eleanor. Why did you not come to me with any of this earlier?"

"I never trusted Mr. Bauer, Father," she stated. "I did not keep that from you."

"But you did keep certain discoveries from me, did you not?" He blew out his air and scratched his fingers over his head. "So is this the real reason for Mr. Rowe's presence here?"

"I told you I saw him in London. Mr. Rowe was already watching Mr. Bauer on behalf of one of his clients, but he was also concerned that Mr. Bauer might try to take advantage of the Society. Over the course of the last few days, we uncovered more evidence against Mr. Bauer, and then today the most condemning evidence arrived." She still had the obituary in her possession from when she and Gabriel had been talking in the conservatory. She took it from her pocket and shared it with her father.

He accepted the slip of paper, retrieved his spectacles from the welt pocket of his loose waistcoat, and propped them on his nose.

"Our symposium speaker, whoever he is, is *not* Thomas Bauer. He tricked Mr. Hawthorne into believing he was a phrenologist. He tricked everyone."

After reading the paper, her father removed his spectacles, pinched the bridge of his nose, and exhaled noisily.

She could sense what he was thinking. How could something like this happen? How would they be able to explain this to the Society members? In a few hours the members would wake and find that their guest of honor not only had played them all for fools but also had stolen money from them.

"What a predicament," he said at last. The fire's light cast shadows, emphasizing the deep lines of worry in his brow. "I fear what will happen when this news spreads. This could very well spell the end of, well, *everything*."

Without warning, the door flung open on it hinges, nearly slamming the wall behind it. Ella jerked and whirled around in her chair.

Mr. Hawthorne stood in the doorway, appearing every bit as disheveled as her father. Instead of sad contemplation, anger darkened his round face. His heavy jowls shook with each word, and outrage narrowed his eyes. "She's gone, do you know that? And that Gutt fellow too. Their things are gone. Completely!"

Confused at the onslaught of information, Ella asked, "Who's gone?"

"Miss Sutton!" he cried, incredulous. "Her chamber's empty. Everything's gone."

Stunned, Ella looked at her father. Suddenly even more of the pieces lined up.

Miss Sutton had always been supportive and enthusiastic about Mr. Bauer, but Ella had thought she was simply in awe of the man's talent. Never did she suspect that the woman might be involved somehow. It almost made sense. According to Phoebe, Miss Sutton had been instrumental in facilitating and encouraging the friendship between Mr. Hawthorne and Mr. Bauer. She had likely been manipulating Mr. Hawthorne's affections this entire time. She even encouraged Phoebe's infatuation with Mr. Bauer.

"Someone needs to answer for this." Mr. Hawthorne's indignant words pulled Ella back to the present.

Pointing out that this entire situation was his decision wouldn't be easy, but truthfully, Mr. Hawthorne had been swindled. And in that regard, she felt sorry for him.

What her father said was true—when word of this got out, it spelled the end of everything they all had worked so hard for. Ella covered her father's withered hand with her own. She had no idea what the next several hours would bring, but the sense that their entire world was about to shift settled heavily on her shoulders.

Chapter 35

IT WAS A couple of hours after midnight when Gabriel stood outside the door to Miss Hawthorne's chamber, preparing himself for what might await him inside.

His clothes and hair were still damp from his foray into the nighttime air in search of Bauer, and the rugged scent of horses and the forest still clung to him. He and two footmen had ridden to the village. The woods. Over every bit of meadow and field within several miles of Keatley Hall.

They'd found nothing. Not a single trail or trace of Bauer.

Gabriel would not waste time being frustrated or questioning the decisions he'd made up until this point. He had to stay calm, rational, and focused, for he had to stay ready for anything that might come next.

Gabriel rubbed the back of his neck and shook out the tension gathering in his shoulders before he tapped his knuckles against the door to announce his presence before entering Miss Hawthorne's chamber.

Before Gabriel could say a word, Mr. Hawthorne jumped from

his chair near the fire, his finely tailored coat askew on his torso, his eyes wild. "Well? Did you find him?"

Gabriel quickly assessed the firelit room. Mrs. Chatterly and Mr. Parker sat on the far side of the canopied bed. Ella was seated beneath the window. Mr. Wilde was absent. Gabriel shook his head and closed the door. "No. How is Miss Hawthorne?"

Ella stood and tightened her shawl around her shoulders. "No change."

His gaze fell to the bed where the normally vibrant, energetic young woman now lay motionless, her paleness emphasized by the dried blood on the bandage over her forehead.

Mr. Hawthorne forged ahead, the pitch and volume of his voice unusually high. "Are you aware that Miss Sutton has vanished? Her chamber is completely empty! Every single item is gone. Gutt, also, is nowhere to be found."

Gabriel glanced toward Ella to gauge her response, and she nodded slightly. It made sense to him that Gutt was gone. But Miss Sutton?

Hawthorne continued, "Also, the magistrate has arrived. A fellow named Moore. He's in the great hall speaking with the servants and Wilde. He said he wanted to wait to go through the boxes and trunk Bauer left behind until you were here to give a statement since you were the last to see him. We should head down there as soon as you're ready."

After a brief discussion, it was decided that Mrs. Chatterly and Mr. Parker would stay with Miss Hawthorne, and the others made their way down to the great hall. Once introductions had been made to Mr. Moore and a constable by the name of Jones, they continued down to the basement-level storage area.

Candle lamps had been deposited around the chamber that

Bauer had apparently been using for storage. Blood still stained the stone floor—an eerie, uncomfortable reminder of what had occurred just hours earlier. Nothing had been disturbed. The other two boxes were still where they had been positioned, and the trunk, which Gabriel presumed belonged to Bauer, remained.

Gabriel explained everything he knew about the man calling himself Thomas Bauer to the magistrate—including his client's interest in Bauer, the belief that Bauer intended to make money while at the symposium, the purchase of personal information to use in demonstrations, the discrepancy of his eye color, and, finally, the obituary.

The room fell painfully silent.

Hawthorne was the first to add his thoughts. "If you were aware that Bauer was a threat, you should have informed us immediately."

"As a licensed solicitor I have a duty to my clients to maintain confidentiality. I was concerned that he might be targeting the Society, but initially I had no proof. Miss Wilde and I spoke briefly of our concerns in London, which led to my attendance here. I did attempt to speak with you on this matter in the breakfast room, but, if you recall, you refused to receive it."

"And you." Hawthorne turned the brunt of his frustration to Ella. "Shame on you. Phoebe is your friend. How could you not speak up?"

Ella jerked. "I've been very vocal about this to anyone who would listen!"

"She's right," Gabriel added. "This is hardly Miss Wilde's fault. No one is at fault here except for Bauer. Or whatever his name is."

"And the other two people who were mentioned?" inquired the magistrate. "A Mr. Gutt and a Miss Sutton?"

Gabriel nodded. "It appears they are likely accomplices. I know for a fact that Gutt has made purchases on Mr. Bauer's behalf in the past. Manipulations of this degree are rarely done alone."

The magistrate motioned toward Gabriel and Ella. "You two witnessed Bauer causing physical harm to Miss Hawthorne, which is enough to warrant an arrest, but what are the other crimes?"

"Bauer stole a substantial amount from our members, and he lied about his identity! What more is needed?" Hawthorne cried.

Gabriel folded his arms over his chest and nodded to the boxes. "Miss Hawthorne might be able to share more information when she wakes, but I assume that whatever is in those crates might tell us more."

When no one protested, Gabriel knelt and opened the first box. As he did the light fell on a mixed jumble of silver items, from cookery to utensils to an array of pieces.

"Those are from Keatley Hall!" Ella cried. "Did he intend to steal them?"

Gabriel let the lid fall once again and moved the entire box aside to uncover the one beneath it. No one spoke as the second box was opened to reveal several small, rare paintings and leather-bound books that had been stolen from the library.

Gabriel turned to the trunk and popped it open. This was the trunk with Bauer's clothing, a few personal items, and a handful of letters.

"The money. Where is the money? Look again!" demanded Hawthorne.

Gabriel pressed his lips together and exchanged glances with the magistrate. "There's nothing else here, Mr. Hawthorne," Gabriel said in a stronger tone. "I'm sure the magistrate will agree with me when I urge you to remain calm. We can track down the addresses on these letters and see what Miss Hawthorne can add, but we need to turn our attention to locating him."

The magistrate looked at the constable and then motioned to the door. "It's late, and we'll search more tomorrow to see if we can find tracks or find out if anyone in the village saw anything. If three people left, someone likely saw something. Notify me when Miss Hawthorne wakes and can talk. We'll be back then."

"That's it?" cried Hawthorne. "That's all you're going to do? This man just deceived every single person in this house! We told them he was a legitimate man of knowledge and education. He took their money! We'll be laughingstocks!"

Mr. Wilde stepped toward Hawthorne and placed a hand on his shoulder. "Rowe and Moore are not the enemies here, Hawthorne. We've been deceived, but not by them. Come, let's get some air."

They all exited the basement chamber, and after the door was secured and locked, the rest of the men dispersed, leaving Gabriel alone with Ella.

Chapter 36

WHEN THE RETREATING footsteps were finally silent and they were alone in the basement corridor, Gabriel took Ella's trembling hand in his. How small it felt, and yet what a tremendous role she'd played in putting the puzzle pieces together. He leaned close and whispered in her ear, "Come with me."

He lifted one of the candle lamps as he led her toward the stairs. The only sound as they climbed the same narrow staircase they'd descended a few hours earlier was the crisp rustling of the fabric of her gown. Once they were finally in the still solace of the conservatory, he could finally release the tension he'd been carrying. He exhaled and turned to face her.

She was mere inches from him. The candle lamp's light highlighted the wisps of her honey-hued hair and the gentle slope of her nose in its amber glow.

After the harrowing hours they'd just endured, he paused to take in just how beautiful she was to him.

How beautiful and brave.

He wordlessly smoothed her hair from her face, allowing his

fingers to linger on the side of her cheek. Perhaps it was his exhaustion, or maybe it was the emotions from the day. Normally he'd be more concerned about her reputation were she to be discovered in such a situation. But what did that matter now? All the rules had been broken. No one knew what the next day would bring.

He could only imagine what Ella was feeling.

Ella looked up at him, and in that moment, his heart ached for something he didn't even realize he had been missing. He had been fighting for justice for a long time. But now he was doing it for another reason—not just for justice, but for *her*.

He folded his arms around Ella in the early morning shadows, and she melted against him. He relished her warmth against him—the steady rise and fall of each breath.

"I think I already know the answer," he said in a low voice, "but are you all right?"

She drew a shuddery breath and looked up at him. "I am. But I'm worried. For Phoebe. For my father. What do you think is going to happen?"

Predicting such a result would be impossible. Even with the best of information, so many of the elements were completely uncontrollable. But she wanted reassurance. Perhaps she *needed* reassurance.

"Well," he began, "if Bauer did indeed take the money, it will be up to the Society as an organization or, at the very least, Hawthorne or one of the Society members to bring charges. They'll likely have to engage the services of a thieftaker or someone of the sort. I'll continue to seek Bauer on my client's behalf, but before anything can really be done, we must locate him. Locate *them*."

She sighed again.

"I wish I could make this fair for you," he added.

She smiled. "You are doing more than that, Gabriel. My whole life, most people have assumed I'm erratic and haven't taken me seriously. You did. You *do*. And you listen to me without judgment. You have no idea what that means to me."

"And I will continue to do so."

"I'm worried about Phoebe," she said as she leaned fully against him and rested her cheek against his shoulder. "What if she doesn't wake up?"

He tightened his arms around her. "She will. But she'll require a great deal of support, I imagine."

Ella groaned. "Tomorrow morning is going to be an awful shock when the members gather for the lecture and there is no speaker."

"How do you think they will take it?" he asked.

She inhaled deeply and leaned back so she could look at him again. "Someone will have to be honest about what happened. The last time the Society suffered a scandal, it nearly did not survive. This is so much worse. And if the Society does not recover . . ." Her voice faded.

He understood. If the Society were to disband, Keatley School would likely not have enough families who wanted to send sons to a school with such focus on the natural philosophies, and it might have to close its doors. If the boys school did not survive, then Ella's dream of a girls school would not come to fruition.

He wanted to take away the concern and disappointment, the uncertainty and the unknown, but he could not do so.

Still, he could support her. Encourage her. And maybe . . . even love her.

He shifted, and she lifted her face up toward his. The night had been so long, so difficult, but he also felt more confident than he ever had. He brushed the hair from her face again and cupped her cheek. He lowered his face to hers and kissed her. When she did not pull away, he deepened the kiss and pulled her tighter.

She wrapped her arms around his neck, and as she did he knew he could never be content until he was sure she was happy and safe. That meant her concerns would become his, and in that moment he knew he'd do whatever it took to right the wrongs she was experiencing, no matter the cost.

Chapter 37

ELLA STOOD AT Phoebe's bedchamber window. Through the ancient, wavy glass, dawn was breaking, and the faintest blue light crept over the verdant landscape. The pastoral view was the same as it always was—peaceful, lush, and calm—blissfully unaffected by the turmoil that churned within Keatley Hall's walls.

Phoebe had not yet woken, and Mrs. Chatterly was asleep in the wingback chair by the waning fire.

Ella's thoughts drifted to Gabriel. Comfort at the memory of his embrace enveloped her, and despite the seemingly unending difficulties, a robust flame of hope and optimism burned.

Gabriel cares about me.

He hadn't needed to say the words aloud. The support of his arms around her, the tenderness of his touch, and his very presence emboldened and infused her with assurance she'd never imagined she could possess.

Ella had thought she knew exactly what she wanted out of life: She wanted to be at Keatley Hall. She wanted to open a girls school. She wanted to follow in her mother's footsteps. It was her destiny. But what if she had been chasing the wrong path? What if her future were to include love and marriage? Not because those things furthered the family's interest, but because they were right for her?

A moan sounded from the bed behind her, pulling Ella from her thoughts.

"Phoebe!" Ella cried.

Mrs. Chatterly jerked from her slumber and joined her at the bed.

Phoebe mumbled, and her eyes fluttered open. She touched her head. As she became more aware of her surroundings, she paled and then struggled to sit up. "Thomas, he—he—"

Ella placed her hand on Phoebe's shoulder to keep her from trying to stand. "Please be calm. Stay in bed, dearest. You've had a fall."

"What? How?" Panic twisted her face, and she tried again to sit up. "Thomas, where is he? What has happened?"

"Shhh," soothed Ella, looking to Mrs. Chatterly for assistance. "He's left. I don't know where he's gone."

Fresh tears rushed Phoebe's eyes. Unsure of what else to do, Ella embraced her friend and let her cry. Ella, too, struggled to keep the tears from flowing. She hated what this man had done to Phoebe—what he had done to her family.

"He lied to me, Ella," Phoebe sobbed. "How could he do that?"

"I wish I had a good answer for that, but I don't. He lied to many, many people."

Phoebe jerked away from Ella's embrace. Her brows furrowed. "What other lies did he tell?"

Ella hesitated, wishing she hadn't said her last words, but even though Phoebe was weak, she deserved to know the truth. After all, she was as much a victim in all of this as anyone else. In a matter of hours everyone would know all the details, whether they liked it or not, and she would rather Phoebe hear the specifics from her in a calm and rational manner instead of Mr. Hawthorne's angry recounting.

As gently as she could, Ella told Phoebe everything she knew—about her mother's journals, Mr. Rowe's investigation, the obituary, and what she knew about Mr. Gutt's and Miss Sutton's involvement.

Ella's heart broke as pain shadowed Phoebe's face.

"So he was not even a phrenologist?" whimpered Phoebe.

"No, dearest. He was not."

"And Miss Sutton? She was playing a part all this time?"

Ella nodded. "I don't know the details, but she's gone from Keatley Hall. No one knows when or why she left. Not even the servants."

Fresh sobs shook Phoebe's shoulders. "I—I just can't comprehend this."

Ella held Phoebe's hand in her own. "At the moment you don't need to comprehend anything. The answers will come soon enough. Right now, you need sleep."

Phoebe shook her head, then winced at the resulting pain. "How can I ever be all right again? How could I have been so stupid?"

"You're *not* stupid, Phoebe. Don't say that. Don't even think that. You're trusting. And why wouldn't you be?"

"But you tried to warn me, Ella," Phoebe protested. "Several times, and I've been so awful to you. How could you ever forgive me?"

"You are my dearest friend, Phoebe. Of course I can forgive you. I know you would forgive me in a heartbeat."

Phoebe sat still for several moments. Then she sniffed. "Have you seen my father? What is his reaction?"

Ella looked toward Mrs. Chatterly again. "He's understandably angry. But don't worry about that now. I want you to rest."

She stayed with Phoebe until she again drifted into a restless sleep, but as the morning's gentle light stretched into the chamber, Ella knew it was only a matter of time until they would all need to face the harsh realities that were waiting.

The tall case clock just outside Ella's father's study door chimed the eight o'clock hour. Outside the window the clouds had begun to gather, and the sky grew quite ominous—perfectly matching her mood.

She had yet to go to bed. Her eyes burned with the need for rest, and her limbs and fingers felt heavy. Even if she were to lie down and close her eyes, though, she knew she'd never be able to sleep. Even in this exhausted state, her stomach churned with restlessness, and her heart raced as if danger was imminent.

Within the next half hour, her father and Mr. Hawthorne would inform the Society members about Mr. Bauer's deception.

And she felt sick.

The members' response might be one of outrage at Mr. Bauer for taking such advantage of them, but more likely they would be angry with Mr. Hawthorne since he was the Society's leader and had reintroduced the topic to the group. Regardless of how the members reacted, her father needed support, and she'd provide it.

Ella found her father in his study. He was seated behind his desk, staring blankly out the window to the quiet forecourt. He appeared to have aged a decade in a matter of hours. Dark shadows lingered under his red-rimmed eyes. He needed a shave, and despite his fresh change of clothes, he looked in disarray.

What could she say in this instance that would bring any comfort?

There was no way the impending discussion with the members could result in a positive outcome. As soon as word of Bauer's fraud spread, the situation would be out of their control. Even so, she owed it to her father to attempt to find a bright side.

After calling for a tray of tea, she carried it to her father and set it on his desk. As she poured him a cup, she forced as much cheer to her tone as she could muster. "Father, I was thinking. Perhaps the members will surprise us. Maybe when they hear the truth and learn how the Society will endeavor to recoup the money, they will understand that they were not the only ones deceived, but Mr. Hawthorne and you as well."

He shook his head, exhaled loudly, and offered her a smile. "My darling, I do appreciate your optimism, but you know the personalities that will be in that room as well as I do. I'm only glad that your mother and grandfather are not here to witness what has befallen their beloved Society."

"No, no. That sounds as if you are giving up!" She pulled a chair nearer to his with as much stamina as she could summon, sat down, and leaned in. "What if Mr. Rowe spoke to them and shared what he knows? It might help them to understand that Mr. Bauer's—or whatever his name is—deception went far beyond our event. Surely that way they would—"

"No, Ella. These members are our friends. Our colleagues. I will not stand in front of them and position this as something less serious and personal than it is."

"What do you mean that *you* will not position it? Mr. Hawthorne is the Society's leader. Surely he'll be the one to address the members."

Her father scoffed. "You saw Hawthorne. He's in no state for such an undertaking."

"Neither are you! Father, you're taking too much responsibility for this. It was Mr. Hawthorne who—"

"Hawthorne is also our friend. At the end of the day, Keatley Hall—and everything that happens beneath its roof—is my responsibility. A responsibility I take very seriously. They will hear from me. It is decided."

Her father stood and stepped to the looking glass opposite the window, where he smoothed his hair from his brow and attempted to straighten his crooked cravat.

Her heart ached as his hands trembled while adjusting the folds of the cravat. She sighed, stood, and moved to help him with the task. She then kissed him reassuringly on the cheek.

As they walked together to what was to be the final morning's lecture, Ella held her breath, fearing what awaited them behind the door to the long gallery.

Chapter 38

SHOUTS ECHOED FROM the plaster walls and ceiling. The sharp wail of scooting chairs and shuffling feet drowned out the tumultuous claps of thunder from the storm raging outside.

Ella stood at the back of the long gallery and watched hopelessly as Mr. Hawthorne and Mr. Shiveley—two educated, normally well-mannered gentlemen—engaged in a screaming match. Another less animated group of members demanded answers from her father. Across the chamber, Mr. Moore and Gabriel were both attempting to explain the details of what was happening to various clusters of men. Members who already tended to err on the side of drama and sensationalism were working themselves into a frenzy. As the volume increased, the tones became more pointed, the echoes escalated, and the general atmosphere grew more volatile. There was only one thing to do: Send all the members away from Keatley Hall as soon as possible.

While her father, Gabriel, and the others attempted to appease the crowd, Ella and Mrs. Chatterly organized the servants, including the valets and ladies' maids who had traveled with the guests, and began preparations for the members to depart. While the confusion and mayhem continued in the long gallery, Ella worked methodically, instructing the stable hands to ready the carriages and horses, sending the footmen to town to arrange for public coaches, instructing the kitchens to prepare food for the guests to take as they traveled, and so forth. Normally such an undertaking would take the entire last day of the symposium, but somehow they had managed to accomplish it in a matter of hours.

Ella was so busy and her attentions were so divided that she didn't have time to be tired. She fixed her sights on one goal: Clear the guests. Then once Keatley Hall was quiet, they could refocus and formulate a plan.

It wasn't until late afternoon that the last carriage conveying the last guest pulled away from Keatley Hall, leaving behind it an odd, uncomfortable silence that, in many ways, was worse than the shouting. It was not until this point that she realized Mr. Abernathy, who had been so intent upon leading Keatley Hall, was gone. She'd been so engaged during the day that she hadn't noticed his departure, and he'd not taken the initiative to bid her farewell.

While Phoebe continued to sleep in her chamber, Ella, her father, Mr. Hawthorne, and Gabriel gathered in the White Parlor.

"I will be going to the home office the minute I return to London," stated Mr. Hawthorne, interrupting her thoughts. "I will be satisfied on this matter. I don't care what that magistrate—what's his name, Moore?—says. Bauer will pay for what he did to us. Miss Sutton and Gutt will pay as well. I don't care if it's midnight when we arrive—I will be heard."

Ella winced as she thought of Phoebe's weak state. "Surely you don't mean to leave yet today."

"Of course I do!" Mr. Hawthorne shot back.

"Well, then Phoebe will stay here, surely," she stated. "She needs to recover. Her head—"

"My daughter can recover in London just as well as she can here. The journey is not that far."

Ella stiffened at the harshness in his tone. "I wish you would recon—"

"Are you an expert on my family now?" he hurled. "She will come home. I think we've all had quite enough of Keatley Hall for the time being."

Ella snapped her mouth shut and blinked away the forming tears. Everyone was tired and on edge. Was this what it had all come to?

As Mr. Hawthorne continued to spew his angry rhetoric, she looked over at Gabriel, who stood in front of the bank of east-facing windows. He was leaning back against the windowsill with his arms folded across his chest and was blankly staring at the rug covering the planked floor. He'd abandoned his coat at some point of the day, and his sleeves were rolled up to his elbows. Dried mud covered the toes of his calfskin Wellington boots, and the shadow of a beard hugged his jawline.

Ella was not so tired that she didn't notice how attractive—how rugged—he appeared. Even so, his usual easy smile was gone. The laughter and amusement that normally resided in his bright expression had faded.

He glanced up at her and saw her watching him.

Her chest squeezed within her as their eyes met, but not just because of the way he looked at her. It jumped with sadness. His departure was imminent—there was no reason for him to remain. The symposium was over, and Gabriel still had a job to do. He would likely leave yet that evening and make it back to London by nightfall.

As her father and Mr. Hawthorne continued to discuss details, Ella approached Gabriel, a bout of unexpected shyness overtaking her. After all they'd experienced together, she should feel more confident, but the day had been unlike any other. Nothing seemed normal. Nothing seemed right.

"Thank you for helping to organize things as everyone was leaving. I know it was chaotic. I—I appreciate your help."

He straightened from the windowsill as she stepped closer and pivoted toward her, closing the space between them. His voice was tired but alluringly soft. "There's no way I'd leave you to handle this alone."

She swallowed hard and diverted her eyes. Surely this heightened emotional state she was experiencing had to do with her lack of sleep and the dramatic events of the last twenty-four hours. It was easier to blame that than to admit the vulnerable truth.

Could she be falling in love with him?

Eager to fill the heart-wrenching silence, she tucked her hair behind her ear and tried to force lightness to her voice. "I suppose you will be headed back to London soon."

He nodded slowly. "Yes. Given that Bauer is out there somewhere, time is critical."

He glanced up and Ella followed his gaze.

Her father and Mr. Hawthorne were exiting the room.

She and Gabriel were alone.

He reached forward and took her hand in his. He slowly rubbed his thumb over the back of it for several moments. "Are you going to be all right? I hate leaving you here. Alone."

Alone.

The word rattled in her tired mind. She was always alone, really. Even when the school was full of students, she was usually by herself. Normally it didn't matter. But after being with Gabriel, knowing what it felt like to be truly understood by another person, the idea of solitude was almost frightening.

"Please do not worry for me." She forced a smile. "There is going to be plenty to do to keep my mind occupied."

His concerned expression did not change. "You say that, but I am still going to think of you. Often."

His words stole her ability to respond. To breathe. The heat of impending tears burned her tired eyes. She blinked them away.

"Ella, I'm not exactly sure what happened these last couple of days, but I don't think I am the same man I was when I arrived here a few days ago. I know I'm not."

"What do you mean?"

"I mean . . . I know you now. You've captivated me. I don't know what the future holds, but I will promise that I'll return as soon as I am able, if you'll allow me. I'll be with you as we get to the bottom of this and right the wrongs that have occurred here. Do you believe me?"

With both hands he lifted her hand and kissed it. The warmth of the touch flooded through her, igniting every emotion.

Gabriel did not depart in a carriage as he had arrived.

Instead, Ella watched from the White Parlor window as he thundered through Keatley Hall's iron gates on horseback, with his oilskin coat flapping behind in the night's gathering darkness.

Each second increased the distance between them, and her

breath shuddered. Her soul longed to believe that he would be returning soon to Keatley Hall as he had said, but such a thought seemed far too romantic, given the task ahead of them all. She had to rely on what she knew how to do, and that was to be practical.

As she turned from the window to the excruciating darkness of the empty chamber, a tear slipped down her cheek. Whether she liked it or not, he had taken her heart with him. And she hoped he would bring it back.

Chapter 39

ELLA LEANED BACK on the sofa in the White Parlor and stared into the popping fire. Even at this distance the glow of it warmed her face and hands. Outside, a cold rain fell against the paned windows in a soothing rhythm.

With the exception of the pattering rain and the occasional gust of wind whistling over the chimney, Keatley Hall was quiet.

Eerily quiet.

She closed her eyes, trying to pretend that the entire interaction with Mr. Bauer—or whatever his name was—had never happened.

But it had happened.

She opened her eyes. The symposium had shattered her family's life as they knew it. Bonds had been broken. Trust had been obliterated. Friendships had been destroyed.

And now the silence in Keatley Hall would remain for a long time.

She assessed her father, who was reading by the fire. She was proud of the way he'd handled such a dramatic event. Whereas Mr. Hawthorne had dissolved under the pressure and scrutiny, her father had excelled. He'd always been the sort of man who found strength when it was needed most.

They'd spent the entirety of the last two days writing to all the students' parents to inform them that, for the first time in decades, Keatley Hall would not be open to students. Not only had the Society's reputation been compromised, but Mr. Abernathy refused to return to the school as a teacher, and the other teachers had similar responses. As a school they would not have enough people to adequately educate and care for the young men. Ella stretched her aching fingers, noting the ink stains on her thumb.

The familiar sound of Mrs. Chatterly's footsteps just outside the parlor distracted her from her musings, and Ella turned as the housekeeper entered. She extended a letter toward Ella. "The boy just brought this around."

Ella squinted and recognized the handwriting. "It's from Phoebe."

Three days had elapsed since Phoebe had departed from Keatley Hall, and eager for an update, Ella slid her finger under the seal, popped it open, and eagerly read the words.

After allowing Ella time to read the letter, her father paused his own reading and removed his spectacles. "How is Miss Hawthorne faring?"

Ella finished the short missive and refolded it. "I'm happy to say that she feels much stronger, but her father has been away from Hawthorne House ever since they returned to London. She said he set out to find Mr. Bauer and has not returned."

Her father clicked his tongue. "Hawthorne needs to mind himself. The way he handles this could ruin him if he's not careful."

Ella placed the letter on the table next to the sofa. "My heart breaks for how much this has devastated the Hawthornes. I wonder if they will ever truly recover from it. Phoebe asked if I'd come and stay with her for a while."

Her father propped his elbow on the chair's arm and pivoted to face her, as if taking fresh interest in the conversation. "Will you?"

She shook her head. "I don't think I should."

"Why not?" he countered.

She searched for words. "I'm needed here. You need me, and I just—"

"Ella." His word silenced her.

"My dear child." His piercing blue eyes were fixed on her, and she glimpsed the strength in her father that he'd not displayed for some time. "I know you worry about me, but like you, I'm still always learning. This has not been an easy event for any of us, but you saw truth when I did not. As much as I hate to admit it, I'd become complacent, but you were sharp. You saw the danger before anyone else. Now your work is done. Your friend needs you. I think you should go to her. And your future—it's still ahead of you. Don't forget to act on that as well."

"My future?" She frowned. "Without the school, I'm not even sure I know what that means anymore."

"Oh, I think you do." For the first time in a long while his eyes twinkled. "The more I think about Mr. Abernathy, the more I realize you were right. What a fickle man he turned out to be. But Mr. Rowe—now there's a fine young man."

Chapter 40

ELLA DREW A sharp breath and summoned every ounce of courage she could muster as the Keatley Hall carriage drew to a halt. She looked through the dirty window and across the sun-drenched London street at the Rowe Solicitor Office. She might be one to shirk convention generally, but even she knew that it was brazen, if not scandalous, to call on a man without at least a chaperone.

She squeezed her eyes shut, as if by doing so she could drum up more confidence. But she needed—wanted—to see Gabriel, and if she did not take advantage of this opportunity, she did not know when the next one would present itself.

She gathered her reticule and gloves and prepared to place her bonnet back gingerly on her head. The Keatley Hall carriage driver opened the door and helped her down. The afternoon was hot for such a late day in September, and she squinted in the brightness. She was expected at Hawthorne House by nightfall, which left her plenty of time for a quick visit.

Once at the office's main door, Ella turned the doorknob firmly, which jingled a bell and captured the attention of the clerk, whom she recognized from her first visit.

"Miss Wilde!" he exclaimed with a bow. "To what do we owe this pleasure?"

She fought the nerves firing through her. What might Gabriel think of her showing up unannounced and unchaperoned? She did not need to respond, however, for as soon as she spoke, the door to Gabriel's office opened.

"Miss Wilde!" Gabriel exclaimed, his light brown eyes wide. "I was not expecting you! Come in, come in."

Feeling oddly bashful, she stepped in farther, fussing with her reticule as she did.

As if sensing her discomfort, Gabriel eyed the clerk, who went back to his task, and Gabriel approached her and lowered his voice. "What a surprise to see you! Is everything all right?"

"Yes, it is." She suddenly felt foolish, as if following her heart here had been a huge mistake. What if she'd misconstrued their time together? What if his attentions toward her at the symposium were for naught but sport and he truly had no desire to see her?

Even with these concerns, the sight of him reignited her desire. She steadied herself. She would do exactly what she did every time she was faced with such a situation. She would feign confidence until she felt it. "I'm on my way to Hawthorne House, but I couldn't resist coming by to see if you had learned anything else about Mr. Bauer."

"Oh."

She tried to read his expression. Was he appalled? Shocked? Disappointed that he was not the reason for her visit to London?

"Actually, there is something I'd like to show you," he said with a grin. "Come with me."

She followed him through the door to his office and assessed the dark chamber afresh. How different it felt to be in his personal space now that she *knew* him. The first time she had been in this chamber was brief, but now she took a fresh note of the painting on the wall and the oilskin coat hanging on a hook right inside the door. The satchel he had been carrying when he left Keatley Hall was on the floor just beneath it.

His words recaptured her focus. "Just this morning I visited with one of the staff at the gentlemen's club Bauer frequented—a man by the name of Blanton." He lifted a piece of paper from the top of his desk. "Apparently he'd seen Bauer home on a couple of occasions when he was too incapacitated to make it on his own. He gave me the address."

"So this is the address of where he is living in London?" Ella clarified, looking at the paper.

"Well, where he *had* been staying. I doubt he'd return after what has happened, but I'm going to visit it later today to see if there is anything I can learn."

Her nerves fell by the wayside as the injustice of what had transpired flared afresh, and she pushed away a bonnet ribbon that had fallen in front of her face. "I'll go with you."

He chuckled at her enthusiasm and tucked the paper in his pocket. "I'd expect nothing less, but this one I should do by myself. It's in an area of town you should probably never see."

"Oh no," she protested eagerly. "I'll be fine."

At this his smile faded. "Are you not expected at Hawthorne House?"

Even though he was probably trying to protect her, his resistance seemed like rejection. She felt . . . silly. She tried to decipher his countenance but couldn't. She'd never seemed to have a problem reading him while they'd been at Keatley Hall. "I understand. If you prefer me not to go, then I—"

"It's not that I don't *want* you to go," he stammered. "Of course I want to spend time with you. It's that the area is dangerous. I have no idea what or who we'd encounter when we arrive, and I don't want to subject you to something we both might regret."

Her opportunity to participate seemed to be slipping away from her. She had to convince him how intent she was on seeing this through. "Gabriel Rowe, this man took advantage of my family. My friends. I fully intend to do everything within my power to help find out the truth about him. Now, you can allow me to assist you, or I will try to find out such information on my own."

He chuckled and tucked the paper in his coat. "I've no doubt you would do just that. And it's only because I think you'd be safer with me than out on your own that I will take you with me. Are we clear on that matter then? Do I have your word that you will not try to track down anything or anyone without me?"

She hated relinquishing any freedom, but perhaps it was an acceptable compromise. "Very well. You have my word."

Chapter 41

VERY LITTLE SHOCKED or surprised Gabriel Rowe. He was always on the lookout for the unexpected—for the twist that would be a clue for his next breakthrough.

But nothing had prepared him to see Miss Ella Wilde in the doorway of his office. She was like a vision—a summoned dream.

He'd been back in London for five days, and in that time he'd visited the passenger agents at the docks every day, attempting to track down any servant or merchant who might have worked with Thomas Bauer. Just this morning Gabriel finally had a breakthrough and obtained Bauer's last-known address.

And then she was here.

Besides his determined focus on finding Thomas Bauer, Ella had been the only other thing on his mind. Her beauty. The feel of her hand in his. Her company and quiet strength.

Yes, it was a shock to see her, but not a total surprise, for she would not be one to stand by and let an injustice simmer. In that manner they were very much alike.

Her gloved hand rested on the carriage seat next to her and

just inches from his own. Everything within him longed to hold it, to press his lips to it.

He refrained, for their current location—a small hired carriage in one of the most repulsive areas of London—was hardly the setting for a romantic gesture.

The stench of human waste, putrid smoke, and rotten produce smacked, and he cleared his throat as the carriage turned a corner. Sharp shouts and dog barks carried on the thick air. Outside the window, dilapidated buildings and broken shelters lined the road. He glimpsed her face for a reaction.

Ella did not wince, but she sighed and shook her head. "This is not at all what I expected."

He raised his brows. "We can turn around if you're not comfortable. I can almost guarantee that whatever we find at this address will not be pleasant."

"No, no. We've gone this far. We might as well see it out."

The carriage slowed to a stop. Someone pounded on the outside of it, and she jumped, startled. He resisted the urge to attempt to dissuade her yet again and stepped down onto the mucky dirt beneath him before turning to offer his hand to help her down.

She settled her hand in his, then hesitated as she looked down for a place to put her foot. Her delicate traveling kid boots were going to be ruined. She lifted the skirt of her traveling ensemble to keep it from sweeping the muck and stepped down.

She took his arm, and together they walked onto the boards that served as a walkway and paused to assess the house. Large sections of paint had chipped away from the facade, and one of the first-story windows was broken.

He was keenly—and protectively—aware of the curious glances at Ella. Not only was she unaccustomed to these surroundings, but the residents here were not used to ladies like Ella gracing their streets. How delicate and refined she appeared in her pristine gown of perse-blue wool with her golden hair tucked beneath the straw bonnet with fluttering ribbons. Determined to keep her close, he tucked her arm more tightly against himself and did not let go.

After double-checking the house number and name on the shingle with the address, he carefully stepped around two broken steps and knocked on the front door.

A pale, scrawny woman with wild, mousy hair and a red-faced baby on her hip answered the door. She fixed her hard gray eyes on him. "What d'ya want?"

"My name is Mr. Gabriel Rowe. I'm looking for someone who I think might live here. May I come in?"

The woman squinted in the late-day sun and then looked at Ella before she stepped back, giving way for them to pass into a dark parlor. The inside of the house was no more inviting than the exterior. Uneven woven rugs did little to mask the dust and dirt scattered on the wooden floor, and the meager sofa and chairs appeared to have been through some sort of fire.

"I dinna want no trouble," she blurted out as she handed the baby to an older girl and wiped her chapped hands on her soot-stained apron.

"Neither do I." Gabriel smiled to ease her. "I'm merely attempting to locate someone who might live here."

She squinted. "Who ya lookin' for?"

"Professionally he goes by the name Thomas Bauer, but you might know him as something different. He's a phrenologist. Dark hair and eyes. Very tall. Often wears a sapphire pin on his cravat."

"Oh," she scoffed, folding her thin arms over her chest. "Pretentious brute, 'e is."

"Is he here?"

She scoffed again and swiped her hair away from her forehead with her forearm. "Mr. Grenshaw ain't been 'ere in nigh a fortnight. And 'e's behind 'is payments too. If'n you see 'im, you tell 'im if'n 'e's not back with me money, I'm selling everythin' in 'is chamber to pay 'is debt."

Grenshaw. Gabriel caught Ella's eye. "It sounds like he's left you in quite a bind."

"A bind? Ha." She sneered. "I've given 'im an extra week on account 'e was wi' me for so long, but I got men linin' up for th' room, an' I've reached me limit."

Gabriel seized his opportunity. "Do you mind if I take a look?"

She eyed him and them looked toward Ella again. "'is room?"

Gabriel nodded. "Yes. I'll pay his back rent for permission to do so."

Her face brightened and she swung out her hands. "Pay th' debt an' everything in th' room belongs t' ye. Ye can burn it for all I care."

"No, no. No need to burn anything. You can dispose of it as you wish."

She extended her work-worn hand, and he deposited several coins totaling the amount she indicated. With her countenance improved she jerked her head to the stairs. "That's it, first on th' left. Don't be long, though. Th' others'll be back soon, and they don't take kindly t' strangers."

Gabriel took Ella's gloved hand and led the way, testing each step to make sure it was safe before she followed. The walls of the narrow stairwell nearly rubbed each of his shoulders as he ascended, leaving him to wonder how Bauer, who was much thicker, could make it up and down these stairs. Once on the landing, Gabriel identified the indicated chamber and pushed open the splintered, creaky door just far enough for them to fit through.

Once they were both in the room, he closed the door behind them. The small square chamber punched with the scent of rum, dust, and perhaps a deceased mouse or rat. The floor groaned as he crossed over to the window and pulled back the threadbare curtain to let in light. Gabriel propped his hands on his hips and assessed the dirty room around him. "This is . . . a shock."

"It is." Ella stepped farther into the room and lifted a book that was atop the room's makeshift table.

Gabriel stepped to the wardrobe and swung open one of the crooked doors. Several meticulously tailored pieces hung haphazardly inside, and some had fallen from their hooks and lay in crumpled heaps at the bottom. "It appears he either left quickly or did not mean to return."

"What are those?" Ella moved behind him and pointed to a stack of three boxes under a blanket.

Gabriel pushed the blanket away with the toe of his boot, retrieved one of the boxes, and placed it on the table. He chuckled, attempting to lighten the heavy mood. "What's your guess as to what's in here?"

She exhaled and raised her brow. "I'm almost afraid to look."

Gabriel lifted the lid to reveal several bound stacks of letters. He loosened the twine securing the first stack, handed half the stack to Ella, and began flipping through the other half.

"They are all addressed to Timothy Grenshaw," she stated, angling the missive toward the light filtering through the tattered curtain. "Do you think that's him?"

"I would think so. Let's take these with us." He handed his stack to Ella and retrieved a much heavier crate. It thudded as he dropped it on the table, sending up a cloud of dust and debris. There was no lid, and inside was a collection of books, pamphlets, and papers on phrenology. He reached for a portfolio and opened it to find a collection of newspaper clippings on Thomas Bauer. Like the obituary, several of these had a drawing of the man.

Ella's sigh echoed from the low ceiling. "So this is how he learned about Thomas Bauer and his work. There must be a dozen pamphlets here by him."

"And look, here are some clippings on the Society."

Ella groaned. "It just makes me so angry! How gullible we all were to believe him!"

Gabriel returned the items to the box and packed them back up, eager to get out of this room as soon as possible. "Unfortunately, it appears he did his research and knew exactly what to do. But don't worry. Even the most detailed criminal will slip at some point. We just need to figure out how to be there to catch him when he does."

By the time Ella and Gabriel returned to the office with the boxes of letters and correspondence, the afternoon had grown late. Night would soon arrive, and Ella had originally informed Phoebe she'd arrive by dusk. They enlisted the help of Gabriel's clerk and began the tedious process of laying out letters and sorting documents. Individual bits of information were scattered like puzzle pieces.

She stood from her chair, placed the letter she'd been reading on one pile, and reached for a different letter. As she did so, she snuck a peek at Gabriel.

He'd shed his jacket in the heat of the day, and he was leaning back against the table as he read. A striped tan waistcoat hugged his athletic torso, and a watch fob hung at his waist. His blousy white linen sleeves were rolled up to his elbows, exposing his muscular forearms.

He glanced up, caught her looking at him, and grinned.

How that grin, combined with the careless manner in which his dark hair fell over his forehead, affected her. She pivoted to mask the giddy smile that threatened.

He lowered the letter he'd been reading to the desk and approached her. "Did you find anything of interest?"

She propped her hand on her hip and shrugged, trying to ignore the effect that his nearness had on her. "A great deal of correspondence but not a single word that even speaks to phrenology."

He looked toward the window and tugged at the edge of his waistcoat to straighten it. "It will be dark soon. Shall I call a carriage and escort you to Hawthorne House? I don't want them to worry if they're expecting you."

She pressed her lips together. That was the last thing she wanted him to do, but he was right. She might not be opposed to testing the boundaries of social convention, but her reputation was already at risk.

With a sigh she refolded the letter. "Yes, thank you. I am sure Phoebe is already wondering where I am. I can take some of these letters with me and continue searching for clues."

Across the room the clerk, whether by accident or by noticing that his employer might want privacy, lifted a box and moved through the corridor to disappear completely.

Keenly aware of Gabriel's proximity and the fact that he and Ella were alone, she battled an onslaught of feelings. His nearness catapulted a fire through her, invigorating her every sense. His scent of sandalwood weakened her resolve.

Before Ella had met Gabriel, she'd never even considered allowing another person to get truly close to her. Her focus on preserving a legacy had left no room for thoughts of romance, but a new, exciting dream was emerging. Now that she'd glimpsed it, was there any possibility of denying it? Gabriel had to feel it too—this overwhelming attraction. The pull was far too strong to be one-sided. How could such an attraction develop so quickly, so intensely?

The late-afternoon shadows were gathering, bathing the office in a soft glow. Gabriel reached for her hand. He swayed toward her. Or perhaps she'd swayed toward him—it was impossible to tell. The line between them was blurring.

The intimate inflection of Gabriel's tone made her feel giddy and girlish. "I'll call a carriage whenever you are ready, but in case I didn't tell you earlier, I'm so glad you're here. When I first saw you I thought I must be dreaming. I hated how I left Keatley Hall, how chaotic it was. I was worried about you."

"I've told you before that there's no need to worry about me, Gabriel."

"I know, I know. Believe me, you've proven yourself more than capable, but I *wanted* to be there. To *help* you. The last few days can't have been easy for you and your father."

As he took her other hand in his, she found it difficult to concentrate on his words. She swallowed hard and managed to whisper, "It is nice to have a friend to talk to about things."

"A friend?" he exclaimed, as if surprised by the word. He dropped one of her hands and slowly, gently touched his forefinger to her chin. Each subtle movement brought him closer to her, and he tilted her chin upward, forcing her eyes to meet his. "My dear Ella. I am, of course, your friend, but is that the extent of your affection for me? If it is, I'd accept it, but I'd be lying if I said what I felt for you stopped at mere friendship."

His fingers dropped to her shoulder, and the warmth of his palm radiated through her gown's sleeve. Her breath caught, as if her lungs refused to breathe, and her heart beat in half measures, hanging on his next word.

She leaned even closer toward him.

As she did, Gabriel pivoted and his other hand stole around her waist and pulled her tight. The warmth of him, the strength of him, weakened Ella's defenses and paralyzed every rational and calm thought she had.

"It's not like you not to have a quick response," he teased, his face inches from her own.

The door flung open as the bell chimed.

Startled at the interruption, Ella jumped back. She whirled toward the door.

There in the office threshold stood Mr. Clancy.

Embarrassment overcame her.

Mr. Clancy had the ability to affect her reputation perhaps more than anyone else in all of London. He knew everyone. One word from him could destroy a woman's entire future.

What on earth had she been thinking to let her guard down in such a manner?

"Oh dear. I'm interrupting," announced Mr. Clancy. "Timing never was my strong suit, I'm afraid."

"No, no." Gabriel dropped her hand and motioned for the larger man to step farther in, completely calm and nonchalant, as if the moment had had no effect on him. "Come in."

"What's all this?" Mr. Clancy's round face scrunched in curiosity as he stepped toward the desk and lifted a stack of letters. "What a mess!"

"Remember this morning when I told you I obtained Bauer's address? We paid it a visit today. This is what we found."

"We?" he asked, raising a brow. "Am I to understand you have taken up this cause as well, Miss Wilde?"

At the refocus of attention on the letters and papers, Ella's pulse began to resume a normal pace. "Of course. This man robbed my friends and made a mockery of my family. I will help however I can."

"I see." Mr. Clancy nodded, and as he dropped the letters back to the table, he grinned. Was he amused by her? Intrigued? Did he think her ridiculous?

He returned his attention to Gabriel. "I've been doing a little probing of my own. I really do think I have a knack for this line of work, Rowe."

Gabriel chuckled and leaned casually against his desk. "Do you, now?"

"Indeed. And I think you will be very impressed with what I've found. Or, rather, *who* I've found."

Gabriel sobered and exchanged a glance with Ella. "I'm listening."

"Oh no. No, no, no. I've been working too hard at this all day to simply tell you. The anticipation must build. You may be the master of this profession, but in mine, presentation is the truest art form. My special guest is in my office, so please, join me there. I'll need you to be quick, though. He's agreed to talk with you, but I'm not sure how long I can convince him to stay."

Gabriel straightened eagerly. "We'll be right over."

Once Mr. Clancy departed and silence once again descended on the chamber, an odd sense of urgency fell over them.

Gabriel raked his fingers through his hair. "What do you think of that?"

"I don't know Mr. Clancy well enough to have an opinion. Do you have any idea who it is?"

"It's hard to tell. Clancy knows everyone." Gabriel reached for his coat and shoved his hands through the sleeves before adjusting it on his broad shoulders. "We'd best go see who it is. Clancy can get quite testy if he feels he isn't appreciated, but he can also be overbearing. Unless you'd be more comfortable going to Hawthorne House instead. It is starting to get dark."

The earnestness in his tone touched her. Her head instructed her to follow convention. She'd already opened herself up to scandal, should word get out of her going to Gabriel's office and spending the day with him. Her heart, however, cried out louder. "That would probably be best, but you and I both know I will never get a moment's rest until I learn who this visitor is."

Convention and propriety were one thing. Pride, passion, and conviction were another.

He smiled as he offered her his arm. "Well then, let's go."

Chapter 42

ELLA PUSHED HER disappointment aside. She and Gabriel had been having the conversation she'd been longing for since the day he left Keatley Hall. The alluring sensation of his hand holding hers eclipsed every other thought, and his affectionate words teased her senses.

She'd have to wait for another time to finish that conversation, though, for the stark reality of responsibility beckoned. She had joined Gabriel in this venture and committed to it.

There would be time—she hoped—for more tender moments soon.

Twilight was falling over London's streets as Ella and Gabriel made their way to the Clancy Assembly Rooms. She had no idea what to expect with this visit. All she knew was that Gabriel was giving her a glimpse into his world, his livelihood.

As they stepped into the very masculine world of Mr. Clancy's study, however, Ella's confidence faltered.

Dark crimson paper hung on the walls, and the distinct scents of linseed oil and tobacco blurred with the fire's smoke. Elegant chandeliers boasting an absurd number of candles hung from the high ceiling. Large, intricately carved chairs flanked a sturdy mahogany desk. As for Mr. Clancy, his auburn hair curled with incredible precision, and a wrinkle didn't dare mar his ensemble of elegant wool. A silky snow-white cravat gleamed at his throat, and gold threads woven into his damask waistcoat caught the light.

Gabriel, obviously accustomed to the surroundings, seemed quite at home as he motioned for Ella to be seated in one of the wingback chairs before he sat.

"So, Clancy, we're here as requested," Gabriel announced casually. "Are you going to tell us? Who is this mystery guest?"

Mr. Clancy rubbed his hands together, as if preparing to divulge a very great secret. "As you are well aware, I've an extensive network of colleagues, both friends and foes, if truth be told. You've assisted me on many occasions, for which I am grateful and, might I add, richer because of it. That being said, when you informed me of your search for Mr. Thomas Bauer, I called in a favor. Before I share my findings, though, I need to have your words, as a gentleman and as a lady, that what is said here and *who* you see here is confidential."

"You have my word," agreed Gabriel.

"And mine," added Ella.

"Good." Clancy stood from his chair and disappeared to the antechamber. When he returned, Mr. Gutt was at his side.

Ella held her breath as shock and anger rippled through her. She felt she would be sick. She dared not look toward Gabriel.

How dare he!

Mr. Gutt's light hair, which had always been tidy and combed, was dirty and wild. Smudges and soot covered his coat. A red cravat was about his throat.

She finally flicked her gaze to Gabriel. Whereas she felt ready to erupt with anger, he appeared aloof and calm. When he did speak, his eyes did not leave Mr. Gutt. "As usual, Clancy, you never fail to surprise."

Clancy sat in his chair as calmly as if it were a pleasant parlor visit. "This was no small undertaking, I assure you. He's departing for America in the morning. I told him that if he shares what he knows with you, I'll personally guarantee he'll not be apprehended."

Ella pressed her lips together to prevent a protest from slipping. Why would they agree to allow him to flee the country after what he'd done? Was there to be no justice for the role he had played?

"So I ask," prodded Mr. Clancy, "do you both agree with this arrangement?"

Gabriel nodded.

Ella begrudgingly followed suit. "Yes."

"So." Gabriel leaned forward, resting his elbows on his knees. "What do you have to tell us?"

"About Timothy Grenshaw?" Mr. Gutt's brow rose.

The familiar moniker struck her—it was the name from the letter.

"Are you surprised to learn his true name?" Mr. Gutt shifted. "I began working for him a year ago. He told me he was Thomas Bauer. He was having trouble getting people to attend his demonstrations, so about five months ago he instructed me to find out information from the servants of where he would perform demonstrations. At first I obliged, but when it became a pattern, I confronted him. He said if I told anyone, he would insist that I'd acted on my own."

Ella could no longer keep quiet. "And Miss Sutton? How is she a part of this?"

"Her name's not Miss Sutton," he scoffed with an incredulous smirk. "It's Elizabeth Grenshaw. She's his younger sister. Did you not see the resemblance?"

Ella mapped the similarities in their appearances—they were both uncommonly tall. Dark hair and eyes. Pale skin. How had she not seen it?

Gabriel's tone remained flat. "How did you come to know this?"

Mr. Gutt cleared his throat and wiped his palm on his coat. "Just before the symposium I overheard them talking about their mother. When Grenshaw realized I knew the truth, he told me that if I kept their secret, he'd pay me handsomely from the collection they were planning to take. So I stayed quiet."

Gabriel finally spoke. "How did you and Clancy connect? How did you know he wouldn't turn you over to the authorities?"

Mr. Clancy responded to the question intended for Mr. Gutt. "Why do you sound so suspicious, Rowe? When you told me what happened, I spoke with my footman. The footman knew Gutt was trying to leave the country but had no money for a ticket. I orchestrated an exchange. It's as simple as that."

Ella frowned and struggled to follow the story. "Are we to understand that both Mr. Grenshaw and Miss Grenshaw were manipulating the Hawthornes all this time? For months?"

Mr. Gutt shrugged. "Apparently the Grenshaws had been planning this heist for years. Miss Grenshaw wooed Mr. Hawthorne so she could influence him. She also encouraged Miss Hawthorne to spend time with Mr. Grenshaw. By the time the symposium started, they were deeply entrenched in the Society. He always said that if anything ever went wrong, they would go to America."

America.

"Is that what he intends to do?" inquired Gabriel. "Go to America?"

"I haven't seen them since the day I left Keatley Hall, but a mutual friend said he intended to sail from Liverpool."

"Liverpool, you say?" confirmed Gabriel.

Mr. Gutt nodded.

Clancy beamed at Gabriel and rapped his fingertips on the chair's arm, as if he himself had just solved the entire mystery that was Thomas Bauer. "There, Rowe. I said I could help you."

Gabriel smiled. "Yes, you did."

Gutt stood from the chair. "Are we done here?"

"I think that sums it up, don't you?" added Mr. Clancy.

Gabriel nodded again. "Thank you for your time, Gutt."

"Come on." Mr. Clancy motioned for Mr. Gutt to follow him back through the door. "I'll get you your money and show you out."

By the time Mr. Clancy and Mr. Gutt left the chamber, Ella's frustration was mounting, and she could not stay quiet. She whirled toward Gabriel. "Are you just going to let him leave?"

Gabriel nodded. "I am."

"But why?"

Gabriel's voice was low. "Because he's lying."

"What?" She twitched. "How do you know that?"

Gabriel leaned back in the chair. "I've heard confessions from dozens of people. When it comes time for someone to recount an event, there are telltale signs when something is not right."

Panic continued to swell. "But how can you be certain? He could get away! And the Grenshaws could be getting away too!"

Gabriel turned to her. "He stared at me too boldly when he spoke. His torso was rigid and he didn't move, except when he rubbed the back of his hand against his mouth when I asked him about Liverpool. He was blinking either too much or not at all. That man was lying, Ella. I'd stake my reputation on it."

Ella could not believe what she was hearing. She wanted to trust Gabriel, but if Mr. Gutt was lying, why was he not doing something?

Gabriel continued, "Gutt clearly wants me to follow his suggestion and go to Liverpool. Which means he certainly does not want me to stay in London."

"That doesn't make sense."

"Of course not. That's the whole point. Consider, Ella. What loyalty does Gutt have to Clancy? Clancy may be securing him passage from England, but that doesn't ensure honesty. Gutt probably has much bigger issues to contend with other than how he is going to get out of the country. You must trust me on this."

Ella could not. "Then why did you not say as much when he was here? When he realized he was caught, he might have told the truth."

"Clancy is one of my informants, and most of the time he does have good information. This time he's wrong, but I don't want him to stop communicating with me. The relationship is too valuable. You must be patient. Gutt is not the man we want. He's a pawn, just as Miss Grenshaw is a pawn. The person we want is Timothy Grenshaw."

Gabriel's words were irritatingly calm. How could he be so relaxed?

Mr. Clancy reappeared, his proud grin wide. "So when will you add me to your employ, Rowe?"

Gabriel chuckled as naturally as if they were discussing the weather. "Anytime you are ready to give this all up, you can come work for me."

"Where to now?" Clancy asked eagerly. "Liverpool?"

"Maybe, but not yet. First I'm going to stop by the docks for the passenger list. Gutt says Liverpool, but it never hurts to double-check those here in London. And, of course, I must see Miss Wilde back to Hawthorne House. I'm sure her friend is wondering where she is."

"I'll go with you." Clancy reached for his black beaver hat. "We can take my carriage. You don't mind, do you, Miss Wilde? We can drive by the docks, Gabriel can visit the docks, and then we can deliver you safe and sound to Hawthorne House."

Mr. Clancy's eagerness reminded her of that of a child. The whole conversation had taken an odd turn—a turn in which she no longer felt as if she was part of the plan.

Gabriel looked toward her. "Is that all right with you?"

No, it was not all right with her, but she was in no position to protest. She'd already shared that she did not agree with the way things were handled, but the decision was already made . . . regardless of her input.

The carriage drive from the assembly rooms to the docks was relatively short. There were so many things Ella wanted to say to Gabriel—that she wanted to ask him. Admittedly, she did not understand his reasoning. And it frustrated her.

Gabriel had been right about one thing. The docks were not a safe place. The buildings around her reminded her of the street where Mr. Grenshaw's boardinghouse had been located.

The carriage pulled to a stop beneath a flickering gas lamp that spilled just enough light to illuminate the wet cobblestone walkway beneath it. To the carriage's left, another road stretched forth, lined with smaller buildings and houses. A heavy fog hung in the air, and it caught the lantern and gas light, resulting in an unsettling glow. Shouting and bouts of raucous voices echoed from the brick buildings, making it seem as if the sounds completely surrounded them. Two scantily clad women leaned against a wall not far from the carriage, and a body—either sleeping or intoxicated—sprawled not far from where the carriage had stopped.

Gabriel touched her hand and refocused her attention on him. "I'm going down to the building at the end of this dock. I won't be long. You'll be safe here with Clancy. Just don't get out of the carriage, all right?"

She nodded wordlessly.

Gabriel exited the carriage, and the gusty wind caught the folds of his tailcoat and billowed them behind him. She watched as the heavy fog enveloped him.

Once the door was closed and Gabriel was walking down the street, Mr. Clancy said, "I take it you've never graced the London docks before, have you, Miss Wilde?"

She turned her attention back to Mr. Clancy. "I have not, sir."

"It's a different world here among the rabble." He laughed and rested his thick hand on his knee. "I hope you're not offended. I doubt you ever have reason to encounter such environments at Keatley Hall."

Unsure of how to respond to the disparaging comment, she remained silent.

Mr. Clancy continued, "Does it surprise you to know that I have friends here in these buildings and on this very street? Ah yes! I see in your expression that you don't believe me, but just ask Mr. Rowe. Ask nearly anyone in London. I interact with people from all walks of life. It is my gift."

The unusual pitch of his voice and the subtle narrowing of

his eyes cautioned her. He was clearly awaiting a response, so she swallowed her discomfort and said, "I only knew you as the master of ceremonies at the assembly rooms. I had no idea you were so connected."

"It is an art. In order to be able to speak with anyone, I must be able to understand them while maintaining an appearance of gaiety and nonchalance." He tilted his head to the side. "I have another gift. Can you guess what it is?"

Ella shifted and glanced again out the window, hoping to see Gabriel approaching, but was met with darkness. Shouting outside the carriage intensified, grating on Ella's already raw nerves. "I cannot guess."

A crooked, portentous smile curved his lips. "I have a very, very long memory. I remember the details that others forget. I keep careful account of every credit and every debit, and like a bookkeeper, I keep a tally of them in my mind."

She squirmed uncomfortably. She couldn't quite put her finger on it, but the contrived words that came out of his mouth felt almost like a masked warning. She told herself it was her imagination—an irrational fear brought to life by their ominous surroundings.

He leaned forward and put his elbows on his knees so his face was not far from hers, denying her the option of looking away. "In fact, are you aware that I knew your mother?"

The air fled her lungs, and in that moment she could only stare.

"Yes. I knew her," he repeated slowly, "only I knew her as Miss Leonora Keatley, before she married your father. Such an impressive woman. Fiercely outspoken, as I recall."

Normally the news that someone had known her mother would excite her, but the darkness shifted around her. Gabriel had indicated that danger lurked outside the carriage, but something in

Mr. Clancy's tone and his unnerving constant directness suggested the danger might be closer.

She searched for words. "Were you interested in natural philosophies, then?"

He laughed easily. "Oh no, no, my dear. I am far more interested in the social aspects of life—why people behave the way they do. Why they say what they say."

She racked her brain, trying to think of any other topic she could introduce to shift the conversation, but her thoughts seemed to be stuck.

"I remember the pamphlet," he announced bluntly.

She jerked as if struck.

Either he did not notice her lack of verbal response or he did not care.

"I was a young man just rising in the ranks during those years. I longed to join the prestige associated with the Society, but I did not come from wealth and privilege, you see. I didn't exactly meet the criteria for the sorts of men they deemed appropriate for such a group. Even so, your mother was always kind to me. So much so that I recall speaking with a woman—a Mrs. Chatterly—about engaging my sister as one of your mother's personal servants. My sister had made some questionable choices in her young life. I believed that if she could be under the care of a reasonable, intelligent, responsible family's roof, she might just be able to turn things around."

Ella froze at the mention of Mrs. Chatterly. She desperately searched her memory, wondering which woman on the staff had been his sister, yet she could remember no one with the name of Clancy.

Her voice cracked as she attempted to portray a placid demeanor. "And how is your sister now?"

"She's dead, Miss Wilde." His tone sharpened. "She was the other servant in the room when your mother died. A 'fit of rage,' I believe the pamphlet said."

His statement stole her ability to speak. To respond.

Was this man accusing her mother of killing his sister?

Silence would make her appear intimidated, so she forced words from her parched mouth. "Whoever wrote that pamphlet was greatly misinformed. I daresay the events of the last couple of weeks have proved that phrenology is hardly a reliable measure."

"How odd it is, Miss Wilde"—he rushed his words out, speaking over her—"that there is only one woman whose name is recalled from that horrific event. One woman whose fate was documented, as if the other two women didn't matter."

She refused to cower, despite her escalating trepidation. "Why are you telling me this?"

"Because your mother murdered my sister!" he shouted in an explosion of fury. Moisture spat from his mouth with the sudden force of his words. He leaned forward in the confined space with his eyes wildly latched on her, unblinking and towering over her. His voice grew eerily calm. "And as I just told you, I have a very long memory. When you combine that gift with an extraordinary sense of justice, one might call that retribution. And the people who know me, really know me, know that I am a man to be feared. I keep them in line by it. And you are about to find out why."

Spurred by his words, Ella lunged for the door handle, determined to leap out and put as much distance between herself and Mr. Clancy as she could.

He stopped her. He grabbed her wrist with such force that she thought he might crush it. He spoke through gritted teeth. "A word to the wise, my dear. Do not scream or cry out or take any of the other actions that might be running through that pretty head of yours. You are in unfamiliar territory. I tell you with certainty, the poor, prosaic people here will not care one speck about the sight of a woman lying lifeless on the ground."

He pushed open the door and somehow got out without releasing her. Then he jerked her, forcing her to step down on shaky legs.

His warning not to scream ran wild in her head, for she did believe he would hurt her. Or worse.

Mr. Clancy motioned to the driver, and in a matter of a few slippery seconds, the carriage that had transported her here—the very one she had believed would shield her from the dock's dangers, was leaving. Each second sent it farther away into the night.

She was exposed. Trapped. Caged.

She blinked to see the conveyance through the foggy night, beneath the light from the sputtering gas lamp on the corner.

Mr. Clancy pinned her arm around his. No doubt to anyone else it looked like a gentleman escorting a lady across the street. She lifted her eyes to what was undoubtedly the destination . . . a public house across the street, light beaming from the windows and raucous laughter and rough voices bursting from within.

Chapter 43

GABRIEL GLANCED BACK at the Clancy carriage as he walked down the cobbled street toward the smaller, run-down buildings at the dock's edge. Pungent odors of fish and refuse hovered in the misty night air, and the nighttime seabird cries added a familiar backdrop to the laughter and music emanating from the public houses and taverns. The Clancy carriage was well marked, with a cloaked driver sitting atop the bench and a footman next to him.

Ella was quite safe, yet he was on edge. For all her gumption and spirit, she was, in effect, sheltered. She would be secure with Clancy, but Gabriel would not be comfortable until she was safely delivered to Hawthorne House.

By the light of the small, controlled fires burning on the edge of the street and the gas lamps shedding a meager glow on the unsavory conditions below, Gabriel sidestepped a sleeping man and ignored a group of dockworkers clustered outside a public house as he made his way to the manifest office at the edge of the docks. A few lights burned in the filthy window, and even though the office was likely closed, he knew with whom he needed to speak.

He knocked on the door. When no answer came, he knocked louder.

Eventually, James Prior, the office's principal agent and a long-time friend, appeared. "What are you doing here? And at this time of night?" Prior shoved his fingers through his tangled black hair and propped his hands akimbo. "Are you aware of the hour?"

"I am, but I need help. I'm looking for a man who is departing on a passenger ship tomorrow. I need to find out which one and if he is traveling with anyone else. So, of course, I came to you."

"Ah." Prior scoffed and hastily motioned with a scrawny hand for Gabriel to enter. "You couldn't think to come during the day like a person of sense? No matter. Come in. We'll have a look."

Gabriel joined him in the office. There was no legal requirement for the passenger ships leaving from London to maintain official passenger manifests, but sometimes they worked in his favor and he would find what he needed.

Prior stepped to a desk, flipped through a large ledger, stopped on a specific page, squinted his wide-set eyes, and then extended it toward Gabriel. "There's one ship scheduled to depart tomorrow—the *Augusta Maria*. Embarking for New York."

Gabriel angled it toward the light from the meager candle lamp and searched down the names.

"The next passenger ship headed to America is scheduled to leave Wednesday at dawn," Prior continued. "The *Obsidian*. That one's bound for Philadelphia."

Gabriel was not surprised that he couldn't locate Gutt's or Grenshaw's names. He pointed to the bottom section of the list. "Are these the most recently purchased passages?"

Prior looked over his shoulder and pointed to an entry. "Yes. The names below this name have been purchased in the last week—and those below this entry have been purchased in the last two days."

Gabriel studied the ledger more closely. It listed not only the purchaser's name but how many tickets were purchased. Only one group of three tickets was purchased in the last week. "What do you know about this name? A William Warner?"

Prior shook his head. "It's difficult to remember. All these folks look the same. One blends into the next. If you're not finding what you need, you can always check the cargo ships. If you want, I'm friendly with one of the clerks, so I'll accompany you. They'll expect a fee, though. They don't have my giving nature."

Gabriel accepted the offer and started toward the other offices, but as they passed where he'd left Clancy's carriage, Gabriel slowed.

The carriage was gone.

"What is it?" Prior asked, slowing his own pace to match Gabriel's.

Gabriel shook his head, confused. "The carriage I arrived in, and the people I was with, have gone."

He attempted to rationalize it. Perhaps Ella needed to leave this area for some reason and Clancy escorted her. He could understand her being ill at ease here, for it was an unsavory area, but she was not one to admit discomfiture.

Gabriel jogged to where the carriage had been and up and down the dark cobblestone street. There was no sign of them.

Surely something happened and Clancy thought it best to move to a safer location. The thought temporarily eased him. Still, it didn't make sense. Ella was far too loyal. She would not leave him here without an extremely compelling reason.

He considered his options for a bit before he turned back to join Prior. "Something's not quite right."

"Do you want me to call for the watchman?" Prior offered.

Gabriel looked across the street toward The Lark & the Gull, a public house well known for providing rooms for passengers who intended to sail. It was also known for its tavern—a dubitable gathering place for the merchants and sailors who were docked here.

As he took notice of the sailors, tradesmen, and East India guardsmen milling about, a flash of red fabric under the gas lamp across the way caught his eye.

The same red of Gutt's neckcloth.

This was Gutt.

And he was walking with Grenshaw.

"There!" Gabriel grabbed Prior by the shoulder and turned him. "Those are the men I'm inquiring after."

Prior squinted in the darkness from their safe distance. "The tall one in the beaver hat bought passage for the New York ship. Two days ago, as I recall."

Suddenly, the bits of information began to form a picture.

Gabriel had been right—Gutt had been lying about the location, undoubtedly to throw him off their scent.

Clancy had been doggedly insistent that Gutt was believable—Clancy had *wanted* Gabriel to leave for Liverpool.

And now he was alone with Ella.

But it was more than that. Grenshaw was here.

And Clancy knew.

The pieces, while not completely together, were lining up quickly. If he followed Gutt and Bauer, would they lead him to Ella and Clancy?

"I need your help." Gabriel licked his lips and swiped at the perspiration beading his brow. He quickly apprised Prior of the events before asking, "Which watchmen are here tonight?"

"Not sure. I can find out, though."

"Gather up whatever watchmen and constables are here. We'll need as much help as we can get. I'm going to make sure I don't lose track of them. I'll meet you back here, perhaps inside." After finalizing the hasty plan with Prior, the men parted.

Gabriel was angry—with himself. How had he missed it? He knew Clancy was connected and integrated into seemingly every one of London's social classes. It had always given him the appearance of power, how he could make things happen. But something like this?

Gabriel headed toward the inn.

Then searing pain jolted through the back of his head. And everything went black.

Chapter 44

ODD, MUTED COLORS flashed under the night's murky shadows. Foreign accents that Ella had never heard met her ears. Agonizing pain radiated from where Mr. Clancy gripped her wrist as he pulled her past the strangers in the tavern.

Did those people not see what was happening—what this man was doing to her? She struggled to keep her feet beneath her as Mr. Clancy hastened his pace down one of The Lark & the Gull's low-ceilinged corridors.

Ella strained to organize her thoughts and formulate a plan. She had but one goal: to free herself from Mr. Clancy. As he pulled her farther back into the public house, past the carousing men and rough women, and into the darker, smaller, less populated passageways, her options for freedom were dwindling.

He forced her around a corner and up a narrow staircase. The sharp tavern sounds were fading to a muted hum. The light dimmed. She tried to keep track of their path so she could get out when she finally freed herself, but the twists and turns disoriented her.

Her shoulders bumped along the corridor's rough walls until

Mr. Clancy stopped abruptly and she collided with his back. He opened a wooden door and shoved her inside.

Once he finally released her, Ella blinked to adjust her eyes to the light. A fire burned in the grate to her left. A bed was to her right. A small table with a chair was under the two windows straight before her. She was in one of the inn rooms.

Then she noticed the man in the corner.

Timothy Grenshaw locked eyes on her. He stood from the chair and swore. "What is she doing here?"

Mr. Clancy snatched the wooden chair from next to the table and pushed her down by the shoulder, forcing her to sit. Before she could process the movement around her, he was wrapping a rope around her arms, securing her to the back of the chair.

"This young lady could not mind her own business." Mr. Clancy grunted. After securing the rope he stepped to face her and ducked, resting his hands on his knees and looking her directly in the eyes. "I did attempt to warn you, my dear."

She winced.

"Have you gone mad?" Mr. Grenshaw hissed, his black Hessian boots heavy against the wooden floor as he approached. "Someone will miss her. The last thing we need are people poking around."

Mr. Clancy chortled and straightened. "She'll not be our concern for long."

"But, Rowe," protested Mr. Grenshaw, his tone gritty. "He'll come for her. Gutt said—"

"No he won't."

The men continued bickering, and the reality of the situation struck her. She'd assumed Mr. Clancy had been on her side and the side of justice, but somehow he was as much a part of this heist as Mr. Grenshaw.

"We must make haste if everything's to be arranged by morning," instructed Mr. Clancy. "Get Elizabeth to watch her."

The scene quickly shifted. The men exited, but sounds of shuffling and footsteps from outside the closed door ensued.

Refusing to devolve to helplessness, Ella took quick stock of her surroundings, searching for something—anything—that might facilitate an escape. Besides the door, the window was the only other way out. She had to be at least one story up, but a cloth covered the window, obscuring any other clue as to exactly where she was.

She swung her attention toward the fireplace, where she noticed a utensil hook. The poker and the brush were on the floor.

Ella strained against the ropes, attempting to dislodge them, but they were too tight. Her fingers and hands were free behind her, but her arms were restricted in a way that rendered her hands useless.

Muddled voices came from outside the door, and she froze. The voices intensified—a male voice and a female voice. *Mr. and Miss Grenshaw.*

Ella held her breath to hear over the blood pounding through her.

"She's in there." Mr. Grenshaw's voice came first.

"This has gone too far, Timothy. You know it."

"There's naught to be done for it."

"This is kidnapping. And possibly murder! What were you thinking? We did *not* agree to this. *I* did not agree to this."

"I know. I know!" spat Grenshaw. "Just do as we're told. It will be over soon."

"I refuse to participate in this, Timothy. No."

"He'll kill you if you don't. He'll kill both of us."

Bile rose in Ella's throat. Her head throbbed. All this time she had assumed Mr. Grenshaw was the driving force behind the entire plot. But was it . . . Mr. Clancy?

His words about her mother and retribution smacked. This was never about phrenology. This was never about anything other than making her family pay for a crime that was never actually committed—and Ella feared she might pay the ultimate price.

Searing pain radiated from the back of Gabriel's head. His head lolled forward. The sharp ache intensified, and he shuddered. He'd been clubbed with something. It was the only explanation.

With eyes still closed, he attempted to lift his hand to touch his head. But his hand would not move.

Gabriel opened his eyes and blinked, furrowing his brow as his eyes adjusted to the weak glow of a lantern hanging overhead.

Where was he?

He looked down. Ropes bound his forearms to the arms of a wooden chair. His ankles were secured to the chair legs. He tugged against the ropes, but they did not budge. Gabriel searched his memory, desperate to remember what happened and where he was.

He hurriedly assessed his surroundings. Two barrels were to his right, and a side of salted ham hung to his left. Bottles were stacked along the far wall, and various other crates and boxes filled the empty spaces.

In a sudden flash, his memory roared back to life.

He'd just finished talking with Prior. He'd seen Gutt and Grenshaw.

Ella is gone.

Fresh motivation fired through him, and he reevaluated the ropes binding him. Satisfaction flickered. Whoever had tied these erred. He should have been secured at his wrist—the narrowest part of his arm. But the rope crossed the muscular part of his forearm over his coat sleeve. If he could slide his arm backward so the rope was over his wrist, he'd be able to work his hand through and free it.

He repeatedly jerked his arm backward, attempting to move the rope. The last thing he remembered was the street outside The Lark & the Gull, and judging by the dissonant music and muted voices, he was likely inside that same public house. If his captor had taken him here, then Ella was probably here too.

The thought of Ella here, in this dangerous establishment, spurred him to quicken his pace. He did not have a lot of space to work with between his elbow and the back of the chair, but with each sharp, angled jerk of his arm backward, he felt slight movement of the sleeve fabric against his arm.

Encouraged, he inhaled a deep breath and wrenched his arm back with all his might. The rope gave and slid down to his wrist. Perspiration gathered on his brow. He folded his thumb toward the other edge of his palm, making the broadest part of his hand as narrow as possible. The rope scraped and tore against the skin on his hand as he jostled it free.

He was almost there . . . he just had one more arm to free. He only hoped he would not be too late.

Chapter 45

ELLA FIXED HER eyes on the hook near the mantel and bit her lower lip in concentration. She held little hope that the pointed iron hook at the fireplace could pierce through the rope and weaken it, but she had little other choice. Right now it was the only option. She had to try.

The voices outside her door had subsided, and she forced a long, slow exhale. Everything within her screamed to give in to hysterics, but she thought of how calm Gabriel had been when he'd encountered Mr. Grenshaw with the pistol. She would be calm too.

She pushed her feet against the wooden floor to scoot the chair closer to the hook. The legs caught on the uneven floor planks, nearly tipping the chair to its side. She tried again. Then again. Regardless of her effort, she could not get enough leverage to lift the chair leg over the plank without tipping.

She had no idea how much time had passed. Half an hour? An hour? She desperately searched the space again for something she could use to free herself. She *would* formulate a new plan.

Footsteps—light ones this time—stopped outside her door. Ella stilled.

The door squeaked on iron hinges.

And there stood Elizabeth Grenshaw.

The women locked eyes in a wordless exchange. How different Elizabeth Grenshaw looked than the polished Miss Sutton. Her dark, stringy hair was secured in a hasty chignon. Long wisps hung around pale cheeks. The flickering fire emphasized the dark hollows beneath her eyes and cast shadows on her high cheekbones and high-bridged nose. She appeared older now, as if she'd aged a decade in less than a fortnight. A plain brown gown of rough muslin hung on her much thinner frame.

Ella was not frightened of Miss Grenshaw. Perhaps it was naive to consider her innocuous, but the woman appeared more sad than threatening, more defeated than triumphant.

Miss Grenshaw stepped into the room and hastily drew the door closed behind her. "You shouldn't be here."

Ella met her gaze fully. "I daresay neither should you."

"How did you manage this?" Miss Grenshaw's words seemed more an accusation than a question.

Ella would display no emotion. Miss Grenshaw might not be much of a physical threat, but she was far from trustworthy. "Perhaps you can tell me, Miss Grenshaw. It's all very curious."

A curse flew from Miss Grenshaw's thin lips, and her normally elegant accent was far less refined than Ella recalled. "You should have left well enough alone, Ella Wilde. You don't know how much danger you are in."

Ella's ears rang at the insinuation, yet she'd admit no fear. She steadied her voice. "Then from one lady to another, you should tell me so I at least know what I'm up against."

Miss Grenshaw pressed her dirty hands to the sides of her flushed face and began to pace the room. Ella could see the battle raging in her as plain as day, and it gave her hope that she might be willing to help.

But seconds passed. Miss Grenshaw did not respond. Instead, she huffed and paced like a caged animal trying to figure out how to break free. "You should not be involved in this."

"Then help me," urged Ella in a strained whisper. "Help me! I have no idea how you're involved with this, but if you help me get away from him, I will return the favor. I swear it to you. And I would call upon our time together at Keatley Hall for you to know that I am good for my word."

For a moment Ella thought the woman was having a change of heart. But in a sudden burst of energy, Miss Grenshaw spun from the room, leaving Ella once again in isolation.

Fresh panic clawed in her chest, and Ella resumed her search for a plan to free herself. But as quickly as she'd disappeared, Miss Grenshaw reappeared and closed the door behind her. She retrieved an item from her pocket, and as she withdrew it, the fire's light glinted on metal.

Miss Grenshaw's harried voice was barely above a whisper. "It was never supposed to be this way." She stepped to the chair and, using a small pocketknife, sawed at the rope securing Ella to the chair.

The rope gave way.

Miss Grenshaw retreated, her stoic expression unchanging. "I doubt I'll ever see you again, but if I do, remember what I did for you today." She turned to leave and, without turning around, said, "Mr. Rowe is in the cellar."

And then Miss Grenshaw was gone.

Stunned, Ella instinctively rubbed her arms where the ropes

had frayed the fabric of her gown and abraded the soft skin beneath. She hesitated in her disbelief, as if this had been a jest of some sort and she was going to be captured anew.

In the silence the truth registered—Miss Grenshaw had set her free.

Ella did not take time to contemplate it. Miss Grenshaw had said Gabriel was in the cellar. It would not make sense for her to lie about that after freeing Ella. So that was where she needed to go.

She searched the chamber for something she could use as a weapon. She gripped the poker that was on the floor in front of the fireplace. The sounds of laughter and voices emanated from the floor below, and she approached the door and held her breath, listening for the sound of footsteps or voices.

When she was sure she heard nothing, she eased the door open just enough to see into the corridor. A single candle sconce flickered at each end of the hallway, and the staircase she'd ascended was to her left.

She hesitated—once she stepped foot from this chamber, she would be exposed. Clancy's warning to kill her if she tried to escape terrified her, and the iron poker was heavy in her hand. She'd never needed to defend herself before.

But she had to get away. And if Gabriel was here, she needed to find him.

Chapter 46

ELLA RACED DOWN the corridor, demanding that her mind recall the directions she'd turned when Mr. Clancy was dragging her to the room. Her breath seemed far too slow to fuel her movements, and her feet could not carry her fast enough.

When she reached the end of the corridor, Ella hesitated at the top of the steep, narrow staircase. What awaited her at the foot of this staircase? Miss Grenshaw had said Gabriel was in the cellar, but where was the cellar?

She reasoned that whatever awaited her downstairs would rival the danger if she'd simply remained upstairs. She knew Gabriel would never leave without her.

She would not leave him.

The music and voices were growing louder, indicating she was moving in the right direction but also making it impossible to hear if someone was approaching. Once she reached the ground floor, Ella turned and looked down the perpendicular corridor and saw it—a closed door with a key hanging outside of it.

That had to be the cellar.

She adjusted her sweaty grip on the poker, moved toward the door, and reached for the key.

"Who is there?" boomed a voice.

Ella whirled.

Timothy Grenshaw was approaching from the opposite direction.

Large. Angry. Dark.

He reached into his coat.

Ella didn't think—she clutched the poker with both hands, squeezed her eyes shut, and swung. Hard. The impact fired pain through her, as if she'd been struck by stone. She opened her eyes.

The giant man dropped backward. The pistol he'd retrieved from his pocket clattered to the stone floor.

An entirely different kind of fear seized her. Had she killed him?

Was she a murderer, just like Clancy claimed her mother had been?

No. She couldn't let her thoughts get away from her. Her mother was not a murderer, and neither was she.

Blood oozed from Mr. Grenshaw's head. She froze, staring at what she'd done. She could not stop now. Gabriel was right behind that door.

When she was able to force movement to her limbs, she reached over his still body for the key. Her trembling fingers would barely wrap around the key ring. She stepped over Mr. Grenshaw's large boot and steadied the key enough to insert it into the lock.

Once done, she turned the key.

And it clicked.

Gabriel grimaced as he wrestled with the knots in the ropes around his ankles. He had to be getting close.

A masculine shout stopped him.

He jerked his head up, ignoring the sting of perspiration dripping in his eyes.

Another shout was followed by a loud bang and a thud.

Frantically, he bent over and tore at the ropes. If someone was coming in, he needed to be free.

The door jingled.

The lock rattled.

He braced himself. Was it Clancy? Grenshaw?

The door opened.

There stood Ella. Pale. Disheveled. The whites of her eyes gleamed in her panicked expression. "I—I—I," she stammered.

Her sleeves were torn and her hair hung in haphazard clumps around her terrified face.

"Shhh," he soothed. "Just stay calm."

"I struck him with a poker," she blurted. "He isn't moving. He—"

"Ella, Ella," he repeated until she stopped talking. "It's all right, but you must trust me and do what I say, and quickly."

She nodded with twitchy, wide-eyed movements.

"Open the door wider to see if anyone is coming."

She did as bid.

"Good. Now, go back to him and check for weapons. Check inside his coat, his waistband, and his boots."

She disappeared just outside of view. Shuffling ensued. She reappeared with a pistol in one trembling hand, a blade in the other, and a fresh tear that had slid down her cheek.

"That's good," he continued, keeping his voice low and swiping his cheek against his shoulder to wipe the perspiration from his eye. "Point the pistol to the ground and then use that knife to cut this rope here." He nodded at the loose rope on his second wrist, and she cut through it quickly.

He took the blade from her to cut the ropes at his ankles, and within moments his legs were free. He took the pistol from her and tucked it in his waistband.

He recognized the dazed panic in her expression—she was stunned and out of her element.

"Stay right by me. We'll be out of here soon." He stepped in front of her, then paused at the door. He inched out slowly to survey the space. Once he was certain no one was approaching, he knelt by Grenshaw.

No wonder Ella was frightened. Blood dripped from a gruesome cut on his head. After checking for his pulse, Gabriel assessed the wound more closely. It was not deep but was bleeding profusely, which made it seem worse than it was. "He'll be fine, Ella, but hand me that rope. He could come to at any moment."

He bound Grenshaw's ankles and wrists. He'd not make the same mistake that was made with him and double-checked the ties. He stood and turned back toward her. He needed so much information from her, but time was not on their side. "What happened?"

Her words jumbled out, hasty and unchecked. "It was Mr. Clancy. He told me that his sister was one of the maids who was killed in the fire that also killed my mother. He said he wanted retribution. He's been working with Mr. Grenshaw and is behind this whole thing. I saw Mr. Grenshaw upstairs, and he was frightened of Mr. Clancy."

Anger seized him.

Clancy? How could that be?

There would be time to figure out the details later. Now, he needed to get Ella to safety.

"Is anyone else here?" he asked. "Gutt? Miss Grenshaw?"

"Miss Grenshaw is here, but she is the one who helped me get away."

"And Gutt?"

"I've not seen him, but they talked about him."

Muffled noises echoed from the tavern. They needed to act—and fast. He placed his hands on her shoulders and stooped to look her directly in the eyes. "When we were at Keatley Hall, you told me that you trusted me. Do you still?"

She blinked as if surprised by the question. "You know I do."

"Then I need you to do exactly as I say. I sent for the night watchmen earlier. If they're here, they will likely be in the tavern. I'm not sure what is going to happen next, but if anything happens to me, you get as far away from here as possible. Do you understand? Don't wait for me or try to help me. You just get yourself to safety as quickly as possible."

Her brow furrowed. "Gabriel, I—"

"I'm serious, Ella. Do you promise me?"

She nodded.

Gabriel retrieved the pistol with his right hand and gripped her hand with the other. "Good. Let's go."

Chapter 47

AS GABRIEL LED her down the dimly lit corridor, Ella glanced back to the large man on the floor. His hands and feet were bound, and he was lying awkwardly on his side. Gabriel had said he was alive, but he didn't *look* alive.

She shuddered and tore her gaze away. She couldn't think about that now. Gabriel was right. There was no way to know what was going to happen next, and she had to keep her wits about her.

When they reached the corner at the corridor's end, Gabriel stopped and released her hand. The distant light glistened off the sweat on his brow and illuminated the heavy rise and fall of his chest with each breath. He pressed his back flat against the wall, and with his pistol pointed upward, he inched to see around the corner.

As soon as he looked down the corridor, Clancy's voice thundered. "Drop your weapon, Rowe."

Ella watched, helpless, breathless, as Gabriel held up both hands, as if in surrender, and stepped out into the adjacent corridor.

Who was he facing? Only Mr. Clancy? Mr. Gutt?

Gabriel did not look back at her. He stared, unblinking, expressionless, straight ahead.

"What have we here?" The amusement echoing in Clancy's tone sickened her. "How did you get out, I wonder?"

When Gabriel did not respond, Clancy continued, "Go ahead and put that pistol down. Slowly now."

Ella searched for any clue she could. She might not be able to see what was going on, but judging by the sound of Mr. Clancy's voice, he was very close . . . likely right around the corner.

Gabriel, his hands still in the air, eyes locked on Mr. Clancy, slowly bent down to place the pistol on the ground.

As he was moving, Ella crouched close to the ground and pivoted to see farther out. The light from the main room was behind Mr. Clancy, and as she leaned closer, she spied his long shadow.

Her breath caught. There was only one shadow.

Her optimism soared.

Clancy was alone.

It was the two of them—she and Gabriel. Against one man.

Close to her ankle was a wooden bucket with a rope handle. Just as Gabriel's weapon clinked on the stone floor, Ella, determined to distract Mr. Clancy, grabbed the bucket and hurled it out into the perpendicular corridor, just behind Gabriel.

Mr. Clancy swore, and in that singular moment of diversion, Gabriel lunged in Mr. Clancy's direction.

Ella leapt forward and snatched Gabriel's pistol from the ground. She turned in time to see Gabriel push Mr. Clancy's arm with his pistol straight up.

Mr. Clancy's pistol discharged.

Ella screamed, and the sound incited cries of alarm from the main room.

Gabriel pinned Mr. Clancy's arm behind his back and then

shoved him against the wall, but then Mr. Clancy spun out from the hold and slammed a heavy fist into Gabriel's jaw.

Ella did the only thing she could think to do. She pointed the gun at Mr. Clancy with shaking hands. "I'll shoot!"

Mr. Clancy jolted his head toward her.

Gabriel took advantage of Mr. Clancy's momentary bemusement and spun away from his hold. In mere seconds Gabriel was at Ella's side. He took the pistol from her and turned it on Mr. Clancy. "Against the wall. Now!"

As Gabriel laid hands on Clancy, men rushed from the tavern.

One of the men, who was obviously familiar with Gabriel, helped him subdue Clancy. "What do you need us to do? We've already sent for more constables."

"Good." Gabriel nodded toward the corridor. "There is a man around the corner. Apprehend him. He's injured. He'll need attention."

The space was suddenly alive with activity—men rushing to and fro. Chaos ensued, but a calm settled over Ella. Could this really almost be over?

Once two of the men escorted Mr. Clancy away, Gabriel faced her, red-faced and breathless. "Where did you last see Miss Grenshaw?"

"In one of the chambers on the first floor."

"This is Prior," Gabriel said, introducing the man with black hair and a pudgy nose who'd spoken when the other men arrived. "I want you to go with him and stay with him until I get back."

She hesitated. Considering all that had happened, she should do as he said. The men around were fully capable of wrapping up all the loose ends, but she didn't want to leave. She needed to see this through to the end. She'd regret it if she did not. "No. I'll go with you."

"It could still be dangerous. There's no way to tell if—"

"No," she interrupted. "I need to go, Gabriel. I'll show you right where they are."

In the next few seconds time slowed. Gabriel looked at Ella. Really looked at her. "All right. But if I say you need to come back here, you must do it."

"It's up these stairs." Confidence replaced her fear as she retraced her steps and led the men to the chamber where she'd last encountered Miss Grenshaw.

Ella paused at the door to wait for Gabriel and the watchmen to gather. Even though she was determined to see justice done, a battle raged within her. Miss Grenshaw needed to be apprehended. She'd deceived many people and was an accomplice to a crime. But Ella had seen the sadness and regret in Miss Grenshaw's eyes. It already haunted her.

Once Gabriel was at the closed chamber door, he looked back to the other men, held up his fingers to count down their entry, and then in a sudden burst, he kicked in the door.

The men rushed in. Shouts and shuffling, cries and curses, echoed in the space. Ella could only watch as the men seized not only Miss Grenshaw but also Mr. Gutt.

Ella drew a shuddery breath. It really was over.

The people who had deceived her family and friends were no longer roaming free—they were going to face justice.

Chapter 48

THE REST OF the night passed in a sickening, overwhelming blur for Ella. Mr. Clancy, Mr. Grenshaw, Miss Grenshaw, and Mr. Gutt had been secured in the gaol at the justice of the peace office, and they would be held there until charges were officially filed. Ella had given her testimony to several constables. She repeated her testimony over and over, recounting every detail she could recall.

Her arms ached, her head throbbed, and despite the warmth of Gabriel's coat, which he'd given her to guard against the night's chill, her shivering did not cease. She detested women who were weak, and yet on more than one occasion she felt the room spin and wondered if she might faint.

Gabriel, on the other hand, thrived in this environment. His assurance, his confidence in dealing with the aftermath of this bizarre nightmare, impressed her. This was, no doubt, what he was born to do. He never questioned his memory; his composure never wavered. He possessed a strength of mind and a dedication to justice she'd never witnessed in another.

After what seemed like hours the commotion finally lulled. Little by little the watchmen and constables dispersed until only a few remained. Calm gradually replaced havoc, and silence replaced the mishmash of voices.

She sat on a bench just inside the door of the office, waiting for Gabriel to complete his tasks. Extreme fatigue pulled at her, and more than once she had to jerk herself awake. At length Gabriel joined her and sat next to her on the bench.

He took her hand in his. "You must be exhausted. The justice of the peace has called his personal carriage to take us home. It will be here any moment."

Home.

Where was home at the moment? She was almost too tired to consider the answer. "Where are we going?"

He leaned close. "We'll go to my house. My sister is there, and before you protest, consider that it's four in the morning. I can't take you to Hawthorne House at this hour."

He was right, of course. What other option did she have?

The carriage arrived, and they stepped out from the justice of the peace office into the inky night. Damp fog covered London's empty streets, and an unusual tranquility hovered. Gabriel assisted her into the carriage, spoke with the driver briefly, and joined her inside.

He settled next to her on the tufted carriage seat, wrapped his arms around her, and pulled her close.

Ella inhaled the scent of the outdoors and even the pungent scent of gunpowder that still clung to him. She closed her eyes and melted against the safety of him—the stability of him. He pressed a kiss to her forehead, and she leaned wordlessly against his chest.

The night had been the most terrifying of her life. Never had she felt so vulnerable, so in danger. She'd also never felt so protected and cared for. She never wanted to be in that situation again, but in it she learned where her heart really belonged—it did not belong in a building; it belonged to a person. All thoughts of Keatley Hall floated to the back of her mind, and nothing was before her except Gabriel.

Ella awoke as the carriage jerked to a halt. She lifted her head from Gabriel's shoulder.

"We're here," he whispered close to her ear.

Pulling herself from her sleepy state, Ella straightened to look out the window at a brick row house.

Gabriel's home.

After he assisted her from the vehicle and talked briefly with the driver, he tucked her hand in the crook of his arm and escorted her up the stairs. He unlocked the door, they stepped inside, and he closed the door behind them.

They were alone.

For several moments they stood in the peaceful silence, mere inches from each other in the foyer. A faint glow from the gas lamp outside the window and the fading fire in the parlor grate provided a sliver of light, but otherwise all was dark and serene.

Propriety would say that she dare not be alone with Gabriel, but after all that had happened to them that night, did propriety even matter? This was the most natural place for her to be.

He drew her close, and she pressed the side of her face against his shoulder. His arms tightened around her. "I'm sorry for what you went through tonight. I wish I could have prevented it."

She sniffed and gave a little laugh. "I never *ever* want to go through anything like that again."

"And you never shall. The fact that you even went through it at all will haunt me until my dying day."

"No, no." She shook her head, pulling away just enough to look into his eyes. "If anyone is to blame, it's me. I insisted on getting involved, didn't I? I really didn't give you much of a choice."

He chuckled but quickly sobered. "I can't believe I didn't figure out that Clancy was involved earlier."

"And how would you have known that?" She smoothed the lapel of his coat before she let her hand rest on his chest. "Like you said, the two of you have worked together for a long time."

"I missed something along the way. Tomorrow we will be questioning them, and we'll know everything soon enough, but right now"—he readjusted his arms around her waist—"I don't want to think about Clancy. Or Grenshaw. Or Gutt. There is only one person I want to focus on right now."

Her heart sputtered in her chest, and she awaited his next words with sweet, breathless anticipation. How was it possible to feel so happy, so giddy after what they'd just endured?

Gabriel brushed her hair from her face, and his fingers tenderly skimmed her cheek. "I reckon you saved my life not only once but twice today. So tell me, my dear Ella, how does one go about repaying that? A simple word of gratitude hardly seems sufficient."

Emboldened by the passion in his expression, she moved her hands from his lapels and wrapped her arms around his neck. "We never did get to finish our conversation earlier, in your office."

"Hmm?"

"If you'll remember, you asked me if I thought of you as more than a friend."

"Ah yes." He lifted his head playfully, as if finally recalling the interaction. "And if I remember, we were, uh, interrupted."

"I'd like to revisit that, if you don't mind."

He leaned down so his forehead was nearly touching hers. "I'd be happy to. Before we were interrupted, I believe I had already shared my thoughts on the matter. I was waiting for you to respond."

She could no longer resist the lure of his nearness and stroked her fingers through the curls at the base of his neck. "I fear, Gabriel, that my feelings on that matter have been decided for some time."

"Have they?"

"They have. I think—no, I know—my feelings for you have far surpassed mere friendship. I fear, Gabriel Rowe, that my heart is now hopelessly involved."

A smile curved his lips. "If we are to speak of hearts, then allow me to say that my heart, and everything I am, belongs to you if you will have it. Whether you knew it or not, you took possession of it weeks ago. In fact, when I was faced with the thought that I might lose you forever, I came to realize . . . that I love you."

How sweet the words were. How beautiful and sweet.

He kissed her softly, gently.

She pressed against him and tightened her arms around his neck, reveling in the new and captivating sensation.

He deepened the kiss.

Never had she felt so safe, so happy, so connected to another person. She could stay here forever in his arms.

They remained there, together, for several blissful moments, until commotion sounded from somewhere in the house.

Startled, Ella pulled away. She turned just as a woman clad in nightclothes and carrying a candle descended the stairs. "Gabriel! I thought I heard something. What is going on?" Her confused gaze fell to Ella.

"Mary," Gabriel said, taking a step back, "this is Miss Eleanor Wilde."

"Miss Wilde!" she exclaimed. "I have heard so much about you. But what has happened? Why are you here at this hour?"

"We've had quite the experience." Gabriel stepped back to put more distance between them. "I'll explain everything in the morning, but Miss Wilde will need to stay the night here. Can you show her to the spare bedchamber?"

Reluctantly, Ella bid Gabriel good night and allowed his sister to help her settle in for the rest of the night. Despite all the fear and anxiety they'd experienced, happiness flared.

He loved her.

And in that moment her heart knew: She loved him too.

Chapter 49

ELLA AWOKE TO a long sliver of white sunlight filtering through the space around the filmy curtains on the far wall. She winced as she rolled over onto her arm, and the previous night's events swept over her.

She bolted upright in bed. Images rushed her: Mr. Clancy. Mr. Grenshaw. The pistols. The ropes. But then the memories of softer, gentler, promising moments with Gabriel washed over her.

The heavy painted door to the corridor creaked open, and Mary poked her head in the doorway. "Oh good. You've woken."

Ella pushed herself farther up in the bed. She'd not spent much time with Mary the previous night—just long enough for Mary to help her prepare for bed and wash the rope abrasion on her arm—but she'd been so considerate and attentive. "Thank you for your care last night."

"Think nothing of it. I'm just pleased you are doing well." Mary motioned to the window. "Shall I open the curtains for light?"

Ella nodded, and the trim young woman turned to pull back the cream-colored curtains, allowing an abundance of exhilarating light to flood the space.

Being in Gabriel's home was such an intimate sensation. This chamber, which she learned last night was called the Rose Room, was small but pretty, with high ceilings and pink-and-cream wallpaper adorned with delicate white roses. An oak wardrobe chest was in the corner, and two east-facing windows ushered in the morning light. A small writing table stood beneath the window to the left, and the small fireplace harbored a cheery light on the north wall.

How peaceful she felt.

"I am sorry about the noise from the street. This part of London is quite loud, I'm afraid." Mary tied back the curtain with a tasseled golden cord. "But there's not much to be done about that, is there?"

Mary fidgeted with her hands as she approached the bed. "Can I get you anything? I brought some tea up earlier while I was waiting for you to awaken, but it might be cool by now."

Ella's throat ached from the tension and dryness. "I would be grateful. Any temperature would suit me. Thank you."

"I'll have the housekeeper bring up a fresh pot momentarily, but hopefully this will suffice for now." Mary poured the tea into a delicate teacup.

After handing Ella the tea, Mary returned to the chair by the bed. Ella wasn't exactly sure why, but she was struck by how young Mary seemed. She must have been quite young when she married. How closely she resembled her brother. Her hair was dark, and although it was secured in a chignon, curls escaped at her temples and at the nape of her neck. Her eyes were soft brown, just a little darker than Gabriel's, and she had the same thick black lashes. Her skin was remarkably fair, as if she hadn't seen the sun in ages, and shadows hung under her eyes.

Mary perched daintily on the edge of the chair. "How is your arm feeling, Miss Wilde?"

Ella smiled. "Please, call me Ella." She glanced down at the white bandage visible under the fabric of her nightgown. "It will be sore for a while, I'll wager, but nothing that won't heal."

"Oh, Gabriel asked me to tell you that he took the liberty of sending a message to Hawthorne House to let Miss Hawthorne know where you were. He didn't want her to worry."

Ella's heart leapt at the mention of his name. "How thoughtful. Is he here? At home?"

"No, he's not, I'm afraid. He left early this morning to see the justice of the peace. He didn't want to disturb you."

Disappointment surged through her. She longed to see him, even if just to confirm that she hadn't dreamt the interaction in the foyer. Furthermore, with her energy restored, she wanted to know exactly what was going on. She could feel Mary's eyes on her. "Did he tell you what happened?"

"He did. Such a horrible experience for you both. I declare, I don't know how Gabriel finds himself in such situations, but as sorry as I am for your ordeal, I am pleased to meet you. Gabriel has spoken so highly of you."

"I'm very fond of him as well," she offered, perhaps too eagerly. "He's a courageous man."

"I understand you are a courageous woman!" Mary countered, her tone brightening with emphasis. "He shared how you distracted a man by pointing a pistol at him. I'm sure I could never have been brave enough to do such a thing."

"I'm sure you would have in the moment. Looking back, I'm surprised at it myself, but I was so frightened that something would happen to him, I . . ." She let her voice trail off.

"You mentioned his bravery." Mary leaned forward in her chair as if growing more comfortable with the conversation. "I, too, was the recipient of his bravery a few years ago. Gabriel has an honorable, unwavering sense of justice that I do not necessarily understand, but for which I am grateful."

Ella didn't want to pry, but she was curious. "Gabriel told me a little bit of your story. It is a sobering one, to say the least."

Mary's eyes took on a far-off expression. "I thought my life was over. I truly did. I'd been accused of committing a crime during a fit of delirium and was institutionalized. My father sided with my husband, but Gabriel—he did not. He fought long and hard for me, and, oh my, what a cost he paid."

Ella tilted her head to the side. "What do you mean?"

Mary looked confused. "Do you not know?"

When Ella shook her head, Mary softened her tone, as if preparing to tell a secret. "When Gabriel defied my father and started to work toward my freedom, my father disowned him, stating that he was foolhardy and lacked judgment. Even when the truth of my husband's actions came to light, my father would not relent. My mother begged and pleaded with them both to resolve the matter, but Gabriel would not betray me. In truth my father's anger had much more to do with the fact that he was wrong when he sided with my husband, and his pride will never permit him to admit fault. Even to this day he will not speak or even write to either of us.

"Gabriel has an inheritance from my mother's side of the family, but it is a pittance in comparison to what he would have received from our father. As it is, poor, dear Gabriel is stuck with me."

Even though Ella did not know Gabriel at the time this had happened, her pride swelled. How she admired his determination and loyalty. She was not sure it was even possible, but his allegiance to his sister made him all the more attractive. "I'd hardly say he's 'stuck' with you. It's clear he respects and cares for you very much."

"That's kind of you to say, but my reputation is in shambles, my husband is a prisoner in Australia, and I've absolutely no money. I'm completely dependent upon Gabriel. If that isn't being stuck with me, I don't know what is."

Emboldened by the level of personal details she'd already shared, Ella lowered her voice. "Do you ever hear from your husband? A letter, maybe?"

Mary's expression soured. "Heavens, no. And I'm grateful for it. I don't know what I would do if I ever had to see him again."

A distant knock echoed from the floor below. Mary stood and stepped to the window to look at the street below. "I wonder who that could be?"

The door could be heard opening, and indecipherable feminine voices followed.

They did not have to wait long to learn the visitor's identity, for within moments Phoebe burst through the bedchamber door, a bundle in her hands, her vibrance reaching to every corner of the room. Panic lit her round face, and her cheeks flushed nearly crimson. She raced to the bed, her satin bonnet ribbons streaming behind her, and dropped a bundle on the floor next to the bed.

She snatched Ella's hands, which had been folded on top of the coverlet, and pressed a kiss to her cheek. "Oh, my dear, dear Ella! How on earth did this happen? Are you all right? You must tell me that you are all right this very minute or else I might burst. I really will."

Ella laughed at her friend's dramatic display. "I am fine, you see?"

Phoebe blew out her breath, dropped her shoulders, and plopped onto the bed. "Well, *I* am not fine. Not one bit. I've been an absolute nervous mess ever since I heard about this appalling business. First you never arrived when I was expecting you, and then I get such news when I wake up. You must tell me everything. Start with the moment you arrived in London and omit no details."

Ella glanced to Mary, who'd been observing the reunion patiently. "Phoebe, you've not met Mrs. Mary Fife. She is Mr. Rowe's sister."

Phoebe whirled around, as if just now aware of the other woman in the chamber. "Oh, forgive me."

Ella turned to Mary. "This is my dearest friend, Miss Phoebe Hawthorne."

Once she had finished their introductions, Ella recounted everything—from searching Mr. Grenshaw's chamber and discovering his real name, to meeting with Mr. Gutt at the Clancy Assembly Rooms, to being kidnapped by Mr. Clancy. She did, however, keep her romantic interlude with Gabriel a secret to herself, but with every new detail Phoebe's eyes grew wider.

"I'm in shock. Absolute shock!" The excitable timbre of her voice resonated from the plaster ceiling. "I simply cannot believe how we all fell for his lies. Every single one of us. Except for you and Mr. Rowe, obviously. Now, I will tell you what I know."

Phoebe made a great display of getting comfortable on the bed, as if preparing to relay a remarkable tale. "The very first news I heard when I woke up this morning was that Mr. Clancy had been arrested. Charming, distinguished Mr. Clancy! Not long afterward, one of the Society members, who is the brother of the justice of the peace, arrived at Hawthorne House with news of Mr. Bauer's, or rather Mr. Grenshaw's, arrest! He told me everything, including about your involvement. I thought surely he was mistaken, but about that time I received Mr. Rowe's most surprising message, and the entire world seemed to come crashing down around me.

The house has been nothing less than mayhem with all the Society members visiting and demanding answers. Of course I had none to give. Oh, it is all such a mess!"

It was an odd sensation to know that so many people knew of Ella's personal trials, but at least the truth was finally coming out. Her family was being vindicated.

Phoebe's story continued. "My father finally returned just an hour or so ago, and what a bluster he is in. He's already been summoned to the justice of the peace office to provide a testimony. He's seething!"

Ella sat up straighter in the bed, determined to glean as many details as she could. "Is everyone angry?"

"No—not angry. I would say they are more surprised than anything. Many of the Society members are just happy to have answers. No one likes to be taken for a fool, and everyone—me included—feels better knowing that justice will be served in one way or another. And, of course, everyone wants to know if they will get their money back, but I suppose that will take time to resolve. Oh! I almost forgot. I took the liberty of writing to Mrs. Chatterly and your father. Don't worry, I did not alarm them, but I thought you would want them to know."

Her dear father. And dear Mrs. Chatterly. "Thank you."

"Also"—Phoebe paused to draw a breath and lift the bundle from the floor—"I brought you a gown and some things. I heard that your belongings were found in Mr. Clancy's carriage this morning, so I thought you might need these."

Mary, as if taking advantage of the break in Phoebe's chattering, stood abruptly from her chair. "If you'll excuse me, I'll go see about getting you ladies some more tea and give you some time to talk."

When the door closed and they were alone, Phoebe spun back around, her eyes wide. "Tell me everything, right this minute, about Mr. Rowe. About what really happened, because I know there is something you are not telling me. How did this all come about? How did you reconnect with him?"

Giddiness rushed Ella at the mere mention of Gabriel's name. There was so much she wanted to confide, but she hardly knew where to begin. "It seems unfathomable to say that something good has come out of this entire ordeal, but oh, Phoebe! I think my future is going to be very different than I planned, and I have the most wonderful suspicion that Mr. Rowe is going to play a significant role in my future happiness."

Chapter 50

BY THE TIME Gabriel returned home, Ella had bathed, washed her hair, and dressed in the gown of pale mauve that Phoebe had brought for her. It was a lovely gown with small primroses embroidered on the bodice, but the frilly gown felt far too elegant for the task ahead of her.

After donning a fawn-colored pelisse and a straw bonnet and gathering up a blanket and a basket of food, Ella placed her gloved hand in Gabriel's as he assisted her into the carriage. The soft purple light of dusk was beginning to settle over the bustling London streets, but it was the first time Ella had seen Gabriel since he'd returned from the justice of the peace office. It was the moment she'd anticipated all day—to confirm that their time together the previous evening had not been a dream and that he really did care for her. That he really did love her.

Once they were seated, Gabriel tapped on the ceiling and the driver urged the horses forward. Before she could say anything, he leaned over, cupped her face with his hand, and kissed her. He then held her gaze. "My Ella, you are the very best part of my day."

At this close distance she saw the exhaustion in his red-rimmed eyes. "Have you even slept?"

He shook his head and ran his fingers through his dark hair. "Not really. I went down to the justice of the peace this morning to see if there had been any developments, and throughout the day, no fewer than twenty Society members stopped by to state their cases. It will be quite the undertaking to get it all straightened out."

She smiled affectionately and touched her fingertips against the prickly shadow of a dark beard forming on his jawline. "In case I've not said it, I am proud of you and what you've done."

"Don't be too proud yet. We can barely get anything out of Mr. Gutt and Mr. Grenshaw, and Mr. Clancy refuses to say a word and has more wealth behind him than anyone with whom I've ever worked."

"What do you mean?"

"As much as we like to think our systems are fair and just, corruption is always present. Many people would be happy to turn a blind eye or tell a lie if Clancy pays enough."

"And Miss Grenshaw?"

He lifted a shoulder. "I don't think anyone's talked to her. Maybe she'll talk to you."

Ella placed the basket of food and the blanket at her feet. In a few minutes they'd arrive at the justice of the peace office, where the gaol was located that now housed Miss Grenshaw.

Ella had never seen a gaol before and had no idea of what to expect, but she knew nothing was going to prevent her from speaking with Miss Grenshaw again face-to-face. For all her faults, she'd done Ella a great service. Who knew what could have happened to Ella had Miss Grenshaw not intervened.

When they arrived, the office was even more crowded than it had been the previous night. She recognized several Society members, but there were also many people she did not know. They seemed to be staring at her. Feeling sheepish under the attention, she leaned closer against Gabriel's arm as he guided her through the crowd.

Ella whispered, "Am I imagining it, or are they all staring at us?"

Gabriel chuckled as he opened the office door with one hand and guided her through with the other. "I believe everyone is staring at *you*. And I don't blame them. Everyone is amazed at how you struck a man with a poker and then intervened when Clancy had a pistol pointed at me. You really are remarkable."

"Remarkable? If anything, my actions give those who believe that I suffer from insanity ammunition. What sane person hits another with a poker?"

"A very brave one."

She nodded at a few familiar faces as they made their way through to the back of the office where the gaol was located. The low-ceilinged chamber was exceptionally dark, and she wrinkled her nose at the musty scent of a space that had been damp for far too long. There were no windows, and intermittent lanterns provided the only light. As the bars and the iron latches on the door came into view, Ella's anxiety heightened.

When Miss Grenshaw's and Ella's eyes first locked in the gaol's shadows, neither of them spoke. Ella stooped and placed the basket on the ground outside the cell. When she did finally speak, her voice felt hoarse. "I brought you a few things."

Miss Grenshaw stood from the narrow bench and approached the bars, her plaited dark hair draped in front of her shoulder. "I wasn't sure if you were going to visit or not."

Ella smiled, hoping to ease the woman's anguish, even as her stomach flopped within her. "I told you if you helped me I'd do what I could to help you."

"And is that why you're here, then? To help?"

Ella faltered. "I would like to, but that is hard to do when I don't know the truth."

Miss Grenshaw slid a suspicious glance toward Gabriel, who was standing quietly behind her.

When she didn't speak, Ella continued, "I've been asked for my testimony, but I can only speak to what I saw with my own eyes. I know Mr. Clancy orchestrated much of what I observed last night, but if you tell me your story, perhaps we could find a way to absolve you of some charges. In order for me to help you, though, I really must know everything."

"I will tell you, even though I hold little hope of it being helpful." Miss Grenshaw sighed and wrapped her arms protectively around her waist. "You know by now that Timothy is my brother, but what you don't know is that we are from a family of actors. As children we traveled with my parents around the country, performing at fairs and acting in traveling troupes. Our parents died when we were young adults, so my brother and I set out on our own. It was all we ever knew.

"Several years ago my brother met Mr. Clancy at a gentlemen's club, and they became fast friends. Over the years Mr. Clancy's prestige and wealth grew, but he remained congenial with our family, despite our lower status.

"About a year and a half ago, Mr. Clancy approached Timothy with an idea. He told us about Thomas Bauer—the phrenologist. Mr. Bauer had died earlier in the year, and Mr. Clancy said that if Timothy were to learn this theory and pretend to be Bauer, we could have an entirely new act.

"Mr. Clancy knew the right people to talk to—and that was Mr. Hawthorne of the Society. He made the introductions, and we took it from there. It was all an act, but it embodied a life we were aspiring to. For the first time in our lives, people took us seriously. People respected us and wanted to be around us. I was even developing a true attachment to Mr. Hawthorne. I can honestly say that we had no idea of the scale the scheme would take, and we certainly didn't know how influential the Society members were.

"Once Timothy and I realized how dangerous this could be if we were found out, we wanted out. But Mr. Clancy—he was too powerful. He threatened us with a great number of things. So when our task was complete, we were going to set sail for America. Unfortunately, my brother's inability to avoid the gambling tables drew Mr. Rowe's attention. Once the two of you were onto Timothy, we knew we were in trouble."

When Miss Grenshaw had finished her recounting of events, Ella exchanged glances with Gabriel. There. They had the answers. But she felt worse than she had when she arrived.

Ella turned back to Miss Grenshaw. "If this is all true, I will do my best to help you, but you must be willing to testify."

Miss Grenshaw nodded. "Yes, I know."

After the conversation concluded and Gabriel and Ella walked toward the carriage, Ella took his arm. "It's just so sad."

"It is, but don't forget that even though she was unaware of the full extent of Clancy's plans, she knew enough to intentionally deceive, and she did so for a long time. Such fraudulent actions do not usually end how criminals hope they will."

Ella frowned. "What will happen to her, do you think?"

Gabriel exhaled a long breath. "It all depends upon how serious the actual charges are that are brought against her and who oversees the case. My guess is she'll be tried for fraud and the intention to steal property, with transportation for a period of years as recourse, but if you speak on her behalf, the magistrate might be lenient. As for Gutt and Grenshaw, I think they will be tried the same. But Clancy will be different. Complainants are coming out from seemingly nowhere with accusations against him."

"What kind of accusations?"

"Oh, every manner of them. Fraud. Manipulation. Intimidation. I hate to admit it, because I did count him as my friend, but deception like he and Grenshaw attempted does not usually begin on such a scale. Don't worry. You have already done your part, and the rest, really, is out of our hands." A grin curved his lips. "But do you know what is not out of our hands?"

She smiled at the sudden shift in his demeanor. "What?"

"Our future." He covered her hand with his, and as they reached the carriage and he prepared to open the door, he paused to face her. "We have had enough of these dramatic and portentous events. Now I want to think of nothing more than you and of all the days we have before us."

Chapter 51

Ella watched the pastoral landscape flash past her from the carriage window. Endless rolling meadows and fields and groves of alder and silver birch trees replaced the noisy, dusty ambience of London. Gone was any trace of summer. In the past fortnight autumn had arrived to the countryside—and with it the scenery now boasted vibrant hues of amber and mahogany glittering beneath the brilliant blue sky.

In just a few miles she would be back home—back to Keatley Hall—where her father and Mrs. Chatterly would be waiting for her.

Keatley Hall—and all that it represented—had always been a beacon of stability and freedom for her, but she, admittedly, was no longer the same young woman who had left less than a week prior. How could she be? Perilous and unbelievable circumstances had forced her to examine herself and had opened her eyes to a world far different from her sheltered existence at Keatley Hall.

And without doubt the most enthralling part of all was Gabriel.

She paused in her musings to glance over at him. He wore no hat, and how carelessly his dark umber hair fell over his face. How she hoped she'd never tire of smoothing it back into place and that his grin—easy, light, and hopelessly alluring—would make her feel this way forever.

Ella had always been too practical to think of romance. Too practical to assume that happiness could indeed be found in anything beyond the walls of academia and duty. Facts and empirical truths might offer security, steadiness, and predictability, but true felicity was found in opening her heart to what might lie outside of what was secure. Now she realized that a true home did not reside in a place, but in loving another person wholeheartedly—and being loved in return.

Before long the carriage turned and jostled through Keatley Hall's familiar iron gates, and a plethora of memories rushed over her. The long, mirthful summers of her childhood. The hopeless devastation of her mother's death. The disappointment of her failed engagement to Mr. Rawlston. The sickening anticipation of the symposium. Every experience had ushered her to this moment.

"You're sure?" Gabriel tightened his grip on her hand. "You're absolutely certain this is what you want to do?"

Their plan blazed clear and solid in her mind. She leaned closer to smooth his hair from his brow and let her hand linger on the side of his face. "I've never been so certain of anything, with the exception of knowing that I want to marry you."

He smiled and pressed a kiss on her lips. "I will support you in whatever decision you make regarding Keatley Hall, you know this, but I want you to make the decision because it makes you happy. Not for any other reason."

As the carriage drew closer and her father came into view, Ella's heart leapt. Before the footman even opened the door, she pushed it open, jumped out, and ran to her father's arms.

He laughed—his familiar, coarse laugh—and hugged her in his fatherly embrace. She pressed a kiss to his weathered cheek.

"My darling daughter," he exclaimed upon releasing her, "how I've been worried for you."

"Oh, Father," she responded playfully, straightening his lopsided cravat. "You know better than to worry about me, don't you?"

"I suppose by now I should. It does me no good, does it?" He looked up as Gabriel approached. "I hear you have had quite an adventure, young man."

Gabriel extended his hand to shake her father's. "Yes, sir. Quite an adventure."

"Ella!"

She whirled at the sound of her name to see Mrs. Chatterly, skirt in hand, hurrying from the front door. With tears in her eyes the older woman embraced her. "Never do that to me again, child! I fear my heart simply cannot take it!" She released Ella and held her at arm's length. "There now, let me look at you. You look well enough. I don't suppose that—"

"Come now, there's time enough for that later," her father interrupted good-naturedly. "Let's get these young people inside. I'm sure they're weary from the journey. They've a great many stories to tell us, I'd wager."

Once they were settled in the parlor, Gabriel and Ella conveyed every detail of what had transpired in London—everything from Clancy's plot for revenge for his sister's death, to the Grenshaws' acting, to the potential consequences for those who had swindled the Society.

Her father shook his head as their accounts concluded. "In all the days I live, I will never understand why some people behave as they do. I have no recollection of Mr. Clancy. How can a man harbor such resentment for so long, and especially against Leonora? Anyone who knew your mother, truly knew and understood her, knew her to be vivacious, vastly inquisitive, and brimming with a zest for life. She exuded passion, yes, but never to the point to which she'd been accused, and never to such a dark level. It pained me—and it pains me to this day—how her gift of wonderment at the world and her thirst for knowledge were reduced to an oddity. But you are changing that, Ella. Your mother would be so proud of you. And now," exclaimed her father with a glint of youthful mischief in his eyes, "I have something I would like to show you. I've been up to something myself."

She exchanged amused glances with Gabriel. "It's not like you to be secretive, Father."

"When talk of having a phrenologist as the symposium speaker first started, months before the symposium, I knew you had reservations. So I wrote to a German gentleman and a scholar by the name of Edvard Reichardt."

She frowned. "I've not heard that name."

"I don't doubt it. He was a friend of your grandfather's, and he was a supporter of the school in those earlier years. I lost touch with him many years ago, but he was one of the phrenologists who, like your mother, saw the error of phrenology and wanted to abandon the study. He's since gone on to both conduct and oversee several studies on brain development. I wrote to him and shared that Thomas Bauer was to visit Keatley Hall. I only received a response a few days ago, but his censure is indeed severe. He knew that Thomas Bauer—the *actual* Thomas Bauer—had died, and he wanted to make sure we knew the truth. He also shared what he knew about the pamphlet that caused us so much trouble. Here is his response."

Ella accepted the letter her father extended, opened it, and angled it so Gabriel could read it with her.

She could hardly believe what she was seeing. Her hand flew to her mouth as the words registered in her mind. "Father, am I reading this correctly?"

He exhaled a long, satisfied sigh and leaned back in his chair. "Apparently, while at a gathering in the Netherlands a few years ago, he encountered one of the men who contributed to the pamphlet. They spoke of their time studying phrenology, and the man confessed, in not so many words, that the damning details about your mother—and, by association, *you*—had indeed been fabricated.

"Those who wrote the pamphlet feared that if a person of your mother's standing and outspoken personality cast doubt on phrenology, that would be the end of it. According to Reichardt, some of the men had become very wealthy by conducting false assessments. So they lied. The fire was, indeed, an accident. Leonora's gown did pass too close to the fire. Two maids had been in the chamber with her and undoubtedly tried to assist, but the smoke overcame them. The door had been locked, and in the confusion, the key had been dropped down one of the grates. By the time their voices were heard and responded to, it was too late.

"The coroner deemed the three deaths smoke inhalation, but the rumors were embellished as they traveled from the Continent, as rumors tend to be. Reichardt said he was appalled that the topic is even still in question, and that he intended to write a letter to the head of the Society clarifying the matter."

Gabriel took the letter from her to read it again. "All of that plotting by Mr. Clancy for all of these years, all because of a lie." He returned the letter and looked toward her father. "You would have been proud of Ella and how she handled the situation at the docks. It really was quite impressive."

"I'm not surprised," her father responded. "Eleanor always did have a knack for finding unusual solutions."

Gabriel cut his eyes toward Ella before refocusing on her father. "Speaking of Ella, there is a matter that I would like to discuss with you, sir. A matter that *we* would like to discuss with you."

Philip Wilde shifted in his chair.

Gabriel continued, "I know I'm probably not the sort of man you had hoped would fall in love with your daughter, but as fate would have it, I have. I'm no scholar, I'm no teacher, and I know very little about the world she's from. But I do love her for who she is—the person she has been every single day. And that is why, sir, I would like to ask for your blessing for your daughter's hand in marriage."

Her father sobered and fixed his eyes on Ella. "What of you, daughter? Do you share this affection?"

"I do, Father." She beamed. "And I know what you are thinking."

He chuckled. "I very much doubt that, my dear."

"You are worried about the school, about Keatley Hall. And I—"

"Ella."

She snapped her mouth shut at her father's interruption.

"I worry about nothing. If marrying young Mr. Rowe will bring you happiness, then who am I to stop it?" Her father stood and stretched out his hand. "You have my blessing, young man. You both do."

Gabriel shook her father's hand, and then Ella pushed through and threw her arms around his neck.

"What have we always taught you?" her father asked. "To be

curious. To imagine new ways of thinking. To challenge expectations and ask questions that will lead to different and more impactful results. You have done that. You are doing that. Just look at where it is leading you. Yes, I had hoped you would continue the work here, but that was so I would know that you were safe, secure, and happy. I now see that you don't need such things handed to you. You are taking what you have learned and forging your own path. That is, in my opinion, success."

Later in the evening, when the sun was setting over the cool meadows surrounding Keatley Hall and the last rays of sun reflected off the conservatory windows, Gabriel and Ella walked through the north garden. The last of the sleepy morning glories had closed their amethyst petals for the night, and the nightingale's tinkling song ushered in dusk's gentle coolness.

"Who would have thought that this time next year there will be no classes starting this term?" Ella adjusted the position of her hand on the smooth wool sleeve of Gabriel's coat. "It's odd to have everything so quiet this time of year. Don't you remember? This time of year the boys would still take their exercise in the garden after dinner."

"Yes, but they'll be back after the Christmas holiday. Fortunately the disruption will be for just a few months, and then all should return to normal."

Ella dragged her fingertips over a boxwood along the side of the path. "Normal? I'm not sure I would call it normal. Some of life here will be as it always has been, but my role will be lessening."

"I heard your father say that Mr. Abernathy is returning next term as well?" he teased, playfully lifting a brow. "Will I have to worry about competing with him for your heart?"

She smiled as the image of the tall, lanky man came to mind.

"Oh, I don't think so. One day Father will need someone to run the school, and for all his dull mannerisms, he is even and will be able to take the helm one day. As for my heart, though, I have other plans."

Gabriel slowed his steps and paused at a secluded area of the path not far from the oak tree. How easy it was to fall against him, to relax into his embrace, and to lift her face to receive his kiss. How easy it was to imagine a whole new future by his side.

"You'll not miss it too much, will you?" he asked.

She inhaled and looked at the canopy of branches above them. "I spent so many years holding on so tightly to the idea of this place and what it represented to me. Little did I know that it was simply preparing me." She returned her attention to Gabriel. "I will always value what I've learned here, but it's time for me to do exactly what was expected of me . . . to travel my own path, and that path, with its twist and turns, led me to you."

He kissed her again, and as she wrapped her arms around his neck, Ella knew that her heart had found its home.

Epilogue

KEATLEY HALL, GILLHAM, ENGLAND

SEPTEMBER 1821

MRS. ELLA ROWE pushed the soil around the tender lavender plant and patted it into place. "There." She lifted the pot and handed it to Mrs. Chatterly. "That should be the last of them."

"How many do you intend to take with you to London?" Mrs. Chatterly added the pot to the others.

Ella placed her small shovel on her workbench. "Perhaps three or four. Right now the conservatory at the row house is quite small, but it's cozy. I don't want to overfill it too soon."

"Give it time. This conservatory was not created overnight. Remember what your mother always said? Flowers bloom when and where they will. How much longer will you be staying at Keatley Hall?"

"Perhaps another week." Ella pulled her work gloves from her hands and used her forearm to swipe her hair from her face. "At least until the term starts. Gabriel and I have work to tend to back at the office."

Mrs. Chatterly shook her head. "How strange it seems for you to be the wife of a solicitor."

"His business is growing faster than we ever imagined. When news got out of our tracking down Mr. Clancy last year, Gabriel had to take on two more gentlemen to help with the work. I could simply burst with pride at all he has accomplished, although I fear his sort of work is a far cry from what traditional solicitors do. But then again, I cannot imagine Gabriel just sitting behind a desk, can you?"

"Indeed not."

Movement outside the conservatory window caught her attention. In the back garden her father and Mr. Abernathy were walking across the lawn.

Mrs. Chatterly clicked her tongue before returning her attention to the bloom in front of her. "I know you never cared for him, but he certainly has settled into his new role as headmaster well."

Ella studied the tall man as he ambled next to her father. "He really was the best choice. He may not be my favorite person, but Father trusts him and likes him. It's nice that Father can take a step back from the day-to-day duties of teaching and the school but can still be there as a guide. I think the additional rest has been good for him, don't you? His coloring is improved, and he doesn't appear quite as feeble as he did the summer prior to the symposium."

The casement clock in the distant parlor chimed, prompting Ella to glance at the timepiece on her chatelaine. She pulled her gloves off and placed them on the table. "I should probably go change. Gabriel and I are going to visit Mary at the girls school and see how she is settling in."

"Mrs. Fife seems content in her new position. She stopped by the kitchen this morning and was quite chatty."

"She does seem happy, doesn't she? And I'm certain the young ladies will love her. I know some of the parents have expressed concern about her past, but that will all fade away, especially as the Society continues to grow. Phoebe told me that her father can barely keep up with all the new membership inquiries he's been receiving, especially from younger gentlemen around Gabriel's age. It seems that everything with the symposium last year did not damage the Society's reputation as we had feared. If anything, it has increased interest in it."

Movement at the door caught her attention. She whirled to see Gabriel. She hoped her heart never ceased this little leap it did at the sight of him.

"What have we here?" he asked, leaning in curiously with his hands clasped behind his back. *"Lavender augustifolia?"*

Ella laughed. "Close! *Lavandula latifolia.*"

He snapped his fingers, as if suddenly recalling the difference. He grinned, stepped behind her, wrapped his arms around her waist, and leaned forward to kiss her cheek. "Are you ready to go visit Mary?"

"Oh no! You must let me change my gown. I'm a mess!" She brushed off bits of dirt clinging to her muslin gown.

"Nonsense! You're beautiful."

Mrs. Chatterly moved to untie the apron behind her back. "I have a basket prepared for Mrs. Fife if you are headed that way. She had asked me to gather a few things for her. I'll return shortly."

Once they were alone, Ella turned toward Gabriel with his arms still about her waist. He kissed her forehead and then her lips. "Are you happy, Mrs. Rowe?"

She smiled and lifted her face to his. "Immensely."

"And you are sure you aren't sad that you won't be here for the start of the school year?"

No question for her could be easier to answer. She rested her hands on his chest. "Not at all. I love being here, visiting here, and it will belong to us for the rest of our lives, but we are not teachers, and we have other work to do. As much as I adore Keatley Hall, I think I am better suited to life in London. With you."

"It is fortunate, then, that your experience at the docks didn't scare you away from the town forever."

The memory of her escapade with Mr. Clancy, Mr. Gutt, and the Grenshaw siblings had been such a defining point in her life, but now the entire ordeal seemed little more than a nightmare or a distant memory. Even now, though, she sobered at the reality: Mr. Clancy, Mr. Gutt, and Mr. Grenshaw were all en route to Australia to serve out the sentences handed down to them: Both Mr. Gutt and Mr. Grenshaw received sentences of seven years. Mr. Clancy's term was for life. Miss Grenshaw, on the other hand, received a lighter sentence, but even with the less severe charges, she still remained in Newgate Prison, where the conditions were famously deplorable.

Ella shook off the thought's sobering effect. "Do you think we will ever see any of them again?"

Gabriel shook his head. "I doubt it. Even though Gutt and Grenshaw received shorter sentences, they will likely never be able to afford passage back to England. Regarding Miss Grenshaw, I can't say for certain, but Newgate's a dismal place."

After getting the basket that Mrs. Chatterly had prepared, Ella and Gabriel made their way along the brand-new brick path that led from Keatley Hall to Keatley Cottage, which was now officially the Keatley Hall School for Young Ladies. Thoughts of the past faded once again to the back of her mind, and excitement and hope for the future rushed to take their place. With the school finally open, her focus shifted to the dream she now shared equally with her husband—the dream of working together to assist women facing injustices—just as his sister had.

As they walked, Ella drew even closer to Gabriel's side. She gripped his hand and did not let go. Ella had loved her idyllic life at Keatley Hall, but she loved her life with Gabriel even more and eagerly anticipated each new adventure that would come their way.

Author's Note

One of my favorite aspects of writing historical fiction is discovering new and interesting details about the past. When I first stumbled across the topic of phrenology, I thought the idea was too ludicrous to believe!

Phrenology, or the theory that a person's personality traits and intellectual abilities are predetermined by the shape and size of their skull, was first developed by Joseph Gall in 1796.

Shocked that this flawed idea ever could have been taken seriously, I continued my research and endeavored to view the concept from an early 19th century perspective. During the Regency Era (1811–1820), the entire notion of science or "natural philosophy" was rapidly evolving, and people were curious about how the world around them worked. Phrenology was just one way they attempted to explain or understand human behavior.

Today, phrenology is considered a pseudoscience and holds no scientific legitimacy. Even though I knew phrenology was in no way valid when I was writing this book, I enjoyed giving my heroine the opportunity to poke holes in the theory and let the light of truth shine through.

Acknowledgments

In many ways, the process of writing a book is a solitary endeavor. It involves hours of research and time at a computer, alone with your thoughts and imagination. On the other hand, getting a story from an idea to a polished novel takes an entire team! There are so many steps in the publishing process, and I'm beyond thankful for the people who have partnered with me on *An Unconventional Lady*.

To my family: What would I do without you? Your encouragement and support allow me to follow my passion for writing. I am so grateful!

To my editor, Becky Monds, and to my line editor, Julee Schwartzburg: Your guidance and expertise truly is my writing compass. With each book, you continue to amaze me! And I can't forget the rest of the publishing team—from sales to design and everything in between—you guys are outstanding.

To KC and KBR: One of the joys of the writing journey is finding dear friends to walk the path with you. Thank you for being with me every step of the way.

To my agent, Rachelle Gardner: I don't say it enough—thanks for partnering with me.

Last but certainly not least, to my readers: Your enthusiasm and passion for reading inspires me daily. Thank you.

Discussion Questions

1. Her mother, Lenora Wilde, died when Ella was about ten years old. What are ways that her reputation and legacy affect Ella from childhood to present? What are the positives and the liabilities?

2. From what you know about the time period of the book, the early 19th century, what did you see in Ella's upbringing that was atypical to other young ladies of her time?

3. Ella's prospects of marriage and her place in society are affected by the two men: Nathaniel Raulson and her father's pick, Abraham Abernathy, but her prospects are also threatened by men who believe they can destroy her reputation. What are ways that women in the 19th century were affected by men, 'appearances,' society's rules, and dependence?

4. This novel has a tension throughout between the value of security and social standing and a match based on shared values and love. What risks was Ella facing by hesitating in following her father's advice?

5. In comparison to Raulston and Abernathy, what differences does Ella see in Gabriel Rowe from their first reconnection? What about Gabriel immediately interests Ella?

6. Natural sciences were popular areas of exploration in the 19th century. How did phrenology, a pseudoscience, set the stage for the plot and the time setting?

7. Ella and her more traditional friend, Phoebe, are certainly two very different female archetypes. How did their social standing and the ways they were raised influence their decisions? How do they support each other in spite of their differences?

8. How do your impressions of Miss Sutton/Miss Grenshaw evolve through the novel? Does she also represent some of the risks that women faced in her time period?

9. Late in the novel, we meet Mary Fife, Gabriel's sister, who has experienced injustices herself. In what ways is Mary an example of what Ella or her friends feared could happen for Ella?

10. Mrs. Chatterly and Gabriel understand Ella's concerns about her family's legacy and her own identity and responsibility related to Keatley Hall. How do you see that insight as a critical step in moving forward with her relationship with Gabriel as the story comes to a close?

About the Author

Photo by Emilie Haney of EAH Creative

SARAH E. LADD is an award-winning, bestselling author who has always loved the Regency period—the clothes, the music, the literature, and the art. A college trip to England and Scotland confirmed her interest in the time period, and she began writing seriously in 2010. Since then, she has released several novels set during the Regency era. Sarah is a graduate of Ball State University and holds degrees in public relations and marketing. She lives in Indiana with her family.

Visit Sarah online at SarahLadd.com
Instagram: @sarahladdauthor
Facebook: @SarahLaddAuthor
X: @SarahLaddAuthor
Pinterest: @SarahLaddAuthor